Elizabeth,

Enjoy!

May your stories have happy endings!

Dick Tipton

Gifts of the Storyteller

Richard C. Tipton

Gifts of the Storyteller

Cover design by Jacob Kubon

Published by

Splatteredinkpress.com

ISBN 978-1-939294-10-4

Dedication

For Matthew, Rebecca, and Corina,
three of my favorite unfinished stories.

Acknowledgments

I want to give thanks to all of my friends and family who have put up with me and made this book possible. A special thanks to my wife, Kay, who is generally my first reader, and whose eye rolls and puzzled expressions are my first indicators of how well I've done. Thanks also to my friends in Peninsula Writers. Many of these stories were first written for the entertainment of my PW small group: Rick, Sue, Shirley, Chris, Phyllis, Linda, and others who have come and gone over the years.

Most of the names I use in my stories are borrowed from friends and relatives, and the characters are in no way supposed to reflect those individuals—except maybe the talented lady in "Imitation Heartbreak." Borrowing names is just one of my ways of letting folks know they are in my heart, and that I'm too lazy to come up with my own names for characters.

Thanks to Jacob Kubon for the book cover, and Rebecca Tipton for her photography.

Finally, special thanks to Linda Wells, Thora Wease, Shirley Neitzel, and Tricia L. McDonald for their help with editing and production.

Table of Contents

Gifts of the Storyteller

I became a teacher because of a story: my story. It was first conveyed to me many years ago, and I'm long retired now. It began with Carl.

Carl would walk into town, his scuffed high boots sagging, his usual spotted wool trousers held high with leather suspenders. He always had on a gray work shirt with the sleeves rolled to above the elbows. If it was good weather, he took a seat in front of the tavern. Once seated, he began the ritual of constantly working his long-stemmed pipe. It was never long before someone brought him a lager. He was a magnet for the village men, and soon most of them would have gathered round.

He was the most important person in our village, though I doubt anyone would have thought of him that way. He came into town once or twice a week from his cabin a mile away in the wilderness. Soon he would begin telling one of his stories, his low, warm tones mesmerizing all those within hearing. They were wonderful stories, our stories, twice told because the men always passed them on to their wives in the evening. They were stories of our history, of eagles and talking fish, maidens and grand feasts and brave explorers, fools and spirit trees and far off lands. They were stories that would make you laugh or make you cry, but they would never weigh you down. In those hard days, our storyteller was the one thing that kept us all from despair.

It is an amazing thing what a good story can do for a soul on the edge of desolation. It can snatch a person up and provide transport to the most wonderful places.

Of course, I was just a boy when I came to know our storyteller. After school, my friend Eric and I would sometimes sneak off to Carl's cabin. Often there were other children there. Carl was always busy with one chore or another, and yet it never failed that he would draw us in as he worked. He split wood while telling us of the ghost of old Tobias Tuft. He cleaned his chimney as he painted word pictures of the voyagers discovering new lands in the old times. He peeled potatoes as he regaled us with tales of magical floating hands. He taught us to dream. But most important, on a day when no others were around, he would give us each a story of our very own. Each of us in turn promised him we would tell no one else our story. It became a delicious secret, and every child had one.

Neither Eric nor I ever told our story. We couldn't do that. I think I know Eric's, though. He stayed in the village. He went to work for Carl when Carl became too old to do all of his chores for himself. I find it both fitting and a bit comforting that Eric has now become the storyteller in town. I usually see him at the tavern, surrounded by other men. He'll be wearing a camo vest and Tigers baseball cap. Encircling him will be a wisp of smoke curling up from the old, long-stemmed pipe he favors.

I think I can tell it now. The story given to me long ago by Carl was of a young man who left home to look for work.

He began as a field hand hoeing cabbages; he unloaded trucks, and later worked as something of a mechanic. He was restless, and wanted to do something more for both himself and the people around him. He became a teacher, and I have to this day, in my mind, the image that old Carl gave me of that teacher kneeling beside a student's desk. The student has on a blue jumper and her eyes are large, dark and uncertain. The teacher is explaining a poem about a traveler who is forced to choose between two roads that fork in a yellow wood. Later in the story, that student overcomes great family problems and goes on to become a wonderful physician. She carries a copy of the poem with her everywhere, but of course she doesn't need it, because it is forever in her head. The image of that student is doubly clear for me because it came true.

After I was grown, I went back to the village when I could. I always tried to visit our storyteller or take in one of the afternoon sessions at the tavern. It was on one of those occasions that I last saw Carl. There were five of us, and later we would swear, to a man, that what we experienced was true. The story that day was of a school of salmon, glistening and rose colored. The fish had finished their time in the big waters and were working their way back to their spawning grounds. The wonderful sense of urgency was growing, and the salmon knew anticipation in every ounce of their beings. The water shallowed, and then became colder near the mouth of a stream. Gleaming gravel littered the bottom. They were only a short distance up the stream when the salmon discovered that the waters had been dammed with large yellow rock. There was a panic among the fish. They leapt and gasped and darted. At that point in the story old Carl slowly stood and walked into the water. As he did so he was transformed into a magnificent silvery salmon. That salmon led his panicked friends around the dam and up the stream into the distance where tall white pines shaded the shores.

When we realized that the tale had come to an end, each of us began to look at the others. Carl was indeed gone. He had become one with his story. His warm pipe still sat on the side table.

Now, years later, I'm headed back to my former home. My old friend Eric called me this last week and told me he had a new story for me. A new story of my own.

Ride On, Cowboy

Daryll had always dreamed of being a cowboy. Now, here he was, standing in the doorway of a bar in the middle of Wyoming. At one end of the bar was a red-headed woman in a buckskin jacket. As his eyes adjusted to the dim light of the bar she looked halfway promising. There were three men who looked like real cowboys sitting at the only occupied table. Behind him the sun beat mercilessly on barren ground and scraggly sagebrush. Ahead, he was certain, lay adventure. He entered.

Daryll's brand new Wranglers made a scuffing noise as he walked. The sweat pooled under his bright red bandana. He hesitated as he approached the bar. Would a real cowboy ask for a couple of shots of whiskey to start? He glanced at the table. The three men stared back. They were all drinking draft beer. He was relieved, because he wasn't quite sure if he could drink straight whiskey.

"Whatever you have on draft," Daryll said in his deepest voice. He pulled himself up on a barstool and sighed. He'd only walked from the parking lot, but his new boots hurt like hell. He decided that when no one was looking, he'd pour some beer into each of them to quench the fire and hopefully speed the break-in process.

"That'll be a buck," the bartender snapped as he placed the glass down on the bar.

Daryll reached for his wallet. "No problem, pardner," he said as he put a ten down in front of him. The bartender gave him a look of suspicion and padded off to get his change. When the barman returned, Daryll deepened his voice again and said, "I'll have another." The bartender looked at him quizzically and took the empty glass. Under the bar Daryll rolled his ankles, but stopped when he heard his boots slosh.

While sipping his third beer, Daryll finally dared to look at the woman down the bar from him. She looked back and smiled. She was older than he had thought on his initial impression.

On his fourth beer, he looked again. She looked back and winked. She apparently found him amusing. He started having fantasies about courting with Miss Polly, the kind-hearted saloon girl.

Two men walked in and went over to the table where the three cowboys still sat. Daryll heard them talking quietly, then they all laughed. A minute later one sat down on each side of him. Each ordered two shots of whiskey. After the bartender poured the four shots the man on the left pushed one in front of Daryll and said, "What outfit ya with, pard?"

Daryll was both flustered and flattered. He thought quickly. "Lazy G, down in Amarillo." His voice squeaked a little on the o.

"Lazy G, huh? Never heard of it, but I'll drink to it." The cowboy held up his shot in a toast, and Daryll had no choice but to do the same. He swallowed and felt his eyes cross as it burned all the way to his beer soaked toes.

"Sheeit!" exclaimed one of the cowboys at the table. "That dude wouldn't know one end of a cow from the other."

Daryll sucked in a long breath. "Do so!" he retorted. Whiskey, he was discovering, made him uncommonly brave.

"So, pardner," said another of the table crew, "how many teats on a cow?"

"Five," Daryll guessed, closing his eyes and trying to imagine what he'd never seen before.

Everyone broke out in laughter, but no one offered another number.

"Don't you pay them no never mind," said the cowboy on his right. He pushed a shot in Daryll's direction. "So, what kind of horse you ride?"

"Palomino," Daryll said remembering all of the Roy Rogers re-runs he'd watched as a kid.

"To palominos!" the cowboy saluted.

Daryll touched glasses and tipped his head back. This time it burned only to his knees, but he was aware that it took longer to uncross his eyes.

"You been ridin' long?" asked one of the cowboys from the table.

"Born in a saddle," Daryll replied. His head was beginning to swim.

"You use an English saddle then, must be."

Daryll had no idea what they were talking about, but in high school he'd used English Leather cologne, and he imagined an English leather saddle must be manly. "Doesn't everyone?" he snorted.

Everyone laughed.

"You and that palomino been together long enough so you both been gelded, I imagine," another of the cowboys yelled.

"Generally happens that way when you ride English," offered another.

Everyone chuckled.

"You ride in on that Town and Country out in the parking lot?" queried one of the table cowboys.

Daryll choked.

One of cowboy's partners commented, "Never knew a cowboy who drove a mini-van."

"Sheeit! Must be a chick magnet," another offered. They laughed.

"Ohio plates. That's a long ways from Amarillo. S'pose he's on a road trip looking for a new palamino?"

"Woman more likely. You only wear boots like that if you're looking for women."

"Carlene, you judge a man by the size of his boots?" one of the men yelled over to the woman at the bar.

"Up yours, Bob! It's a wonder you can even find your boots or anything else. Take both hands, does it?"

Bob blushed, and everyone laughed.

"Don't pay them no attention," said the cowboy on the left. "Mel, bring us another round of whiskies."

"I'll get these," said Daryll magnanimously.

"Make 'em doubles," grinned the cowboy on the right. "And let's have two apiece."

When the drinks had been poured, the cowboy on the left lifted his glass to the woman at the end of the bar and said, "To wild, wild women!"

She watched the three men down their shots. Daryll sagged on his stool. His ears were ringing. By now his legs had gone numb and it only burned to his navel.

"You go to hell, Ray!" the woman shouted back to the cowboy on the left.

"Give Ray a break, Carlene. You know he still loves you."

Everyone laughed. Even Carlene. It was another inside joke, Daryll figured.

"You ever had yourself a woman, pardner?" one of the cowboys at the table asked Daryll.

Daryll started to answer, but the effort left him so weak he slid off the stool and onto the floor. The best he could do in reply was grin. Soon the five ranch hands were gathered around him whispering conspiratorially. He only heard bits and pieces of the conversation. "Rode hard and put away wet," he heard one say. "Yeah, like it stopped you from tryin'," he heard another say. They kept whispering around him. "...road kill..." "She'll kill him." "...dogfight." "...his wallet..." "...up a dry gully...."

The one called Ray slapped Daryll awake. "How much money you got on you?"

Daryll blinked. "About forty bucks, I guess." He knew he shouldn't have told them. It was Jack Daniels speaking.

"We've got a proposition for you, pardner." another said. We're gonna give you a chance to double your money. We'll bet you forty bucks that you can't pick up Carlene down there and go home with her."

"Fine lookin' man like you shouldn't have no trouble. Carlene's the easiest woman this side of Green River."

Daryll smelled a set-up, but it was five to one. He still had the presence of mind to ask, "Bartender hold the money?"

"Sure thing."

"Can I sleep on it first?"

"Naw, we gotta get back to work. We'll give you an hour." One of the cowboys picked Daryll up and tossed him back onto his barstool as easily as if he were just another bale of hay.

Daryll shook his head, looked down the bar at Carlene, and tried to focus. He wondered if his eyes were permanently crossed. "Now she's got a twin sister. There's two of them! Do I have to pick 'em both up?"

"Your choice. Two women in the sack for the price of one, though...that's hard to pass up."

They all laughed, even Daryll. He reached for his wallet. He figured he was gonna be out this money one way or another, he might as well take a shot. "You all have got to keep quiet and stay out of it," Daryll mumbled.

"Sure, no problem."

"Promise?"

"Code of the West," one replied and held his hat over his heart. The cowboys put their money up and retreated to a corner table.

"I wonder if she's got a gun," he heard one mumble as he walked past.

When Daryll finally looked up, the bartender was standing expectantly in front of him. "You got any coffee?" Daryll asked.

The bartender shook his head to the negative.

"Tomato juice?"

A small can appeared before him. He tossed it down and asked for another. He had to pull himself together. What sort of a pick-up line would a cowboy use? "Wanna see my pistols, Baby?" "Ma'am, that's a nice pair of armadillos you've got in that gunny sack you're wearin'." In truth, he was afraid it would be more like, "I think I'm going to throw up. Could you help me outside?"

Minutes dragged by. He had to pull himself together. Finally he pushed himself away from the bar, got off his bar stool, and began to slosh his way toward the woman at the end of the bar. Visions of High Noon dogged the back of his mind. It was showdown time. He reached his destination. He didn't want to die.

"If I sit down here you won't shoot me will you?" His voice had an edge of whine.

"No promises." She appraised him out of the corners of her eyes.

Daryll sat silently and thought about her response. Minutes passed. She wasn't going to make it easy.

"My name's Daryll," he faltered.

"That your real name, or is it like all that cowboy shit you been flingin' around?"

"It's my real name. So the cowboy stuff was that obvious?"

"Big as the butt on a mule."

"Damn. All my life I've dreamed of being a cowboy. I thought maybe for a few minutes I'd try to let it happen. Guess I'd better just go back to being an accountant."

"As a cowboy, your days are numbered—but I guess you could say that as an accountant, too." She smiled at her joke and her face softened. Daryll suddenly knew he was in love.

"Are you a cowgirl?" It was a dumb question, and he knew it.

"You could say that, but it's kind of a condescending, sexist way to put it."

"Oh, I didn't mean it that way! Please, I'm in awe of the whole idea. I think I'm probably afraid of horses; I've never been much closer to a cow than a glass of milk and a hamburger, and the 'Wild West' is this romantic notion I've had since I was about four years old."

"Ain't nothin' romantic about bein' a cowboy. They mostly work their tails off; they generally smell like horse manure and sweat; most have the manners of a jackass, and damned few of them has the brains god gave a fence post."

"So women don't like 'em? I always thought...."

"Oh, some of 'em can be all right if a girls been drinkin', been gettin' high on country music, and is lookin' for a roll in the hay. They're no damned good if a person wants a commitment or an intelligent conversation that goes beyond the relative merits of different styles of barbed wire."

A dim light bulb of the honest type went off in Daryll's fuzzy brain. He decided to lay his cowboy cards on the table. "Those fellas over there at the table, I think they got me drunk and want to take my money. I'm sorry I got involved...got you involved...but they bet me I couldn't pick you up and get you to take me home. I apologize, and will just leave you in peace."

"They did that, did they? And that big one called Bob was in on it?"

"Yeah, they all were, I think."

"Bob's my brother. Let's teach them a lesson. Can you walk?"

"Maybe if I take these boots off first."

She gave him a funny look. "They still full of beer?"

"I think so. You saw? They hurt like hell, and I was desperate."

A few minutes later they had their arms around each other and were headed toward the door. Daryll imagined he was in heaven until he heard Carlene yell at the men in the corner.

"Bob, you sorry sonofabitch, you can just kiss your money goodbye. I'm taking this tenderfoot home with me right now."

Bob stood up looking mean and angry. Daryll hoped Carlene had that gun. Then Bob slapped the one named Ray on the back, smiled, and said, "You win some, you lose some. Mister, you can just take the money." He walked to the bar and took the stack of bills from the bartender. He strode over and handed it to Carlene, who took forty dollars off the top and handed it to Daryll. She pocketed the rest.

“This guy can't drive, Carlene. C'mon, boys, let’s get him to that mini-van and tuck him in back where he can sleep it off."

The cowboys picked Daryll up and carried him out to the parking lot. They laughed and slapped him on the back, and Carlene gave him a kiss on the cheek before they tossed him in the back beside his suitcase. He was glad the stow-and-go seats were down. He was asleep almost before they slammed the tailgate shut.

It was dark when Daryll awoke. A neon Coors sign in the window of the bar was the only sign of life. He felt in his pockets. His money and wallet were still there. He got out and walked around the van. The sharp gravel made walking in his stocking feet painful. There was something wrong. He shook his aching head and looked more closely through the dark. They had let the air out of all of his tires. His boots were on the hood. He hobbled to them and saw that they were holding down a note. He held the paper up to the moonlight and read in large, elementary script: *Get a horse!*

The Growl of the Bullet

"I give up! Please, don't let him bite me!"

The strange voice woke Richard from a deep sleep. He blinked several times in the darkness of the bedroom. There was a deep grrrrr from behind him, and in the opposite direction, from over by the darkened wall across the room, the voice came again.

"Call off your dog. Please! I give up!"

Richard shook his head slowly, trying desperately to pull his thoughts together.

Grrrrrr.

Suddenly the picture started to come clear. He lay still for a moment. There was another whimper from the far wall, followed by another grrrrrr from behind him. Seconds later he slipped quietly out of bed. Another growl emanated from the rear. He carefully and quietly moved toward the voice. *Please, don't let Kate wake up until this is over*, he thought. He could just see the form in the light from the digital clock.

"Turn around and face the wall," Richard commanded in a low, threatening tone. The command was punctuated by another, louder growl. He heard the man suck in a deep breath and saw him slowly turn around.

"If you've got any sort of weapon, drop it now!" Richard hissed in quiet but unmistakably certain tones. Another growl left no doubt about the threat implied in the command. There was a thunk as something hit the floor. Richard began to sweat; the warm beads rolled down his forehead, and he felt his armpits become damp and hot.

Grrrrrrrrrr.

"Stay, Bullet. Good boy!"

Richard picked up the shoes that were lying beside the bed and stripped the laces from them with quick tugs. There was another growl, this one even more menacing than the last. "Stay!" *Please, don't let Kate wake up.* "All right, fella, put your hands behind your back slowly. Don't even think of turning around or Bullet's going to have his breakfast early."

Richard moved cautiously back to the intruder. There were more growls as he crossed the room. "Get those hands behind your back, and other than that don't even think about moving, mister."

Grrrrrrrrrrrrr!

Roughly he knotted the shoelaces around the man's wrists. They were big wrists. The three hole shoelaces seemed somehow inadequate. Richard was suddenly aware that the perspiration had started to cool in his armpits, and he began to shake. Another growl.

"Bullet! I said stay!"

He tiptoed back to the bedside and picked his robe up from the dresser. Carefully he pulled the belt out of the loops and then returned to the man. The regular growling echoed in the otherwise silent room.

"Put your ankles together and lean up against the wall." Richard pushed the man as roughly as he could and heard the dull thud as the man's head contacted the wallpaper. The man started to protest, but a growl from across the room quickly silenced him. Richard wrapped the terrycloth belt around the man's ankles and knotted it three times. He tried vainly to remember the knots he'd learned years ago as a scout. *Oh, well, three granny knots are worth a bowline any day,* he thought to himself.

The man squirmed as though he wanted to turn around, but Richard stopped him with one sharp command. "Bullet!"

The man whimpered.

From across the room there was a rustling and the growling stopped. The stranger sagged visibly. Richard allowed himself to relax a tiny bit, but he was not at all certain about either the shoelaces or the knots in the belt from his robe. He decided he needed a club, but he couldn't think of anything in the bedroom that might serve. Then he thought of the weapon the man had dropped. A new growl, somewhat higher pitched, came from across the room.

"It's all right, boy. Just watch him." Richard dropped to his haunches and began to feel around. Soon his hand closed on the handle of a hunting knife. It felt strange, cool, and soft against his palm. He stood, his knees popping with the effort.

"You wanna explain yourself, fella?" He waved the knife at the back of the man in a useless effort at intimidation.

"I didn't think there was anyone home. I just wanted to take a couple of things, you know, to make a buck or two. I wasn't going for much. Then your dog...."

"That dog was purchased from a pound after the police found him too difficult to work with." Richard's voice was returning to a normal volume and timbre. "I'm going to go in that next room and call the police now. I would suggest you not make a move. I'm going to give the command for Bullet to stay on guard, but if you so much as blink an eye he'll have your throat out in less time than it takes to switch TV channels with a remote."

"Don't leave me! Take me in there with you. I hate dogs. I can't stand it!" the thief begged. It was a strained, immature man's voice. It was cut off as a deep, undulating growl filled the dark.

"All right, but you do exactly as I tell you or you're dog meat. Bullet, stay! Mister, I think you can hop out into the other room. Once you're through that door I want you to lie down and bury your face in the carpet. Don't even open your eyes. I'm going to turn on the light and make that call. You even breathe funny before the police get here, and you're a dead man. Did I mention, I don't have much use for thieves?" Richard was surprised at how much he was enjoying the situation now. He'd been robbed once before, years ago, and this was beginning to seem a nice turn of events.

The regular growling continued as they moved to the other room. The man hopped noisily, and Richard's thoughts turned to his wife. *Please, don't let Kate wake up, not yet!*

He punched in the number. A deep grrrrrr echoed from the next room, and Richard basked in the comfort its protection made him feel. It was, he thought, the first time he'd ever really appreciated Kate's snoring. And maybe they really should get a dog.

My Name is Gabriel

I wasn't sure how I arrived at the shop. I didn't feel groggy or hung over, only disoriented. I leaned heavily against a counter and surveyed my situation. The only illumination seemed to drift in waves through yellowed windows at the front of the store. In the dim light, specks of dust floated aimlessly. The air smelled of cinnamon and rose hips and fresh tobacco.

I wasn't alone. A tall man, whom I took to be the proprietor, was working quietly along the aisle in front of me. I studied him, looking for clues. The dark skin and large, hooked nose led me at first to surmise that he was middle-Eastern, but a second impression of his face revealed an oriental inscrutability. He wore robes of a type I could not identify with certainty. They were dark blue and trimmed with gold.

The man walked up and down among the jars and boxes on the shelves, stopping occasionally to sniff or lift one to his ear. Some he shook lightly; some he turned carefully; and occasionally, after one of these examinations, he gently placed the container into a basket he carried over his left arm. After some minutes he glanced my way and smiled, but he said nothing. He continued to examine the bottles and boxes. As my eyes adjusted further, I noted that each container was of a different form and color. No two shapes or shades were exactly alike. As there were thousands, all arranged neatly on shelves constructed floor to ceiling, this discovery astonished me.

After a period, I resolved to engage the shopkeeper in conversation so that I might learn more about my situation. I took a deep breath and stood. The room, I noticed, was now tinged with the odor of oranges and sandalwood. I maneuvered to the man's side. I had not realized before how tall he was. He glanced my way and then continued his work. As he did so, he began to speak.

"We must turn them occasionally. They lose depth and definition if they rest too long in one position. Sometimes they resist, but if we let them become flat, it becomes very difficult for them later. One-sidedness does not lend itself to growth; as the light inevitably surrounds them on all sides, they need to be able to utilize it in the most efficient ways."

He sniffed lightly at a golden brown bottle and slipped it into the basket. "When they first show signs of becoming stale, they must be recycled."

"Are they all different?" I asked. I realized as I spoke that I didn't have any idea what it was that I was asking after. I had no clue as to the contents of the bottles and tins. I peered more closely, and it was only in that instant before he answered that I realized that each container had its own label, and that the language and lettering seemed different from one to another.

"Oh, yes," the man chuckled, "they are all different here. That will not always be the case, but these are relatively young yet."

I fell silent again and watched as he continued down the aisle. Once in a while he clucked his tongue as he peered into a container. Occasionally he smiled and moved a jar from one shelf to another. Scents of olive and oregano stopped me for a moment, and the man moved on ahead. As he moved away, I tried to look at him more critically. I explored the veins of his hands, the large knuckles, the folds of skin at his neck, his lined face, the dark beard, the stoop of his shoulders. Still I could not guess his age. My curiosity aroused, I hurried back to his side.

"May I ask your name?"

"You may ask anything you like. My name is Gabriel," he responded without taking his eyes from his work.

I waited a moment before speaking again. "I don't know how I got here, or even where I am."

"Ahh, does that concern you?" His robes rustled quietly as he took a coppery tin from his basket and set it lightly on a top shelf.

"I think so. I'm not sure. I don't think I'm as concerned as I am curious, and that puzzles me a bit, too. There is so much I don't think I understand."

We reached the end of the aisle, and I saw there a number of jars and tins on a broad countertop. Some were opened, some were not. Gabriel reached over and lifted a dark green bottle from among the others. He lifted the stopper and the smell of pine erupted around me. It is a smell I have always loved.

"Mmmm. I like that!" A pleasantly cool breeze brushed my face. "I grew up in the mountains." In my mind I remember at that moment hearing the rush of a trout stream as it churned and frothed its course through glistening boulders. I let my imagination run for a moment, and then returned to the conversation. “What is it that you keep in these bottles?”

“You haven’t guessed?” He reached over and picked me up in his hand. It was the first time I realized I had no body. I was not surprised or frightened somehow, just more aware than I thought I had ever been. “Each of these bottles contains a soul. They just rest here for awhile. Being a soul can be hard work, and they need time off now and again. You do, too. Enjoy!” He carefully slipped me into the bottle and slid the stopper into the opening. The sound of it gliding into place was that of a breeze in the top of white pines.

The Time of Dry Water

It happens, though thankfully it only happens once or twice ev'ry hundred years. Happened to me, it did. It was nigh onto fifty years ago. I got caught in a time of dry water. I was herdin' cattle at the time. We was in the badlands of eastern Montana—worked for the Rocking J. First noticed it when we were camped on a small lake. Shoulda been ideal, but it weren't no good. The water got so dry it took six gallons of it stuffed down tight to make a cup of coffee. You could fish all day with jest one worm, 'cause the water was so dry the worm'd never drown. Fishin' weren't worth the time, anyhow, cause the fish was jest wasted away to scales and bones.

Now I've always had a very strict policy of takin' a bath on the first Sunday of the month, whither I need it or not. It's a policy has gotten me in bad with some of the rest of the boys, 'cause they think it makes me kinda uppity. There's some truth to it, but I can't change my good upbringin'. For a time, though, all that was put behind. Me and the boys took to takin' baths an' swimmin' two or three times a week, 'cause we'd jest jump in and come up more dusty 'n before, an' nobody'd be the wiser for it.

Now dry water times can be real serious when they hit. There's always someone who's willin' ta take advantage of the situation. I remember there was one fella, Vernon Suckoluvich was his name, made a fortune drillin' wells at the time. Seems that with the dry water, nobody could tell a dry hole from a wet one. So old Vernon jest drilled hole after hole, and he raved and ranted and preached about how sweet an' clear the water in each of them holes was, 'til finally folks believed him. He had more business than he could keep up with. When times got better, people started to catch on and demand their money back. That Vernon, he wasn't no dummy; he high-tailed it outa there. Last I heard he was one a them televangelists in California or somewhere like that.

The Potluck

Marv King looked again at the article in the Golden Years Retirement Community newsletter. It was a reminder that Tuesday evening would be the regular potluck dinner followed by as many tables of cards as could be arranged. It had been the schedule for years, though last year Marv had skipped the meals altogether. When Betty was alive, she had always done the cooking and they had attended regularly. After she died, Marv didn't have much appetite.

The January sun felt cool as Marv headed in to town. He dreaded grocery shopping, but, if he wanted a good meal and some euchre, it was a necessary evil. Saltines, canned tomato soup, six TV dinners, a bunch of bananas and a package of hotdogs—his usual items—didn't even cover the bottom of the grocery cart. He wandered the aisles looking for inspiration. People would not be impressed if he took a TV dinner to a potluck, even if he dumped it onto one of his own plates. Most of the folks were polite and wouldn't say anything to his face, but he just knew that there would be a couple of old ladies who couldn't contain themselves and would make some sort of nasty remarks. He wasn't about to let them get started.

The end of the bread aisle opened out into the deli, and there, looking at the brightly displayed salads, Marv had his first inspiration. He could cook, he told himself. He just needed a starting place. Betty had often just added a little something to make a recipe her own. He'd watched her do it hundreds of times over the years. He could handle that. He ordered two pounds of German potato salad.

That evening Marv proudly unveiled his dish. It was beautiful. Betty had always said that presentation was the most important part of cooking. The potato salad now rested regally in a Sterling silver serving dish. Marv had sliced a banana and stirred it in, then topped the dish with a bit of brown sugar and a colorful sprinkling of chili powder he'd found in the cupboard.

Later, several of the widow women had complemented his cooking, raving particularly about his presentation. Three even asked for the recipe, though he shyly demurred. That night his luck at cards was slightly better than average.

When the next Tuesday arrived, Marv met it with only slightly less trepidation. He'd placed saltines, hot dogs, tomato soup and six TV dinners in his cart before a glimmer of inspiration came. He tossed a couple of cans of VanCamp's baked beans in the cart and headed for the door. That evening Marv gently placed a lovely carnival glass bowl on the serving table. In it was a stunning presentation of baked beans to which he'd added a cup of brown sugar and the half a can of sliced black olives he'd found in the back of the refrigerator. The widow women raved! One even asked him what cooking school he'd attended. He took second place in the euchre tournament.

Buoyed by his growing reputation, Marv approached the grocery store with more confidence the next Tuesday. Two hours later, his cart holding only a box of saltines, canned tomato soup, six TV dinners, a bunch of bananas and a package of hotdogs, Marv found himself wandering the aisles aimlessly waiting for a gentle nudge of inspiration. Both his new confidence and his patience had dissipated into nothingness by the time he witnessed a little girl throwing a tantrum on the floor because her mother wouldn't buy her a box of Wonder Woman Sugar Jets. He took a box, smiled at the little girl, and put it in his cart just out of spite. Now, he reasoned, all he needed was to find something with which to mix his Sugar Jets. He found his answer in the pickle section. That evening he served his contribution in a lovely antique bowl with a gold rim. The dish was topped with a sprinkling of brown sugar and surrounded by flowers he'd trimmed from the median at the entrance to the park. The cards weren't so good, but the widow women had gone wild.

His standing as an emerging chef on the line, Marv considered buying a cookbook on his next trip to the store. He thumbed through a book that had the word *Easy* splattered across the front with a big yellow star. Fourteen ninety-five seemed a bit much, and besides, he didn't understand all of the abbreviations. He abandoned the book section and went to add saltines to his cart. Soon tomato soup, hotdogs, six TV dinners and two cans of tuna followed. You could add tuna to anything, Marv reasoned. He turned back to the deli, and this time inspiration took the form of coleslaw. It was a lot of work, but when Marv presented his designer tray of saltines, each covered with a layer of the tuna-coleslaw-with just a dash of brown sugar mix, the widows went gaga. Cooking was a triumph. He broke even at cards.

A reputation is a double edged sword. Marv was nearly panicked as he entered the Piggly Wiggly. Saltines, canned tomato soup, six TV dinners, a bunch of bananas, hotdogs, and a package of toilet paper later he was still panicked. He added a bag of brown sugar. “What goes with anything?” he asked himself. A still, small voice from deep inside answered *ketchup*. He sped down the aisle and threw two bottles into his basket.

The widows raved when they saw his banana slices in ketchup and brown sugar. He served them in a chafing dish adorned with two blue mermaids. He was counting on presentation to win the day. Guy Connors, however, took him aside.

“Marv, I know what you’re going through. It happened to me after Anna passed. I saw it happen to Toby Miller and Doug Brown, too. Remember when I brought that sauerkraut and salmon casserole to the potluck a few years back? The widow ladies fell all over themselves to give me compliments, but it was enough to gag a gopher. I’ve gotta tell ya, this ketchup dish of yours would bring all the terrorists to their knees if the Department of Defense was allowed to use it on ‘em. Only thing is, even George W. and his pal Dick would recognize it as torture. Use your head, Marv. Forget what these widow women are tellin’ you, and give the rest of us a break. A widow has about as much integrity as a hormone pumped teenage boy trying to make it with his latest girlfriend. If you’re honest, you know you’d rather eat cow cookies than ketchup-banana surprise.”

“Your right,” Marv admitted, “but what do I do for potlucks?”

“Same as the rest of us. Find one of those widow women who has a leaky faucet, a lawn to mow, some trim to paint. Exchange a little work to have them cover for you at the potluck. Be careful, through. They’re all dangerous! My advice is to go for the ones over ninety-five. Most of them have lost hope."

Even though Marv was a bit embarrassed, Guy's little talk had taken a load off of his mind—and stomach. On his way out he asked Leota Swanson, the oldest woman in the park, if she needed anything done around her trailer. She said, "No, Guy takes care of my chores." When he got home, Marv picked up the camp directory and started looking for the widow who was second oldest.

The Halo

Adjusting to Heaven had not been an easy thing for Ethyl. But, to tell the truth, adjusting to life on Earth hadn't been easy for her, either. Oh, to be sure, Ethyl thought Heaven a fine place and all; it was just that the strain of avoiding gossip and having to sneak a cigarette after lunch made her a bit edgy. Being an angel is a tedious affair if one has a high strung constitution.

There was one thing that Ethyl missed most of all—Thursday afternoons at The Cut 'n' Curl Salon. It was on those Thursdays that she would have her nails done and her hair done and she would catch up on the entire neighborhood and she would leave feeling like the world was in the palm of her hand. On the way home from having her Thursday makeover, Ethyl would exude an air of confidence no one could dare to question.

In Heaven, having one's nails done was viewed as a kind of extravagant luxury that was not condoned except in the very lowest corners, and Ethyl was clearly aware that she did not wish to be associated with those places. Nails were out. The hair, though—she couldn't give up doing the hair.

The silver shine after a shampoo caused her halo to reflect light in a way that she thought increased the impression of both sexiness and importance. The ego thing was quite possibly a sin, she knew, but she figured she had an eternity to work on it, so she indulged herself.

Time is not a relevant concept in Heaven, so who knows how long Ethyl continued her Thursday afternoon ritual of shampoo, conditioner, rinse, and curl. She always felt better for it, though she had the nagging feeling that some of those around her looked on with slightly raised angelbrows. "Judge not, lest ye be judged!" she would respond to them in her mind. Then she would turn and flutter away from them with just the slightest twitch of her hips.

The ritual went on until one day when Ethyl shampooed, conditioned, rinsed and curled, and forgot afterwards to pick up her halo from the edge of the Heavenly Pool. The Heavenly pool was a small, isolated lake with very soft water—which suited Ethyl just perfectly. It was breathtakingly beautiful, and it may have been the idyllic setting which brought about the lapse. As was her custom, Ethyl had wrapped her hair in a towel and started back to her quarters. When she remembered the halo, she was beside herself. It was like losing her keys to the store where she had worked—only worse. It was like leaving her MasterCard laying on the counter when she walked out of the department store—only worse. It was like forgetting her mother's birthday—only worse. It was like forgetting to change underwear for a whole week—only worse. Ethyl was an instant wreck.

She began to backtrack everywhere she had been. Her heart pounded nervously. She turned red whenever she saw someone she knew. She felt naked, exposed, unworthy, lost. It was just like eighth grade all over again. She was so nervous she even grew a large, red pimple right on the end of her nose.

"Nice turban! We don't see many of those here," she heard someone call as she scurried back to the pool. She turned and saw Emily Waxmire waving to her. Emily looked genuinely impressed, but Ethyl had known Emily since P.S. 47 and third grade. She doubted she could do anything to impress Emily after those years. Ethyl waved, smiled weakly and moved on. She was beginning to feel the old ulcer starting to kick up, and she hadn't known that feeling since Earth days. That thought gave her a headache.

There was no one at the Heavenly Pool when she arrived. That made her feel better. She searched, and the halo wasn't there. That made her feel worse. She sat down and began to cry. Dora Angstreth had always said there was nothing like a good cry to make a girl feel better—and Dora would know. She cried all the time. Ethyl had a good go at it this time, but it only made her feel red and bloated. A stranger walked up. Ethyl felt the muscles in her lower back tighten. She didn't want anyone in the world, much less in Heaven, to see her like this. She became aware of an ache in the back of her neck.

"Nice turban," the stranger said in a soft, friendly way. "We don't often see those around here."

"Thank you," murmured Ethyl, doing her best to look away while not coming across as being rude.

"Are you all right?" the stranger asked after what seemed to Ethyl to be an interminable silence.

There was something about his tone which made her open up. Suddenly the whole story came pouring out. He listened carefully, and then asked what she had done so far to try to find the missing halo. Ethyl thought she detected just a twitch of a smile at the corner of his mouth, and she became a little more guarded as she repeated the search step by step for him. He was a good listener, though, she finally decided as she spoke. She felt a bit of relief.

The stranger rocked back and forth on his heels and thought for a moment. Then, with a hint of a drawl in his voice, he suggested that they call out the Heavenly Hounds. "I remember one time when there was a lost harp up here, and they called out the hounds. Those boys found it in almost no time. Make a lotta noise, they do, but it might be worth a try. Besides, it'd be fun to watch 'em work again," the stranger chuckled.

Ethyl twitched. It was that old twitch on the left side of her face. She'd forgotten about it, but now, with the thought of baying hounds calling everyone to attention about her problem, it was back. She thanked the stranger for his suggestion and departed as quickly as she could. As she went along she began to imagine that she was sinking lower and lower. She could only assume what it meant for someone in Heaven to sink lower and lower, and her ideas only made her feel worse. Old country songs started to play themselves in her head—the kind of country songs that make a person feel more miserable than they really are. "Country songs," she thought, "I'm in worse shape than I imagined, and I'd imagined the worst." She had begun to hum "I'm So Lonesome I Could Cry" when she noticed a store with a large neon sign out front that said CHOCOLATE. "It always worked at home," she thought. She turned and went in.

"I never noticed this store here before," she said casually to the proprietor. She began to salivate as she looked over the magnificent variety of choices. "You have a wonderful selection!"

"We just opened," he replied. "People don't generally need to indulge themselves here in Heaven, but we had an intuition that someone might come along with a need."

Just then the door opened and in walked the stranger from the pool. Ethyl panicked. There was a trash can in the corner and she made a dive for it. "Oops, I dropped something in here!" she said just as her head reached the bottom. The little white lie echoed in the empty container. Hearing herself didn't make Ethyl feel any better.

"Who's the angel with her head in the can?" the stranger asked.

"I don't know," said the proprietor. "Why don't you ask her yourself?"

The stranger glided over and tapped Ethyl on the shoulder. It wasn't an easy thing to do, given the position she had assumed. The sinking feeling began again, and Ethyl knew there was no avoiding the inevitable. She pulled her head out of the can, leaving the towel behind. Then she turned to face the two men who were looking at her. She had thought they would laugh, but they both looked genuinely concerned instead—so much so that she almost felt better.

The proprietor spoke first. "May we be of any help, Ma'am? You seem to be a bit on edge."

Ethyl blushed. Then she sucked in a really deep breath. "I've misplaced my halo. I'm afraid I'm in real trouble if I don't find it. I don't want to cause a fuss, and I doubt you can help."

The store owner allowed a long, respectful pause before he replied. "Ma'am, you haven't misplaced your halo. You can't. Your halo becomes a part of your nature up here. It will always find you. As you grow in heavenly maturity, you'll find you can't even take it off anymore. In fact, it looks very nice on you right now."

Ethyl looked up. She reached up. It was there. It probably had been under the towel all along, she realized. She felt a bit sheepish. She closed her eyes. She became aware that her desire for chocolate had disappeared. She opened her eyes. The two men had gracefully disappeared as well.

Years later Emily Waxmire commented on how nice Ethyl's hair looked. Ethyl just smiled and thanked her. She hadn't done a thing with it in ages.

Uncle Jake

The asphalt of the parking lot shimmered with the mix of oil, rain, and fallen maple leaves. I found no cheer in its iridescence. My mood, like this gray Thursday morning, was full of dull sounds, drizzle, and deep depressions. I locked the car door and headed for the entrance to Mother Hubbard's. I had enjoyed huge breakfasts here as a youngster in the tow of my uncle, but all I wanted now was coffee. It was a quarter to seven, and I had been driving for over nine hours.

I glanced around and didn't recognize anyone. The crowd was mostly men in coveralls and flannel shirts. A few women were scattered about, more noticeable for their laughter than their attire. Several of the patrons glanced up, but none held my gaze. I felt very much the outsider in my suit and topcoat. There were only two empty tables. I chose the one near the back, close to the archway leading to the ladies' restroom. It struck me as the most anonymous.

The motif in the café was geese. From the worn appearances, I surmised it had been geese for twenty-five years, though I remembered chickens and roosters from when I was a boy. Now the limp, vinyl tablecloths portrayed families of geese waddling around their edges. The menu stood in a wire holder formed to look like a goose. A framed print on the wall showed the back of a boy with a stick herding geese down a dirt road. The chipped salt and pepper shakers were ceramic geese. A three foot tall goose with a golden egg stood amidst the philodendron on the room divider.

I had just become lost in the warmth of a mug of strong coffee when a man came over and pulled out a chair. He offered a calloused hand.

"I'd guess you're one of the Crane boys," he said.

"You'd be right. I'm Tim."

"The suit was a dead giveaway. I'm Elroy Birdahl. I was your uncle's neighbor to the north."

"I remember. You and Uncle Jake were like best friends, weren't you?"

"I think you could say that. I think I remember you, too, but you were only six or eight years old the last time I saw you. Spent one summer terrorizing the frogs and squirrels in the woods down by the creek, didn't you?"

"It was the best summer of my life." Images of soft grass, oak trees begging to be climbed, and moss covered rocks flooded back. After a few moments my gaze focused back on the weathered old farmer across the table from me. Conversations overheard and my uncle's off-hand comments had created a lasting impression of Elroy Birdahl in my mind. He had hitched his life on his back and pulled it through the days like a draft horse with a single bottom plow. I could sense that power as he sat across the table from me. He wasn't fidgety or quick with his movements, but he radiated energy. Now he was waiting for me to say something more.

"I know I should thank you for all you did for Uncle Jake and Aunt Helen. Will you be at the memorial service this afternoon?"

Elroy Birdahl did not answer right away. "No need for thanks," he began. "I won't be at the service. Jake and I already said our piece to each other while he was alive. Jake and me, we talked a lot over the years. A service is a necessary thing, I guess, but there'll be some things said and goin' on this afternoon neither he nor I would quite approve of. I'm better just stayin' away, thank you."

"Would you mind my asking what things?"

Elroy dabbed a napkin at a spot on the table. "Would you mind my answer?"

"Would Jake?"

"No. His thoughts and mine sort of came together during time. He'd tell ya the same."

"Then I'd like to hear."

"Part of it you have to feel; you can't just hear it and understand. It starts with the land. You ever smell anything so good as a fresh plowed field? After plowin', Jake and me, sometimes we'd just stand together and inhale that smell. Add a jar of cold water and a bit of spring breeze to that and you just know life is good.

"It was partly those times that led us to the conclusion that the Earth has a soul. We both recognized that, though I think Jake said it first. Then some time back I ran across an article in a magazine where this scientist was explaining that everything moves. Even the tiniest, tiniest particles are in motion, and it turns out all creation is nothing but movement—wave lengths. Everything around us, even us, we're clusters of wave lengths. That's what sound is, too—*harmonics* was one word that scientist used. It's all related.

"Jake, he jumped on the idea of harmonics, Tim. He loved music. You know that. Me, I couldn't carry a tune in a washtub, but Jake, he could play anything on that harmonica.

I remember the afternoon I showed him that article. He took off on a rip-tear! He was pacin' back and forth. We were down in that woods by the stream between our places—where you used to go—and he got so excited.... 'So all creation is music,' he says. 'It's like we're all tied together with music. Like that rock has the time signature; every fish has its tune; those oaks are harmonies. We're all part of the same symphony. We're all like notes!'"

Elroy swirled his coffee and stared into his cup. "Well, he went on like that, and one idea led to another. We talked about bein' in harmony for years. Oh, I know other people use those same words, but for Jake and me it was somehow bigger. We spent a lot of good evenings together, and concluded that at some level everything is related. My soul and your soul are part of the Earth soul. The Earth soul is part of the solar system soul; the solar system soul is part of the galaxy soul; the galaxy soul is a part of the universe soul; the universe is part of the All-Soul. God is the All-Soul, and as Jake would say, 'My God! What music! The final resonance.'"

Elroy had become animated as he spoke, but now he relaxed back into his chair. We were both quiet until the waitress came and refilled our cups.

"Thanks," I said. I had been caught up in his excitement. "I think that memorial service is going to be anticlimactic now. Still, I'm not quite sure I understand yet why you said there'd be parts you and Jake wouldn't approve of."

I watched as Elroy worked to carefully form his words. "Jake and me, we both kind of stopped goin' to church so much, though neither of our wives approved. It just seemed that church kept puttin' barriers between people, makin' exclusions and drawin' boundries. When you can feel and smell and see that the Earth has a soul, and every part of creation here is a piece of that, hearin' about pearly gates and how only those that toe the party line are goin' to have stars in their crowns just doesn't quite satisfy. It's like they cut most of the human race and the biggest part of creation out of God's party. It's just too exclusive. Jake and I figured God loves it all. Bein' close to nature does that. You know, Jake and me used to worry about you and city folks who either left or never knew the land. We were always afraid you'd miss the connection."

"You were probably right, but I think you just helped me make that connection again. I'm hardly a hemidemisemiquaver, but I'm beginning to tune in."

"What?"

"Sorry. A sixty-fourth note. I don't know how I remembered that word. I think a hemidemisemiquaver is the littlest note in music."

Elroy digested that for a minute, then he slowly pushed back from the table and stood up. Before leaving he held out his hand and grinned. "Rock on," he said.

Damn the Cat

People sometimes say that we resemble our pets. Mildred Hoyle would have said that's nonsense. She was eighty-six, long widowed, independent, and feisty. For one thing, her cat would never be a widow. He was a yellow tiger, a tom, who liked to roam. Like many cats, he was loving when he wanted to be, but aloof and arrogant the rest of the time. Mostly he was aloof and arrogant. Mildred saw herself as neither aloof nor arrogant. She was practical, however, and that was why she had named the cat Damn. Her neighbors often heard her out in the yard calling, "Damn! Damn! Damn!" Mildred had to smile as she called. She wasn't fond of her neighbors, so she saw her cat calling as doing a kind of double duty.

Mildred loved her cat in the way that women can love an abusive husband or a delinquent child. She accepted their relationship in pragmatic fashion. She figured that at age eighty-six she needed something to piss her off occasionally just to keep her going. She loved the cat, and Damn did a fine job of keeping her going.

About six months ago Damn disappeared after Mildred took him out with her to check the mail on a Tuesday. By that Friday Mildred began to worry just a little. Disappearance was totally in character for Damn, but he loved regular meals enough so that he was seldom gone more than three days at a time. Monday at mail time Mildred began to worry in earnest. Worry probably is not the accurate word. In the back of Mildred's mind there was also that hope of relief that comes when a divorce is finally over or a cyst is removed from your neck. That sense of relief was tempered by a certain sense of loneliness, however. Mildred, in her way, loved that cat.

On Wednesday the cat crawled back. More accurately stated, most of the cat crawled back. Damn was missing his two back legs. He was also missing the arrogant aloofness he had had when he departed. Now he needed love. That's probably why Mildred called her friend, Mary Foy, to take them to the vet's.

The vet told them that it would take at least six hundred and fifty dollars worth of surgery and antibiotics to save the cat's life. Damn had been a stray held at the Royce County Shelter when Mildred adopted him. She'd paid nine dollars ransom to get him out of his cage. She'd thought of him basically as a free cat. She liked that thought. *What in the hell good is a two legged cat?* she mused now. Kind-hearted Mary, on the other hand, had big tears in her eyes.

The vet looked at her. "It'll be forty dollars if you just want to have him euthanized." Mary broke down altogether and started sobbing. Damn put on his most pleading and pitiful face and looked at Mildred. *Forty dollars for a free cat? With forty dollars I could piddle away a whole day at the casino!* she reflected. Damn rolled over on his back to have his belly scratched. Mildred reached out automatically and scratched it. *Six hundred and fifty dollars?* This was her only baby, after all, and now she felt some responsibility for having dragged her friend Mary into the mix. Mildred muttered, "Damn, Damn, Damn!" and opted for the surgery.

Damn was nothing if not pitiful when he came home a few days later. He pulled himself around on his two front legs and yowled. It was a blood curdling yowl. It was a yowl that on the second day caused the neighbors to stop a passing police cruiser and urge the two policemen to make an arrest because someone or something was certainly being tortured. After the police left, Mildred got out the Scotch and started to think. Something had to be done. Her nerves were on edge. Damn's nerves weren't much better. She needed to help that poor cat.

A couple of stiff drinks and Mildred felt better. She got up and went to the closet for a sweater. In the process she absently started pawing through the box of toys she kept for visiting kids. An old metal Slinky caught her eye. Aha! she thought, and she snatched it up and went to look for the cat. It wasn't easy getting a slinky over the cat's bandaged butt, but Mildred was patient. She would help that cat no matter what! When the screeching stopped, she took Damn to the top of the basement stairs. It would be easier down the road, she reasoned, if he got a feel for the natural motion of a Slinky. He could work out the flatland later. She flipped him down the first stair. Head over Slinky he flipped step by step to the bottom, the sound of the slinky coiling on every other step, a sound like a cat yodel on each alternate contact. At the bottom, Damn lay panting for a moment, and then, like so many thrill riders before him, he retched. This was no mere hairball. This came from his soul. It was so bad that any time from that point on that Mildred so much as got the Slinky out of the closet, Damn started vomiting. Mildred went back to the drawing board. She was determined to give Damn new life.

Mildred was artistic in a crafty sort of way. One afternoon she was going through her craft supplies when, before long, using nothing more than Popsicle sticks, pipe cleaners, glue, paperclips, and rubber bands, she created what she deemed to be a fair set of prosthetic legs. Damn didn't totally trust Mildred any more, and he made a chase of it, but a cat with two legs was in the end no match for old Mildred. At first there was a problem with the legs just spreading out sideways from under Damn. Mildred solved that by putting marshmallows on the feet. That sort of worked until Damn discovered he liked marshmallows better than he liked walking with Popsicle stick legs. Mildred went back to the drawing board.

Saturday morning Mildred flipped on the television and sat down to think. There was nothing on but cartoons, yet she found the noise comforting. After a time she looked up absently during a commercial. It was in that moment that inspiration struck. She called Mary for a ride and said it was time to go shopping. Mary loves to shop.

The cat was behind the sofa when Mildred returned. He'd started spending a lot of time there. It was the safest place he knew. Mildred sat down opposite in her recliner and pulled a big box out of a shopping bag. "Damn, I have something for you. Come on out, Damn!" She opened the box and took out a wildly colored remote control car. Reaching back into the bag, she pulled out a package of bungee cords. "Damn kitty, kitty!"

It seemed to Mildred the perfect solution. Once Damn's rear was strapped into the car, she began experimenting with the controller. The car pushed him stumbling to his dish. Not bad. He ate a few bites. She backed him away, his claws unable to catch on the linoleum. She manipulated the joystick and brought the cat back to her chair. She scratched him behind the ears. She tossed the rubber mouse underhanded across the room. It was Damn's favorite toy. He was all attention now. "Let's see what this baby will do," Mildred said smiling. She jammed the joystick ahead as far as it would go. The car did a wheelie and headed across the room at amazing speed. There was a yowl and a crash and the sound of small pieces hitting all around the room. Apparently the cat was thrown clear of the car and he crawled immediately behind the couch. He stayed there for the next two days, growling and hissing whenever Mildred tried to approach him. It was not a problem. The car was totaled, and Mildred needed the time to return to the drawing board. The cat had become her mission. She would take care of that cat!

In the end Mildred called Mary again. The whole mess, Mildred reasoned, was at least partly old weepy Mary's fault. She should be a partner in the solution. Mary's husband Tom was a handyman and woodworker. When the ladies approached him with plans for a wheeled platform, he jumped at the chance to go to work. He even made improvements to the plan by creating a rotating axle and enlarging the wheels. The next day he held the cat while Mary attached him to the platform—Damn was still leery about letting Mildred near. The platform worked perfectly. After trying it out, Damn almost let Mildred pet him again.

The next day Mildred took Damn down the drive with her to fetch the mail. The platform was working, although Damn was a bit nervous on the down slope. Damn was with her when she opened the box, but by the time she shut it he was half way down the block. She last saw him when he cut across the Crampton's lawn and disappeared behind their house. Mildred walked down the block calling, but she didn't go far. She knew it was no use. He still liked to roam.

The cat never came back. Mildred hasn't totally decided if that is a good or bad thing, but if anyone asks about him, she still says, "He was a damn good cat!"

The Trial

The man sat next to his lawyer and looked down at the slowly swirling patterns in the composite table top in front of him. Several wireless monitors attached to slim patches on his skin gauged his every response, though the responses were not made public. A restless woman stared at the man through the glass which surrounded the Cubicle of the Accused. She felt nothing but anger and hatred. The loss of her husband and son had left her with no capacity for sympathy. When the face of Judge 461 came on the screen at the front of the room, the woman noticed that the defendant didn't move.

"All rise. This court is now in session, the honorable Judge 461 presiding. Please turn off and stow all electronic and protonic devices," a recorded voice commanded.

The woman watched as the lawyer nudged his client and the two stood in unison. The lips of the person on the screen began to move. The face was a composite picture created from thousands of photographs of citizens from around the country. In earlier times judgeship had been deemed too politically sensitive a position, and too dangerous, for any judge to be seen or known personally. Though those times were long past, it had been decided that the composite practice warranted continuance.

"Thomas Jordan Ferguson, inmate 47231E, you have been found guilty of two counts of murder in the second degree. Do you have anything to say before your sentence is passed?"

"I do, Your Honor. I am sorry. I am deeply sorry that my actions have caused so much hurt. I did not mean to take the lives of those two people. I didn't know them, and I bore them no malice. I ask the forgiveness of their family and friends. I have my own family and responsibilities, and I plead for leniency so that those innocent people might not also be hurt. I accept your judgment, and stand open to your will."

The man looked truly penitent, and the woman wished she could see the monitors.

"Your statement is duly noted. Also noted, however, is the fact that this is your third conviction for operating a vehicle while intoxicated. It is further noted that at the time of the homicides you were operating your vehicle while your license was suspended. Your wanton disregard for the rule of law and the safety of others has left this court with little room for leniency. Therefore, you are to be remanded to the Hall of Social Justice for a period of no less than two calendar years, but a date not to be reached until you have experienced the total impact of sorrow known to the family and friends of the deceased. Further, you are, upon release, to return to the Hall of Social Justice yearly for the next twenty years to undergo updates in the grief regimen as appropriate per the responses of the family and friends, or the average of the society in general, whichever is greater.

"The prisoner is now to be removed from the court. Those members of the family and friends of the deceased who wish to have their grief registered at this time may report to room 149 in the Hall of Statistical Equality. For your convenience, Grieving Cubicles are also available at all precinct stations. Records of this trial may be accessed under the code DMJ6923. Please use the same reference when recording grief."

The woman moved with her children, family and friends to exit the courtroom and cross the plaza to the Hall of Statistical Equality. It seemed odd to her that a pleasantly cool breeze should be blowing and that the sun should be shining brightly on this day. They strode woodenly across the artificial flagstone square. Once inside the hall she handed each of her children, a boy of ten and a girl of seven, a packet of recordings and set them in individual cubicles. The recordings contained movies of the family, particularly of the father and brother, the accident scene, the scents of their father and brother, the favorite music of the deceased, and messages designed to stimulate and help the children through the grieving process. After kissing each of the children and hooking them to the monitoring devices, she started their machines. The grief that they felt during the exercise would be recorded and measured against the baseline which had been established immediately following the accident. Her own grief at having to put the children through this process nearly incapacitated her. She moved to the next cubicle and placed her hand on the identification pad. She was aware that up and down the hall Doug's parents and friends had already entered other cubicles.

In the Hall of Social Justice the convicted Tom Ferguson was being dressed in a suit which was woven with wires and diodes and computer chips that would allow him to feel exactly the same mental and physical pain that was being felt by the friends and family of the deceased. Every nuance of their suffering would be his. His hand was placed on a device which activated and controlled the whole procedure.

"You have a minimum of two years during which you will have to take upon yourself the pain of those left behind. Additional pain has been added to the banks to simulate the lifetimes of loss which might have been felt by the two people you killed. You have complete control over how much of the cumulative pain you wish to experience at any time, so you have a degree of control over how long you will remain here. You should know that no one has survived the amount of cumulative recorded pain that is projected in less than 3.752 years. With extrapolations for continued pain as it is added by the sufferers during the years to come, the average time of incarceration for similar offenses is 7.36 years—provided you can endure the pain at an average level for someone of your age and background. The quickest a person has ever been released in similar cases is 4.38 years, but she was too damaged to return to society. One in three persons in your place opts to turn the dial up to the point where suicide by grief becomes the escape, but we understand that you have a family counting on your speedy return."

The custodian turned and walked away on rubber soled shoes. The man turned the dial to one. A wave of nausea and depression overwhelmed him. He was wracked to the point of nearly giving up, but he was a strong man and the thoughts of his family drove him on as he inched the dial towards two. He began to wretch uncontrollably and quickly turned the device back to .32. Tears rolled down his cheeks. For the near future he would have enough difficulty dealing with his own grief without adding to it from the storehouse built up by the family and friends of the victims.

Some years before, brain research had made it possible to quantitatively chart the effects of grief and bitterness by tracing the fingerprints of two trimino acids on the gray matter of the brain. The activities of those acids were rooted in depression, grief, and other negative physical and mental responses. The exact triggers could be identified by noting which areas of the brain they stimulated. Ferguson had read on-line the accounts and understood in laymen's terms how the system worked, but he had not been ready for the effects of its practical application. He understood in his first moment why recidivism from the justice system had dropped from sixty percent forty years earlier to just three percent at the current time. He also understood why the rates of inmate suicide had jumped forty-fold. He was not sure he could hold off that impulse for the average 4.38 year span he had been quoted.

During the first months, Ferguson struggled to bring up happy memories: memories of when he and his wife had courted passionately, memories of bringing their daughter home from the Birthing House, memories of playing ball with his son and listening to music. Each happy thought helped for a moment, but then it was shattered by the force of a crescendo of grief—his own and his victims. He came to understand that it was easier in the long run to maintain a constant level of emotional pain as opposed to the erratic ups and downs of trying to conjure pleasant thoughts.

In time he lost all desire for physical exercise, all desire to eat, think, and even to open his eyes. His wife and children were allowed to visit him once each month, and they were faithful in trying to bring him pleasant thoughts and raise his spirits, but those visits, too, afforded him grief. After a year and a half he began to refuse them. Two months later the officials began to feed him intravenously, as they often did with inmates in his circumstances.

In somewhat over a year, life began to take on a semblance of normalcy for the woman who had been wife and mother to the victims. The surviving children began to chafe against the schedule of going to the grieving chambers. The woman gave in to their wishes well before she entertained stopping her own visits. One day, seventeen months after the trial, she decided to access the case number for an update while she was in the grieving chamber. It was her right, by law, to know what was going on with the killer of her husband and son. She found that he had begun refusing the visits of his wife, and that he had stopped responding to anyone in the environment around him. He had stopped eating on his own and refused to exercise. There was a part of her which felt satisfaction in knowing that he was suffering now in the ways he had caused her and her family and friends to suffer. There was another voice within her, however, that wanted to call out to the man's wife and children to give them comfort. They, too, had suffered a terrific loss. Her update was accessed August 17, one week from the anniversary of her wedding. She was not yet ready to forgive Thomas Ferguson.

On the day of her anniversary, the woman sat in the grieving chamber and looked through her wedding album. It made her cry. She continued by looking through her albums of family pictures, then she began plugging in movies of family events and watching them on the holographic picture cube. For a little while she almost forgot that her husband and son were not right there with her. She carried on a conversation with them as though they were. When the movies stopped she felt emptiness in the pit of her stomach. Her mind ached.

When she finally stepped into the steamy air outside of the Hall of Statistical Equality, she was drained of almost every feeling. She was surprised to find that she had spent thirteen hours in her cubicle. She was exhausted, hungry, and confused. Not wanting to go immediately home, for a time she sat on a bench under the streetlights and watched vacantly as people walked by. She realized she wanted no more. She had had enough of grief. She felt no more need for retribution.

In the weeks that followed, the woman gave no thought to returning to the grieving chamber. When a friend, the friend who usually watched the children for her, asked about the omission from her routine, she was finally forced to evaluate her circumstances.

"I'm finished with that," she said finally.

"Are you over the loss, then?"

"No, but I guess I've reached a point where grief's no longer needed. There'll always be some sorrow, but I don't feel a need to deal with it in a conscious way anymore. And I don't feel any more need for retribution."

"What about your friends and the others in your husband's family? How do you think they feel? What are you going to say to them?"

"Most of them finished going to the Hall of Statistical Equality some time ago. The one or two who still go, do it in support of me, I think. I don't think I need to say anything to any of them. They can do as they feel best. That's that."

The new freedom was a wonderful thing. The woman began to find herself humming as she did her chores, rejoicing at the sunrise as she saw the children off to school, and chuckling at the joke section on the screen as she perused the daily news. Still, a small voice continued occasionally to haunt her. She sometimes envisioned the wife of Thomas Ferguson—still lost in a world of sorrow over which she had little control. She began to worry about his children.

Her concerns about Ferguson and his family began to recycle through her mind, and each time they did it was a reminder of everything past. She knew that she was not yet healed.

Eventually the woman called the lawyer to ask if there was something she might do to shorten the sentence of the man she had hated—the man who had crashed into her life with such violence.

"The law is very clear. Even if no one visits the grieving chambers, he must still work his way through the average amount of grief as computed by the Department of Statistical Equality. That's done for situations when someone causes harm to a person with no family or friends. They don't necessarily get off easier than anyone else."

"But I'm satisfied that he's gone through enough. Isn't there something I can do?"

"You said that he no longer receives visits?"

"That's what the record says."

"Let me see what I can do. I know the judge will say her hands are tied. I'm on pretty good terms with the warden. Would you want to visit if it could be arranged?"

"Can he be forced to see me?"

"I don't think so, but I'll see what the warden says."

There was no message from the lawyer during the rest of that week. The woman found herself more and more intrigued by the idea of seeing Ferguson face to face. She wondered how he had changed since the courtroom. Monday morning the lawyer contacted her. She found herself tense as she took the call.

"The warden says there is no way to force Ferguson to meet with you, and his depression is so deep that it's a foregone conclusion that he wouldn't do it anyway. The warden contacted the judge, however, and she's sympathetic. She says she's watched too many inmates simply waste away to the point where a second chance is not possible. Most come out aged by years and scores of years, even with a relatively light sentence. She said that she would—and the warden is to personally oversee the process—allow you one session for sending positive thoughts to Ferguson through the system of the grieving chambers. Is that acceptable to you?"

"Well, I guess so. But what's that going to do?"

"Hope is a powerful thing. If it comes from this direction it won't have the same backlash that's usually felt when a person tries to fight the system. Wednesday at four o'clock the warden will be waiting for you. Will that work for you?"

"Yes, yes, I guess so. But what will I say?"

"Your thoughts are your own. Just remember that hope is one of the most powerful forces known to man."

It was recorded in the files of Case DMJ6923 that the inmate requested solid food on the evening of Wednesday, November 24, 2145.

A Murder Casing

The cat was lapping at the pool of blood, his whiskers twitching in an odd up and down motion. Every muscle was tense, every sense on edge. He stopped frequently to survey his surroundings. It was easy pickings, but it had its toll.

One would think that living in a sausage factory would be the dream of every cat, but Murdock had a right to be nervous. Years ago he'd lost his tail and two toes in the grinder. He'd seen his mate and three kittens disappear down that same giant, roaring maw. Almost daily, the watchman, old Mr. Vanderhorst, would throw something at him in an effort to get him out of the building. At least three times a week he had to fight other cats that wandered in looking for the good life. After the last visit by state inspectors, he'd been both poisoned and shot at. There had been a number of attempts to trap him. The good life was not easy. In fact, he was reaching the age where the good life no longer seemed fun.

It was a troubling thought. If one is a cat, how does one retire gracefully from a prominent position? He needed a long-term plan. Most cats are capable only of planning in the short term. He needed a confederate—a wise confederate. An advisor. He decided to advertise. No dogs, rats, or mice need apply.

There were few responses, and the weeks slipped by. Then, on a particularly beautiful autumn day, a one-eyed cat wearing a turban showed up outside the main door of the factory and started calling his name, "Murdock! Meurdock! Meourdock!" The stranger would not allow himself to be ignored.

Murdock left through a back window and stole around to the front of the building.

"So, what's with all the caterwauling? What's the story, Mac?"

"You Murdock?"

"Yeah, what can I do for you?"

"The question is, 'what can I do for you?' I'm here in response to your ad."

"So, what sort of qualifications do you bring with you?"

"I'm a channel cat."

"A what?"

"A channel cat. I do séances. With nine lives each and a lot of reproductive power, there're ages and ages of cat wisdom behind the two of us that we can call on."

"And all that wisdom didn't tell you that cats don't walk into sausage factories through the front door?"

"Thousands of years of cat history have proven that being an annoyance for a long enough period of time will generally get you where you want to go. That's right out of the catechism. Now, you see, I've got a guide and escort," the turbaned visitor purred.

"So, nice hat. I can see you're no Puss 'n Boots. Where you from?" Something from the back of Murdock's psyche had become aroused and wary.

"Katmandu, of course."

Later, after seeing that his strange guest was fed and bathed, Murdock got right to the point. "So how does this all work?"

"There is an entire catalogue of options, but none without their dangers. I can either channel, or I can guide you as you make your own contacts with the spirit world. In either case, one of us becomes catatonic while the other must both pay close attention and be ever vigilant."

Murdock was a cat of action, so he said, "All right, let's get started, but if it's acceptable to you, I'll be the watcher the first time."

"As you wish. I'm willing to cater to your every whim for now. Where is the safest place for us?"

"Up near the ceiling. There's seldom anyone or anything there—other than an occasional pigeon—and the visibility is good."

"Very well, lead on."

Murdock noted the eager, covetous manner with which the stranger seemed to glance at everything around him as they made their way.

Several minutes later they were atop a catwalk located centrally thirty feet above the factory floor. Strings of sausages whizzed by below, and the delicious odors wafted dizzily upward. "This is it. So, what now?"

The turbaned stranger gave a hungry leer at the scene below and quipped, "Now all we need is catsup!" Then, turning serious and offering a mysterious smile, he said, "We begin with a cat scan. We check everything around us very closely.

This is dangerous business, and there's no sense tempting fate and chartering a seat on that great catamaran to the sky."

Murdock glanced over his territory and said, "All's clear!"

"No, you don't understand. Extra care must be taken to avoid a cataclysm. Examine the surroundings with extra fineness. You must be able to categorically insure a lack of intrusion."

"Listen," Murdock retorted, "this ain't no ordinary cat house. This is my territory, and I can assure you it's safe. Don't be bustin' a vessel and goin' cataleptic on me."

"You may be good, Murdock, but a catamount you're not. This is no time for catnaps, and I won't continue unless I'm purrfectly assured I will be safe."

"All right, all right already. Don't get a catheter up your butt. I'll take care of it."

Outside a whistle blew, and beneath the two felines the factory eased to a standstill. The cataract of ingredients spewing into the giant grinder stopped. The conveyer wound to a halt like a lazy caterpillar, and soon workers catapulted out the door. In minutes the place was silent.

"It's so quiet now it reminds me of the catacombs," the turbaned stranger mewed in an awed voice. "What's the catch?"

"No catch, it happens about this time every day."

The lights dimmed. In the distance a door clanged shut. The stranger relaxed. He reached into a pouch that dangled from around his neck on a golden chord, pulled out two tablets and swallowed them."

"What was that?" Murdock asked suspiciously.

"You could call it my catalytic converter. It's the catalyst I need to transform myself into a channel cat. From this point on, I'm relying on you, so be alert."

He watched as the stranger's eyes began to glow red like a pair of cathode ray tubes. Suddenly Murdock was seized by a sense of ancient territoriality, of danger, of jealousy. This interloper was a danger to the terrain he'd so carefully marked and defended for years.

The stranger closed his eyes and began to breathe in a deep, irregular way. Murdock crept close to the stranger and gave a shove. There was no landing on one's feet among the razor sharp blades within the giant hopper below.

"Tut tut," Murdock mused. "Another catastrophe." Then he realized he was more relaxed than he had been in months—and happy to be in his place and time. "No," he thought, "maybe not a catastrophe, maybe just the catharsis I needed."

Save the Last Dance

He moved awkwardly, one ear pressed between two pendulous breasts. His partner's dress was a floral print, small violets against a white and green background. The faint smell of alcohol wafted just above the unpleasant smell of cheap perfume. She chanted the time as she led him around the dance floor.

That was his first memory of dancing. The year was nineteen thirty-five. Miss Carter was the only teacher of ballroom dance in town. He couldn't keep time to music, so when the rest of the class paired up to dance he was always left with Miss Carter. She was a woman of large hips and tight dresses, of violent red lipstick and rouged cheeks. Her vain attempts to make herself look attractive left her looking more like a clown than a femme fatale. To a sixth grade boy, she was the rack, the pillory, and the iron maiden. To Ben Keller's mother, Miss Carter was a hope that her son wouldn't be a complete social failure. It was a futile hope, at least insofar as dancing was concerned. Twelve weeks of classes left him more insecure than ever.

Junior high was a blur. Saturday night dances found the boys lined up against one wall of the gym and the girls against the other—except for the girls dancing with each other in the northeast corner. Each week this self-imposed segregation lasted most of the evening, until finally Ben's friend Buzz Faldon and a few other boys worked up enough courage to ask girls to dance. Ben never once found himself in that group. He stood alone, trying to count the time, wishing he were anywhere else in the universe.

Work at Gresham's Grocery provided an excuse not to go to dances during high school. There was only one time, when Buzz got him drunk on a pint of stolen whiskey, that Ben went to a dance. He spent most of the evening throwing up in the boy's lavatory. Buzz and the others got the girls.

After high school, if it hadn't been for Buzz getting around at the dances and setting him up on blind dates, Ben would never have met Stacey. Ben loved her at once. She seemed to understand his shyness. Mostly, when they dated, they went to movies or the concerts in the park. Ben knew she liked to dance, but Buzz had apparently warned her.

Finally, at his wedding, Stacey, this woman for whom he would do anything, coaxed him to dance the traditional bride and groom's waltz. He broke her foot. Stacey had the good sense to never again ask her husband to dance. Forty-five years later she developed cancer. Not once in all of their years of marriage had they ever waltzed again. For most of those years, dancing never entered Ben's mind.

It was a dozen years after his wife's death, on one of his visits to Ohio to spend time with Buzz, that the subject came up.

"Ben, whaddaya say we slip down to the Senior's Center. They're having a dance. It'd be a lot of fun."

"Buzz, you know I never could dance. Hell, I can't even remember how to spell it. It's the last thing I'd ever want to do—wound another unsuspecting victim."

"There are some fine women down there, Buddy. Good company. We could have a shot or two of whiskey first. I sort of told a couple of people I'd be bringing a friend."

"Some things never change. Buzz, you're a horse's butt! There is no way on this green earth I will ever dance. Period!"

"I don't think I've ever known a bigger chicken than you, Keller. Come on and just talk to folks, then. It'll do you good—expand your horizons. Talking's easy. Look at me; I'm in this wheelchair. There was a time I used to steal your women, but how much dancing do you think I do anymore? It's just good to get out."

The Senior Center reminded Ben of Junior High. The single women lined up on one side of the room and the men on the other. A few couples danced, but they were mostly husbands and wives. After two hours of scratchy music and meaningless talk of sports Ben started to really look around. One woman on the other side of the room attracted his attention—he had no idea why, but he seemed drawn to her. Maybe it was the floral print dress. Maybe it was her smile. She had a pretty smile. He watched her as she talked with the other women. He watched her as she went for more punch. He found he was watching her when Buzz interrupted his reverie and tried to reengage him in conversation. Ben blushed. *I'm over eighty years old, for crying out loud,* he thought. *I shouldn't be having these thoughts!* The thoughts he was having had to do with memories and resting his head on supple floral print, feeling a button tight against one ear. Suddenly he wanted to be able to dance.

Buzz looked across the room and then back at his friend. "Awk, bock, bock, bock, bock."

The chicken imitation irritated Ben. He turned back to the conversation, fuming to himself. Soon the talk of spring training bored him again and he returned to his thoughts of the woman in the print dress on the other side of the room. It had been years since he had experienced a woman's soft warmth, and he felt a stirring deep within. At first he thought it was his bowels again. Then he thought of asking his friend if he could borrow his wheelchair. He had never tried the sympathy factor except with his wife, but he imagined it might help. In the wheelchair he'd be at the right height to rest his head on her chest. He imagined the scene and finally decided the chair's footrests would be a problem. It was just a fantasy anyway. He'd have to settle for starting a conversation.

When Ben looked up again, Buzz was smiling at him. They'd been friends too long. His thoughts were apparent. Ben glanced across the room and then back at his friend.

"I bet you haven't got the rocks. You want me to ask her for you?"

"You always were a horse's butt, Buzz."

"Awk, bock, bock, bock, bock!"

The other men all looked toward the sound. Ben got up and crossed the floor, leaving Buzz and the others smiling.

"Ma'am, I wanted to ask you to dance, but I don't dance myself, so I'm not sure what I'm doing here." His words amazed him. It was the closest he'd come to using a pick-up line in almost sixty years.

She blushed. *That was good,* he thought, *a sign of decency.*

"I never could dance myself," she said. "Kind of a tin ear, I guess—just never could quite keep time to the music."

"We'll, I guess that settles it, then. I can't keep time, either. Dancing is out. Problem is, I've got a friend over on the other side of the room thinks I'm about the biggest chicken in the world—and he's right, but I can't let him know that. Would you consider just standing in one place with me—during the next slow dance—and we can sort of sway back and forth like we're dancing. If we just stand in place I can't stomp on your feet, and neither one of us has to worry about keeping time."

She looked at him for a long moment. Her eyes narrowed, and then grew wide as she stood up. "Alright, we can try."

They walked to the darkest corner of the floor and he pulled her to him. It seemed good. After a minute she relaxed. "My name's Ben," he whispered.

"I'm Sarah."

Neither of them noticed that during the third number they had started dancing.

Decoy Hunting

Time comes when a man's just gotta stand up and say, "No!" Problem is, that can be a problem when you're saying "No!" to your wife. One no leads to another, you see. That's why I finally agreed to take my brother-in-law duck hunting. He's not generally a bad hunter, especially for rabbits or grouse, so that wasn't quite the issue. Mostly he's just one of those people who rubs me the wrong way. We don't talk anymore, so it's no longer a difficulty.

I knew better than to share a blind with Harold, so I put him in my favorite spot just out from the end of Brown's point. I got him settled in, and then I went up the shore about a half mile to my second favorite spot. I figured it was far enough away so I wouldn't have to listen to him. A little bit of Harold can go a long ways.

Waterfowl are my specialty. I've been carvin' decoys for over twenty years, and while I don't like to brag, I've got a wall full of prizes to show for it. That morning I set out nine of my babies in a little grouping that was picture perfect. I settled back in the blind to wait. It was a bluebird day, and there weren't many ducks in the air. Once in a while a little breeze would swing by and set the cattail leaves a tappin'. The maples on the opposite bank had turned crimson, and the tamarack were a rich gold.

There wasn't much action, but I just enjoy bein' out. Along about mid-afternoon I considered taking a nap. I was just nodding off when I heard a bit of racket down the shore and movin' my way. I parted the reeds and began watching.

Soon enough I spotted the source of the noise. He was dressed like a mannequin in a Wilderness Outfitters Shop, carrying a machete at his side and a twelve gauge Browning semi-automatic in the crook of his arm. His headgear was a fluorescent orange camouflage hat, the kind with a flap bill in front and earmuffs on the sides. He was straight from the city. You could tell he thought he was bein' sneaky, but for all of the noise he was makin', he might as well have been honkin' a taxi horn.

I was about to take the safest option and make myself known when I lost sight of him in some tag alders. A minute later he jumped out, raised his gun, and blasted every damned one of my decoys plumb where they sat in the water. He even had to reload to get 'em all. I was so astounded I just sat there with my mouth open. Then he amazed me even more when he went out and gathered every darned one of 'em and came swishin' back to shore just grinnin' like a coon eatin' corn.

I can tell you I was right there when he got to shore, and I asked him about his huntin'. Well, he told me about how huntin' hadn't been anything at all until he got the right advice. He said if I wanted some success, I should go talk to the fella about half a mile down the shore. He was an expert. He then displayed for me my hand-carved, pellet riddled decoys as proof of that fella's savvy.

It seems that this city fella had hung around long enough so even my brother-in-law got tired of talkin', and so the dirty bugger told the city slicker that if he'd just go up the shore about a half mile, he'd find some real fine wood duck hunting. The city dude held up my babies and said, "If this here mess a wood ducks isn't proof that fella knows what he's talkin' bout, then nothin' is."

I let my brother-in-law walk home that day. As I mentioned, I haven't talked to him since.

The Vision

Thin and spare, wrapped tightly against the cool of the spring morning, the old man sat, eyes closed, face turned to the sun. A young man, one of his disciples, approached and made the formal greeting.

"Good morning, my father. May Peace and the Spirit be with you."

"And with you." He nodded for the young man to sit.

There was a long silence between the two men. The only sounds were the calls of chickadees and the low voices and rustle of villagers performing their morning tasks. The old man waited, knowing that to rush a question often is to lose it, or to lose the ear of the one who would do the asking. When the silence was finally broken, there were many feelings woven among the disciple's words.

"I slept little last night. My dilemma was in reconciling your teaching with the lives of all people. You have said that we are to love others and give them our hand to help them when they stumble. You have said we should return to them a hundred times a hundred times, and more when they do us wrong. Is there no limit? Is it not best to avoid the man who is filled with lust, the man whose greed consumes all around him? Are we not better off putting the drunken and the lazy behind us? It sometimes feels so useless. Do they not just drag us down, away from the Spirit?"

There was a long stillness as the old man looked deeply into his disciple's eyes. "You are almost of the age where you must go in quest of your own vision. I think, perhaps, it is time for me to tell you of the vision I had as a young man.

"I was three days in search of the Spirit before he caught me up and showed me secrets of what is to come. In my vision I saw the hand of the Spirit reach down to all the men that ever were and ever will be. The Spirit grasped the hand of a holy man on a high hill, and that holy man grasped the hand of one beside him. Soon all men, in order of their holiness, were lifted toward the heavens, each grasping the hand of the one in front of him and pulling the one who followed. And so, in a great spiral that circled the earth many times and ascended gracefully upwards, men were drawn to the Creator who embraced them with loving arms."

The old man sat rocking, his eyes closed as he gently nodded in reverent remembrance. The young man watched his teacher carefully. In time the old eyes opened and the young man felt free to speak.

"I am afraid that I am puzzled. It is a beautiful picture, but I'm not certain how it answers my questions. Do we want the thief and murderer in heaven? Must we accept the harlot and the gambler?"

"Your instincts are good, but judgment is a blade that cuts in many directions. There is much that you must understand, and in the process it is never easy to lay down an old truth in the face of a new one.

"Each man is placed on this earth with his own journey and a set of gifts to help him in his travels. One may be given the gift of building, to another the gift for growing; so are given countless necessary gifts, and no one man may possess them all. Each man is given gifts, but they are not free. With those gifts comes heart knowledge that they are to be shared with all men in a larger journey. Sharing gifts is a way of extending one's hand, and so to each is given a sacred trust. To break that trust is to fail to pay the debt that is owed the Creator.

"As each man is raised in the holy spiral which would lift all men to Heaven, each is responsible for all who would follow. If the one ahead fails to keep his grasp on the one who follows, all behind him are lost. It is the nature of the greater journey. We gather strength from those who go before, and we give strength to those who follow.

"That is a reason why we must never give up on those who seem not to hear the call. Each of them, too, has the heart knowledge given at the start of the journey, and in each of them there is the potential that that knowledge may be awakened and used to the betterment of all. Surely you know of men who have changed in that way, and it would seem that sometimes the one who learns understanding at the end of the line moves most quickly to its head."

The two men sat, each in his own thoughts, until the sun had swept its shadows around the trees.

"Was there more to the vision?" the young man finally asked.

"I was not given more at the time, but I can tell you the thoughts of many nights. I can see now that you wonder about those who are let fall. I see in your eyes and sense in your tone that it is more concern for those behind you than concern that the spiral be broken somewhere ahead. That is as it should be.

"The man who lets go of those behind him will surely be judged on their account. His place is at the end of the line.

"As for those ahead, I suspect there will be great sorrow among them when the chain is broken, as none will be complete in the larger journey without the presence of the whole. But the Great Spirit who reaches down once, will surely do it again and again, for that is the way of love."

THE LOST CHORD

Perfect pitch was what had me wading through knee-deep mud and snake grass. It wasn't my idea, or my perfect pitch. My friend Doug was the driving force behind it all. I was only along because I'd been given a vision of free beer. I'm a grad student. Free beer is important.

Doug had caught a frog along the bank while we were fishing the week before. I'd been with him and witnessed what took place that day, or I never would have consented to the trip to the swamp. As with most of our fishing trips, there had been some beer involved. Doug, being the generous person that he is, decided to share his beer with the frog. Over the course of the afternoon the frog had a number of sips, and Doug noticed a change in his croaking. After he called my attention to it, I thought I could hear the change, too. The froggy voice went up.

"When we first caught this frog he croaked B flat. He's croaking D now. I think it's the Guiness." Doug gave the frog another sip. The frog burped. "Hear that change? E flat. I think you can tune a frog!"

Doug's a science major. He was off and running with the idea.

I saw Doug a week later. That was when he'd talked me into the trip to the swamp. He'd been performing experiments all week. He said he'd come to some interesting conclusions, but he needed more frogs to arrive at a statistically valid result. He added that if his hypothesis was correct, we could get free drinks in just about any bar. He wouldn't tell me more.

We caught nineteen frogs out in Stout's Swamp. They were a variety of sizes and colors. Doug was so happy with our catch that he bought me a beer on the way home. He didn't offer to launder the smelly clothes that I had to stand on the back porch for three days before I could go near them again.

A week later Doug had me return seven brown frogs and one greenish one to the wild. He said they failed the audition. I didn't go back to the swamp, but I did at least get them to some low ground just out of town.

It was another week before Doug declared he was ready. We went to O'Malley's bar after classes that Friday afternoon. Doug already knew the bartender, and after promising to present a show that would both celebrate the Irish and amaze the patrons, he wrangled a free draught for each of us, plus a Guiness for the frogs. Doug pulled an eyedropper and four bright green frogs out of a box that he was carrying. He sat the frogs on the bar and asked for attention from the patrons. Once he had everyone's interest, he adopted a cheesy Irish brogue and launched into his demonstration.

First he pointed out that he had only green frogs. "I've established that green frogs are better singers than brown frogs. Me unscientific observation is that they were probably originally imported from Ireland, and are therefore innately musical and poetic. Brown frogs kin sing, but not so well...

Scotch Irish or Welsh stock, most likely. Their songs sound more like hymns than ballads. To further me observations about the Irish ancestry, I've established that I kin tune a frog more finely with Guiness than any other drink. Bud makes 'em sick. Scotch doesn't work at all, and rum just makes 'em sleepy."

At this point Doug tickled the frog to his left under its chin. The frog croaked weakly. "Did you all hear that? That was an A just an octave below middle C. I'm gonna tune this frog to C. I'll do it by givin' him just a couple of droppers of Guiness." He filled the eyedropper and began putting one small drop at a time into the frog's mouth. After each drop he tickled the frog's throat and called out a note. Nine drops and the frog was at C. He moved to the next frog and began to repeat the process.

"This frog is a B," he declared. "I want him to be at E." It took seven drops of Guiness before Doug was satisfied. "The next two frogs will need to be G and B. Once they've been tuned, we'll have *do, me, so,* and *ti.* The result will be a nice harmony. These boys have been practicin', so they're almost ready to perform the old Irish ballad 'Green Stones of Kilarney.'"

Doug quickly tuned the final two frogs, hummed a pitch, tickled each frog under the chin to get it started, and soon we had a croakfest. There was, indeed, a crude kind of barber shop harmony to the noise. After a couple of minutes Doug touched each frog on the back and the music stopped. Soon we had all the beer we could drink, and Doug was leading the chorus as they went through one tune after another, each followed by great applause.

It was the beginning of a glorious month. Word got out, and no tavern in town would turn us away. I asked Doug how he was able to teach frogs all of the old Irish Ballads.

"I don't know many Irish ballads. I just make up a title. The boys give enough variety to make it sound legit. 'Irish Laundry on the Line,' 'Green Blood in the Hills.' If people think they should know something, they'll go along with anything so as not to look dumb."

Doug kept improving his delivery. He'd throw in lame jokes like, "Ya can tuna fish, but who woulda thought ya could tune a frog?" We had to put a schedule on Facebook listing the bars where we were to perform. The Frogtown Ramblers. It got to be kind of a cult, and my grades started to slip.

There was a nice looking woman who started showing up almost everywhere we went. She usually sat toward the back, but she was hard not to notice. Doug finally asked her to come meet the boys.

"I just think it's interesting. I hate frogs. I don't want to be anywhere near them."

It was only a matter of days before Doug gave me the frogs.

"I'm through. Jeanette says my hands kind of feel like frog slime. I can't have that if I'm going to be spending a lot of my time with her. I think she could be the one...."

And so I took the frogs home. I tried tuning them. It sounded like bagpipes playing backwards when I attempted it. I wound up just keeping them in a terrarium in my living room. I'd stick them in the toilet once in awhile so they could have a swim. On nights when I couldn't sleep I'd slip them a little Guiness, and they'd usually sing me off to dreamland. Most of the time they were as much a nuisance as a help. I started thinking about taking the boys back to the swamp.

With no free beer, I thought, *what's the reason...?* Then my friend Darcey came over one evening. I'd been studying all day and was in a bit of a daze. I barely paid any attention when she went in to the bathroom. Then I heard a flush and looked up at the empty terrarium. There was a kind of harmony in the sound of rushing water. Like the lost chord.

Finding Peace in Marriage

My late wife was something of a nag. Not that I didn't give her reason—I often took a perverse sort of pleasure in giving her reason—but I think mainly she got it from her mother's side of the family. She'd nag me about picking up the dirty clothes from the floor. She'd nag me about leaving the toilet seat up. She'd nag me about taking out the garbage, applying for vacation time, wiping my feet, combing my hair, elbows on the table, and any other little thing that she could think of. It was seldom just one thing at a time. Ours was not a peaceful sort of relationship, though I don't think either of us would have changed anything very much. After thirty-three years, I was pretty calloused from all the nagging. It mostly was just noise to me, a kind of background music for my life.

Betty got the cancer in November, and she was gone by the next June. She spent a lot of that last spring working in her flower garden. She said she knew I'd never keep it up, so she wanted it to be as perfect and easy as she could leave it. She loved flowers, all except for geraniums. She was allergic to geraniums. Lilies were her favorite. On her deathbed she was nagging me about watering the lilies and cleaning out the basement.

Two months before her death Betty started a notebook detailing all of the things I was to do when she was gone. She thought of it as her gift to me. I think the only thing she couldn't face about dying was the idea that her nagging might be over and I'd be on my own. I teased and tried to assure her that God and the angels would be there for her if the urge to nag became too powerful, but I don't think she was comforted. The notebook soon became two. On page forty-one of note-book two she explained how she wanted lilies planted on her grave. That was right after instructions for using bleach when I washed my underwear, and just before the admonition about channel surfing with the television remote.

It was with very little surprise after Betty died that I discovered I enjoyed not taking the garbage out; I enjoyed drinking out of the milk jug, and putting my feet up on the coffee table. The clutter in the basement was comforting. A weight had been lifted. I would also have to admit, though, that I sort of missed Betty's voice filling up the emptiness with one nagging thing or another

Then it happened. I came home from work on a Thurs-day and the waste basket was sitting in the middle of the kitchen floor. I pushed it back under the cabinet and went into the living room to watch the evening news. The remote was not there. I found it an hour later on the top shelf of the bookcase. I thought about calling the police about a break in, but I found nothing missing and there was no sign of forced entry.

Friday I came home from work and tripped over the laundry basket as I went into the bedroom to change clothes. Suddenly I heard the water come on in the bathtub, and as soon as I shut it off I heard the water come on in kitchen sink. I ran back and forth between the two faucets several times before they stopped. During my last trip to the bathroom I stopped to relieve myself. As I walked away from the toilet the lid slammed down. I jumped like it had been a shot. I began to have a suspicion.

"Betty? Betty, is that you?"

There was no answer, but I went back and propped the toilet seat up. I turned my back and it slammed down. I repeated my actions, and soon again the seat slammed behind me. Then the water in the bathtub started running.

"Betty, you had your chance for thirty-three years. Now leave me alone! And no, I will not take responsibility for watering those damned flowers. Period!"

The water started and stopped in the bathtub several times in quick succession. I gave up and went out and watered the flowers. When I walked back in the waste basket was in the middle of the kitchen floor. This was war! I kicked it across the room and left the debris wherever it lay. That was the last night I had a good sleep for the next two weeks.

A few days later I duct taped the toilet lid up. I suffered for that—I didn't like sitting on a cold ring any more than Betty had, but I was mostly able to take care of business while I was at work. Finally I got so tired of the bathtub and kitchen water running all the time that I lost it one evening. I went out and tried to drown the damned flower garden. I came in and dumped all of the waste baskets in the basement. The retaliation was that I never again located the TV remote. Never in her life had Betty been more of a nag.

Then one evening I went in after work, turned on the TV the old fashioned way, and put my feet up on the table. Suddenly one of Betty's gardening magazines went whipping by my head. It fell to the floor and lay open to an article about lilies. Soon the television began snapping off and on. It was in the middle of a Red Wings game, and I'd have to say I felt the hockey aggression rise in my blood.

"Alright, Betty, I'll plant flowers on your grave. You asked for it! I'll see that they get watered, too!"

The next day I bought every geranium I could find—fifty-seven pots. Any farmer would have been proud to claim the furrows I made the following day in the cemetery. Soon the grave was a riot of red. That night I was kept awake by a kind of far away, hollow sound of sneezing and wheezing. It was Betty, I knew, and I must admit I felt a little bad about it. The next night I rented a motel room and got a good sleep, though I must admit my conscience began bothering me along toward morning. I really did miss the old girl, mostly.

A conscience is a wonderful, terrible thing. I left work at noon. By two o'clock I'd dug up all of the geraniums. By three I'd replaced them with lilies. I've not heard from Betty since, and in the year and a half following that time I've never failed to water the flowers once a week. The toilet seat stays up, and I even look forward to taking the garbage out.

Willie

Had an old Banty rooster when I was a kid; followed me everywhere. Aunt Wilma gave him to me, and I named him Willie. He went to school; he went to the barn to do chores; went to church—but mom wouldn't let him sit at the table. Of all the places we went, his favorite place was the lake where we went fishin'.

I took up fly fishin' when I was about ten, and old Willie always had a special fascination for my flies. They must have reminded him of his relatives or somethin'—in fact, now that I think about it, some of them probably were descended from his relations. Anyway, he tagged along and watched me practice castin' for weeks. He seemed as excited as I was if I caught something. He watched and watched, and I guess he kinda got the rhythm and the idea in his head.

One day down by the pond he walked out on a log, stuck his tail feathers in the water, and began flippin' his fanny around. After a bit he stood up, crowed, and ran fer shore. There was a little sunfish had a hold on his tail feathers, and it let go when they got to shore and it began to gasp fer air. That rooster was hooked. From that time on he couldn't pass so much as a puddle of water without backin' up, squattin' down, and givin' the fishing a go. Thought of himself as the world's largest human dry fly, or something near that, I expect.

Got so we had kind of a contest goin' as to who could catch the most fish. When he won he'd crow about it until you could hardly live with him. He came by it naturally, as my Uncle Vernon was like that, too. When I won, I was real gracious, 'cause if I wasn't it made him madder than a wet hen, and he'd sulk fer hours.

On account of his not bein' able to get out to deep water, Willie never caught any fish that were too big. Then, when I was twelve, I bought an old rowboat with money I earned milkin' cows on the neighbor's farm. It leaked a little, and one oar had a bite out of it, but I thought I was captain of the finest ship in the world. At first Willie wasn't sure of that boat, but after I called him a chicken a few times, he started ridin' around in it with me—though at first he sat in the middle and hung on fer dear life.

After a few safe trips he started actin' pretty cocky. Then one day we were out near the island and he decided to try his luck at fishin'. He stuck his tail over the stern and ruffled his feathers in the water. Pretty soon there was a huge splash and he'd disappeared before I could even turn my head to look. I'd have suspected fowl play if we'd been closer to shore, but at that, there wasn't a soul in sight.

A couple of months later I caught a seven pound large-mouth that had both light meat and dark. Tasted awful good with corn on the cob and mashed potatoes, so we reckoned we knew what happened to Willie. I haven't gotten a chicken near a boat since.

Grumbling

My husband grumbles a lot. Mostly it's habit, but every once in a while I get tired of listening. I'll come home from the store and he'll look at the slip and grumble about the price of groceries. It happened again not long ago. He looked at the slip and grumbled and started bragging about how much money he saves us with his hunting. Sometimes he pictures himself a hunter-gatherer, I guess. So I challenged him. He's pretty competitive. I said, "I'll bet you two tickets to the symphony against two tickets to see the Redwings that for twenty-five dollars I can bring home more groceries than you, Bawanna. The only thing we'll exclude is the price of transportation, which will cost you more, anyway, since you'll have to drive farther."

He loves the Redwings, and he loves to go hunting, so I knew I had him.

"Okay, Sweetcakes, you're on." We shook on it.

He spent the day and came home with six rabbits. It was about eight pounds of meat by the time he'd gotten them ready for the freezer. I had two big steaks, ten pounds of potatoes, enough salad fixings to last a week, and a six-pack of beer.

He still tried to weasel out of the bet. “My rabbits didn’t cost as much per pound as your stuff.”

“How much was the license?”

“Fifteen dollars. But I can use it again.”

“Shells?”

“Probably two, two-fifty.”

“Game vest?”

“Thirty, but I can use it again.”

“Shotgun?”

“Six hundred and fifty. Don’t make me use it again.”

I’d have enjoyed the symphony more if he hadn’t grumbled most of the way through it. Even at that, I found that in a perverse way the grumbles provided kind of a satisfying counterpoint to the music.

He likes to grumble about how women talk too much. Oh, that’s a big one. One day I called him on it. We were about to go to a party at Tim and Julie’s.

“I’ll bet you two tickets to the Lions against two tickets to the Civic Theater that we can take a random ten minutes listening in on women’s conversations and ten minutes listening to men’s conversations, and the women will have spent more time talking about things that really matter and that impact our lives in a positive way than the men.

He loves the Lions, and he’s so darned sure of himself, so I knew I had him.

“Okay, Darlin’, you’re on.” We shook on it. I gathered up a notebook and a stopwatch.

“From eight to 8:10 we’ll listen to women. From 8:15 to 8:25 we’ll listen to men. We can’t say a word to anyone about what we’re doing. Agreed?”

“Agreed.”

I admit to being a little nervous, but I shouldn't have been.

Women	Men
School lunches	Golf
Casserole recipe	Dirty golf joke
Quilts	NFL draft picks
Car seats	
Diets	

"Golf is good exercise."

"Child nutrition trumps that for importance, doesn't it?"

"Maybe. Millions of people enjoy watching football."

"Millions of people enjoy casseroles, and they have a much closer impact on people's lives than watching a bunch of rich guys running around chasing a ball. Do I need to go on to diet and child safety?"

"You're just lucky the guys didn't start talking politics."

"Yeah, I'll consider myself lucky there. Like any of you have the ear of the President or an in with the North Koreans."

The play was a good one, and he mostly only grumbled during intermission. I must say, I enjoyed the performance immensely.

My Mr. Columbus likes to take the back roads, the "short cuts." Me, I'll take main roads and highways any time I can. He grumbles about that. Says I use more gas and it takes longer. We go to see his mother every other week. She lives about thirty miles north and west of here. He started grumbling while I was driving. I finally had enough and called him on it.

"I'll bet you a pair of tickets to the Tiger's home opener against tickets to see the touring production of Swan Lake in Detroit. My route is faster and more economical than your route. Rules are we top off the tank at the beginning of the trip and fill it to check gas mileage at the end. We start at exactly the same time of day, and we put a stopwatch on it. Just to make it easier and more fair, we have to stay within the speed limit or there is a disqualification. Fair enough?"

He grinned. A home opener is like the beginning of the world. He loves the Tigers. I knew I had him.

We left at precisely 9:00 A.M. the next Saturday. I'd lost the coin toss, so I was driving first. Traffic was light when I pulled onto the expressway. It's only four exits, but I've always felt it was the easiest route. After we exited the expressway, I heard him give a little laugh when I hit three red lights in a row as we went through town. Thirty-four minutes and twelve seconds after we left, we pulled into his mother's driveway. We got a calibrated can of gas out of the trunk and topped off the tank. 1.4 gallons. 31.1 miles.

Two weeks later we left our house at 9:00 A.M. exactly. I have to say, it took all of my willpower to stifle a laugh when he got behind a hay wagon on Fourteen Mile. When we finally got to a passing zone, he floored it to get around the farmer and I knew my mileage was in the bag. Then the Boy Scout bicycle brigade on Well's Road had him fit to be tied. I, of course, said nothing. Later he grumbled about the grandmother he had to follow when we got into town, but he only hit one red light. He got all of that one, though. Thirty-eight minutes and twenty-four seconds. 31.2 miles. 1.6 gallons. It was a clean sweep. He didn't talk even to his mother for the rest of the day. Just grumbled.

He wanted to give the second ticket to Swan Lake to my friend Ruth, but I made him go with me. The show was outstanding.

I haven't been able to stop all of his grumbling; that would be like changing underwear in the middle of the day for him. But he shuts up pretty quickly when I suggest we make a bet. He doesn't make bets anymore. "What's the use?" he growls.

I know I shouldn't say anything, but it's hard to help it. "You're right. You never mess with a woman."

Side Trip

The anesthetist placed the mouthpiece over my face. It seemed only a distraction. I was barely conscious at the time.

On the other side of consciousness I awoke clutching an armload of wildflowers. I had picked them in a dream on my way up the mountain. With my other hand I was being helped up and over a granite ledge. Flecks of mica sparkled in the pink rock.

The view was breathtaking. Tendrils of fog laced the valleys. The colors in the trees were undergoing their fall transformation, a vivid adieu to the warmth of summer. The reds and greens and yellows of the nearby faded to blues and purples in the distance.

I laid the flowers on a mossy stump and turned to thank my helper. He was a rosy cheeked old man sporting a droopy gray moustache. He was wearing jeans and a brown plaid wool shirt.

"Beautiful view isn't it, young fella?" he offered.

"It is. Where am I?" The surroundings were a new and unexpected change from the dull green of hospital walls. "Is this heaven?"

"Oh, bless me, no. I suppose you could say it's a kind of suburb," he chuckled.

I'm sure I stood there blinking for a full minute. Suddenly I felt exhausted and sat down in the shade of a crimson maple tree. "What am I doing here?"

"Well, that's a pretty good question. You seem to be lost. With any luck you'll find yourself here." The old man's tone was infectious.

"Oh. Well, I suppose I've been trying to find myself my whole life. But to think—this is pretty strange—to find myself here—it seems I'm more lost than ever."

"Ain't that just the way?" He pulled a notebook from his back pocket and began flipping pages. "Let me see. Thirty-seven, social worker, nominally a Methodist. Two kids, wife, both parents still living. Accident on U.S. 37 near Hagarston. That pretty much it?"

"In a small nutshell, I suppose."

"And have you found yourself yet?" he smiled.

"You're moving pretty fast. Hardly a clue. Yet."

The old man crinkled his eyebrows. "How will you know when you do?"

"I guess I just have to trust that it will feel right—that I'll know."

"I'm sure you will."

There was a long silence before a whisper of breeze ruffled through the leaves. I watched the blues of the distance become more intense as the morning shadows receded. My companion didn't seem to feel a need to talk, but my thoughts were racing and curiosity got the best of me.

"So this isn't heaven, and it isn't home. I've got a funny sense that I'm here as much to look for God as to look for myself. I have a little trouble thinking of God as a suburbanite."

The old man took his time responding. "Apt feelings. What you're looking for, yourself and God...I don't know that a person can find one without the other."

"Why do you say that?"

"Unless you realize that spark of divinity in yourself—in all things—it's pretty hard to recognize God.'"

"I've checked out most of the world religions, and I used to be pretty active in my church. Is that why I'm here, because I didn't do enough in church?"

"Oh, dear, no. Religions are fine stepping stones, and they can be exactly the right place for a person to be at a particular time. That's why they're there. Fact is, though, you need to give up religions to find God."

"Excuse me, isn't that just a bit counterintuitive?"

"It would seem. Religions fill your mind with preconceived notions. You need to be in a state of 'not knowing' to be open enough to really know God. At its worst, religion leads to closed minds, and those closed minds are cause for suspicion and division. On the other hand, at their best, each of the religions can give you a little piece, even a little peace, and sometimes those pieces even fit together. But it's like that armful of flowers you brought—if your hands are full of flowers, how can you pick up the gemstones in your path?"

"I really have been looking. That's in the notes, isn't it?"

"My, my, don't worry about the notes." The old man held out the notebook to show that the pages were blank, then continued. "It's a paradox, isn't it? It's hard to find yourself or God if you're always on the move searching, but if you stop searching it means you've calcified, gone stagnant."

"So maybe the search is the meaning?"

"Maybe, in one sense at any rate." The old man pulled me to my feet and placed the flowers back in my arms. My knees were shaking, and I felt suddenly woozy. He said, "Just another minute. Remember that all things are connected. That can't change. It's the nature of the connections that's malleable. Connect in love or connect in fear. Your choice, and your universe depends on it."

There was a sudden void, and then I awoke looking into the face of my doctor. He had rosy cheeks and a droopy moustache. There was the perfume of flowers in the air.

Green River: Gate to the World

I was on my way across Wyoming when I stopped into a bar in Green River. It was a place just off Main Street called Adelle's. I was attracted by the neon signs in the windows, especially the one that said Air Conditioned. The thermometer on the Cattleman's Bank said it was one hundred and three degrees at four ten.

Green River is hardly an oasis. Hills, sagebrush, and a few clumps of sun-blasted grass are about all you'll see for miles. Oh, there's the river, but it looks about as inviting as gangrene. I stopped initially for gas, or I wouldn't have stopped at all. I was driving home from Sacramento and an advertising convention I'd attended. Kalamazoo is home.

Adelle's was long, dark, and cool. There was a pine bar along most of the left, a pool table at the far end, and small tables scattered up the right side. The walls were mostly decorated with smoke faded Charles Russell prints and advertising mirrors from a variety of breweries. Three big guys whom I took to be oil field roustabouts sat at a table toward the front, and there was a blond seated on a bar stool two-thirds of the way towards the back.

The motivational speaker at the convention had pumped us up with all kinds of self-confidence. I ordered a Coors and eyed the blond. She was an attractive woman in a well-traveled way. The bartender noticed my look and said, "Her name is Mary, and good luck."

I moseyed down the bar and stopped just short of Mary. Pointing to a stool next to her I asked, "May I?"

"If you don't mind livin' dangerous."

"Is there any other way to live?" I smiled.

"Good. You see those three guys at the front table? Two of them want to be my boyfriend, and only the third would have a chance—if he wasn't married."

My confidence took two steps backwards, but the convention speaker's voice, *Believe in yourself, and ninety-five percent of your battles are already won. You can do miracles!* echoed in my mind.

"Ma'am, I can see that you would have to fight constantly to have only two boyfriends at once, but if you'll spend just a little time with me, I think I can convince you that the only real choice is to pull up stakes and join my outfit." Half of that was my spiel for asphalt roofing, and the other was mostly from bad Westerns I'd watched as a kid. I figured that when you're in the West, you should talk like a Western.

"Sit. What do you do for a living?" Mary still hadn't so much as looked my way.

I chose the occupation I figured would most impress a girl from Green River. "I'm a rancher," I replied smoothly.

"No shit," she said, and then she glanced down at the shorts I was wearing.

In the back of my mind I knew I was screwed, but the presenter's words, *Believe in yourself,* still echoed. "Yup, most of my life now. And you, ma'am, do you have a job of any sort?"

She ignored my question and said, "I would have taken you for someone who wouldn't know a Limousine from a Holstein."

I was toast if I took a guess, but I pride myself in fast thinking. "Beautiful lady," I said, "that would be a good observation if I was a cattle rancher, but I'm not. I have a raccoon ranch in Missouri, and I can assure you that I can tell one raccoon from another. Missouri raccoons, for example, have black ears, and Illinois raccoons have brown ears. Tails differ from region to region as well." I made it up, but I figured that she wouldn't know and wouldn't question my statement.

"Is that so? Fact is, I used to be a raccoon herder on a ranch in Oklahoma. Oklahoma raccoons have one brown ear and one black. The females always have the black ear on the right side. We ran seventeen thousand head. Rode ostriches and used polo mallets to herd the little buggers."

My self-confidence began to return. The lady was as big a liar as I am. Now the contest really began. "I generally only run twenty thousand head. We gave up on the ostriches and now use kangaroos in our herding. The boys I have working for me say that the coons respond best to old Hank Williams tunes, and they all carry Bose speakers attached to their saddles."

She looked at me kind of askance. "Puts me in mind of when I hired on with an outfit herding green turtles in Hawaii. We rode spinner dolphins and had underwater speakers playing Don Ho music all the time. To this day I'll deck the first S.O.B. uses the words tiny bubbles."

I ordered another beer for each of us.

"That's unbelievable," I said. "We tried Don Ho when we were rounding up alligators in Louisiana, and three of my best men got eaten."

Mary finally smiled and turned my way. "Alligators have pretty good taste when it comes to men."

"And women," I replied. "Have you ever eaten alligator?"

"Raw, baked, and pan fried. Tastes about the same as iguana."

"You, my lady, are a woman of the world. How interesting. How did you find your way to Green River?"

"By way of Tibet and the Upper Congo. You?"

"Sacramento, Prague, and Adelaide. But I got routed through Rio because of a baggage handlers' strike in Pretoria."

"I hate that airport in Pretoria," Mary blurted. "There are so many panhandlers and con artists there."

"Two more beers," I called to the bartender.

Believe in yourself, I heard the convention speaker saying.

I turned to Mary and asked, "Is there anywhere you'd still like to go?"

Mary paused for a long time. She was thinking deeply. Finally she said, "Palo, Michigan."

She had me. I'd never heard of Palo, Michigan, so I lied. "Yeah, I've always wanted to go to Palo, too. What's the draw for you?"

"I've heard the shopping at Joe's Market is excellent."

"Really?" I said. I was headed for Michigan anyway. A couple of hundred extra miles might not hurt. "Want to come along with me? I'm headed that way." This was starting to look almost too easy.

"I really wish I could, but I've got to fly out for a United Nations conference on hunger tomorrow."

"Oh, darn. Well, what about tonight? I was going to get a room at the Motel Six, and we could go out for dinner. Perhaps you could help me with my presentation on job creation. I'm set to brief the President on Thursday."

"That would be delightful, but I have an appointment with my Mary Kay dealer in just half an hour." Mary lifted her glass to me and then headed toward the door.

I followed, but I stopped to ask the bartender, "What can you tell me about that lady?"

"Mary? We call her the Virgin Mary because no one has ever been able to pick her up, and for what we can tell, she has never told a lie."

I shook my head, turned to leave, and two of the roust-abouts were standing there ready to escort me to my car.

Chuck it All!

Call me Expressmail. Move over Ahab! Step back, Santiago. Out of my way, little Arliss! The story about to unfold may become the epic struggle between man and beast. I invite you to watch as the action unfurls.

Allow me to present the back story. It all began with a recent discovery—holes burrowed beneath my barn--big, ugly, unwanted holes. The Devil's doing, by my calculation, but a woodchuck by any other name would smell so foul.

For cunning, meanness, and excavation, there is no critter that will match a woodchuck. *Diablo* I say! But I planned to meet him—tooth and claw. I live in a semi-rural area with houses only on two sides, and those each a hundred yards away. My opponent had the low ground, but I had the firepower.

Sunrise to sunset, for three days I sat in the blistering sun, a six millimeter varmint rifle resting across my knees. The first day I baited the front of his hole with turnips and iceberg lettuce. All I got was a sunburn. The second day I added watermelon and wore a big hat. The third day I supplemented my bait with a pork chop. I went in at three o'clock when the charlie horses became unbearable. The forth day I fell in the hole my antagonist dug under the steps leading to the deck at the back of my house.

I set a trap—staked it to a four by six deck post and baited it with cat food. The man at the hardware store where I bought the trap swore by cat food, reasoning that it worked for coons. I watched all day through a space in the Venetian blind. The sly devil never showed his ugly face. The second day I put out bagels thinking that would catch him in the locks. No dice, gambler! The third day I covered everything with ketchup and went to mow my lawn. Imagine my chagrin when I had to first fill the holes in the middle of my yard. It was looking like my nemesis had recruited his cousins.

No luck with the trap. I became suspicious. Was there a spy in my household? Was she telegraphing my every move? It seemed so, but what can a man do if he doesn't trust his wife? She has the twisted notion that woodchucks are cute—but no! There had to be another answer. Another approach. No one else was there. *Mano e Chucko*. I was not to be out-done! Damn the torpedoes!

I adopted a new strategy. I searched every store in town that sold stuffed toy animals. In the end I settled for a bad imitation of a beaver because it looked a lot like a wood-chuck in both color and form. Whack the tail and I had a clone.

The devil is in the detail, though. How does one duplicate the sounds and smells of a woodchuck? In the end I settled for rubbing my decoy in the compost pile and playing old Chuck Berry recordings at a high volume in the house. It wasn't perfect, but you have to start somewhere. The latest hole was convenient, as it was under my front porch. The location precluded anything like a clear line of fire, so I went to town and bought another trap—a live trap this time. If I could capture him alive, I would make him pay.

I set the trap and headed into the house. I no sooner closed the door than I heard the trap slam shut. Yes! I'd build a rack, a scaffold, an iron maiden. I'd make an example for all of his kind! I paced and planned and schemed for a few minutes, until my wife complained that I was scaring her. Then I went to see my victim—the neighbor's damned poodle. It was, perhaps, the biggest letdown of my life.

While escorting the poodle to the property line, I discovered a brand new hole in the garden. I grabbed the hose, watered down the dog, with which I was still furious, and then began to fill the hole with water. Five minutes later a sad, silly looking woodchuck came sputtering to the surface from a hole twenty yards to my left. I eyed him carefully. He looked a lot like a beaver. I knew I had been on the right track, but I was caught in the open with no weapon save the hose. I did the only thing a grown man could do under the circumstances. I shouted curses at him. He didn't move. I cursed him loud and I cursed him long. I ran out of all the good words I knew and was beginning to repeat myself for the third time when the sheriff walked up behind me. It seems the neighbor lady turned me in for hosing down her poodle and disturbing the peace.

Two days in jail for disturbing the peace seems a lot, but I am not finished. I was not about to pay a fine for cursing a woodchuck. I only wish that now I had one to help me tunnel my way out of here.

Carpe Diem

Sticks and branches littered the yard. Debris from the night's storm littered the sand along the beach. Tom and Miranda sat on the deck drinking coffee and watching as the first morning breezes ruffled the lake's surface. A bright morning sun was quickly raising the temperature, but whispers of fog still caught in the pines on the far shore.

Miranda looked up from the grocery list she was writing and glanced out at the water. "Does it look to you like the boat is riding a little low out there?"

"It's probably just the way the sun is reflecting," Tom yawned.

"Oh, I suppose you're right. I'm going in to make toast. Want some?" She got up and Tom followed her. As he closed the door behind him, he glanced back at the boat and noticed a figure in the water.

"Do you know him?" Tom asked as he pointed through the blinds and back out toward the lake.

Miranda returned to the door and looked out. "No, never saw him before."

The man was walking up out of the lake. He was dressed in cut-offs and a green tee shirt. He had the head of a carp, and was looking sideways at the boat. As he reached the very shallow water it was apparent that he was dragging one leg just a bit.

"I don't like the looks of him," said Miranda. "You'd better go run him off."

"I don't think he looks like much of a problem," Tom replied. "Probably just one of those folks who rent the cottages at Hughes' down the way."

The man hesitated, looked back toward the water, and then started up towards the cottage. Tom stepped out to greet him.

"Morning," Tom said.

Miranda stared through the blinds and glowered.

The fish-headed man stopped and turned at an angle to Tom, as though it helped him to see more clearly. His lips were working open and closed, but no sound came out. Tom noted the red gill slits palpitating just above the neckline of the tee shirt.

"Is there something I can do for you?"

The man said nothing in response, but turned and pointed in the direction of the boat. He held an arm out and cupped his hand. He then lowered his arm slowly.

Tom wasn't sure what to think. "I don't understand. Is there something I can do for you?"

The man looked sideways back at the water, then repeated his gesture. His lips continued to move, but there was no sound. The unblinking eye was beginning to unnerve Tom just a bit. He glanced back at the cottage and saw that Miranda was still watching through the slightly parted blinds.

"Look, I don't know what you want. Are you trying to sell something?"

The man moved his head and shoulders side to side in a negative response.

"If you're trying to sell something, I'm sure we aren't interested." Tom recalled the cupped hand at the end of the outstretched arm and added, "And if you're looking for a donation, we've given all we can to charities this year." He glanced back at the cottage.

Miranda stepped out and called, "Phone for you, dear. It's Mr. Laughlin at the office, and it sounds as though he wants to review all of the accounts." It was a ploy they had used to get themselves away from unwanted social situations in the past. Tom was uneasy that he was being rude, but he was thankful his wife had thought of it.

Tom took a step back. "Um, I've got to go now. Maybe I'll see you around some time again." The man shrugged.

Tom turned on his heel and strode to the door. When he glanced back, the man was standing in the same place and watching his retreat.

"What does he want?" Miranda snapped as Tom shut the door.

"I don't know. He hasn't said a word. He just keeps waving his arm at the boat." He peered out and the man was still standing in the same place, but now he was looking at the lake. Miranda refilled the coffee cups and they stood watching the stranger through the slits in the blinds. The man took a few steps toward the deck and stopped. Tom could see the gill slits heaving now.

"I think you should just tell him to go away!"

Tom winced. "He seems nice enough." He didn't want to be discourteous, but the man did make him feel a bit uncomfortable. They continued to watch. The carp-headed man was beginning to fidget. He cast sidelong glances, first at the lake and then at the cottage. Fifteen minutes passed. Tom was finishing his second cup of coffee.

"I don't like it," Miranda hissed. "Maybe he's casing the place. Who knows? He's not one of us. He might come back some night and murder us in our beds. You'd better make sure all the stuff is locked in the garage from now on. I saw him glance at the lawn mower."

Tom shrugged his shoulders and said nothing. Miranda overreacted all the time, but he wasn't sure what to make of the stranger, either. It had been almost a half an hour now, and the man was still there. His lips moved in little oh's, and he had begun to fidget a good deal.

Suddenly Miranda gave out a muffled scream. Tom looked through the blinds and watched as the man headed toward the house. He dragged his leg a little as he came, and seemed to favor it as he climbed the three steps to the deck. He looked around, and then walked to the umbrella table and picked up the pencil Miranda had been using to make her grocery list. He bent at the waist and began writing on the pad of paper. After finishing, he turned and limped back to the shore. Soon he had waded into the water and disappeared. For a few moments a ripple remained on the sparkling surface.

"Don't go out!" Miranda warned. "He might be watching."

Tom nodded. He reached for the remote and turned on *The Today Show*. They sat and ate toast and watched until an exercise program came on.

"I can't believe he'd still be watching," Tom said. He walked to the door. Miranda was right behind. She was as curious as he was to see what the stranger had written. Tom picked up the note. Miranda looked over his shoulder.

I just wanted to tell you that
the storm caused some damage
to your boat last night. I hope
you catch it in time.

They looked up together. There was no boat in sight.

Evasive Action

Given time, Fate has a way of evening out the bumps in the road of life. For years Al clung to that belief. It helped him find strength when he needed it in his marriage. He clutched to that belief even though he sometimes feared that the pothole in the pavement of his personal cul de sac was big enough to swallow a Greyhound. Lately it felt as though he was running out of patching material. In most ways Al thought Miriam was a good wife, but they had one major area of contention.

Every story, like every street, has two sides. For her part, Miriam admitted that Al was in most respects a good husband. He worked hard. He provided adequately. He was affectionate without being too persistent. He mowed the grass when it was too long. He took out the garbage when asked. He could usually fix the things she broke. One shortcoming, however, had long bothered her. In fact, as she would tell you, it just graveled her butt. It was a major pothole. Miriam was determined to repair the void. For years she had tried. She would make Al love the thing she loved the most, even if it killed him.

Al thought it might—kill him, that is. He was seldom a contentious man, but Miriam's love of shopping, her first love, was enough to give him headaches, backaches, sore feet, indigestion, and psychological hemorrhoids. It bothered him that she didn't care if she bought something. She just loved shopping for shopping's sake.

"Al, honey, would you please go to the mall with me?"

"I'm busy, babe. Can't you get someone else to go?"

It was starting again. Al didn't really hate shopping. Al hated Miriam's version of shopping. Shopping was for going someplace, buying what was needed, and leaving. Tools, sporting goods, groceries—those were things worth shopping for—when you needed them. Wandering aimlessly without buying anything was anathema to any intelligent or ambitious person. It was a sign of both mental and moral deficiency. And shopping for clothes or jewelry or skin-care lotion was about as inviting as frozen underwear.

"I want you to go with me. It'll be fun!"

For Miriam, the noise of the crowd, the feel of the fabric, the minor successes achieved through a never-ending hunt—those things were what life was all about. They were the animating forces. Who needed tools when there were "Sale!" signs? Who could ever want quiet when there was an exhilarating throng of people shouting and grabbing at a table of closeout items? Giving in to impulse was invigorating. Who needed a fishing rod when the greatest trophy could be worn to a gathering of admiring women who wished they'd gotten there first?

"Al, I really wish you'd come with me. You know how much I need your advice."

"Like fish need feathers!" Al mumbled. "Like a drowning man needs to be handed a bucket of shi...."

"What was that, honey?"

"Nothing, dear. I'm really busy. You just go on."

"Al, I want you to come to the mall with me. It's your mother's birthday we need to shop for."

"My mother's birthday isn't for two and a half months."

"But it always takes a long time to find something for your mother. Besides, it all needs to be wrapped and sent, and I may not have the time after today."

"What happens after today?"

"I've got a very full schedule coming up."

Al was beginning to sweat. The old trick of pulling the wires off the spark plugs hadn't worked since the neighbor boy had butted his pierced little head into their business by asking if he could be helpful for the first time in fifteen years. And Al had been more embarrassed than Miriam after he had thrown himself on the floor in Mervyn's and pretended to have seizures. The clerk had called 911 before he'd even worked up enough spit to start to drool. And how was he to know that the two ladies shopping a couple of aisles over were paramedics?

"I'll be in the car, honey."

"I really need to finish working on this drawer. You just go on without me."

"Al, we haven't got all day!"

He had to think fast. She'd grown inured to the sight of fake blood. He'd used all of the Syrup of Ipecac the last time he'd tried to feign sick. No, he needed a new approach. The last time he sneaked out the back she'd reported him kidnapped to the State Police. He'd been run to ground in minutes, and the police were threatening to bill them for services.

She's crazy, he thought as he took his keys off the rack. The stack of maps on the shelf caught his eye. The glimmer of an escape plan occurred to him. He sauntered to the car, slid confidently behind the wheel, and backed out into the street.

"Why are you going this way, honey?"

"Trying to miss the traffic, dear."

"But the mall is the other way, Al."

"This is a more interesting route, and not nearly the traffic. You'll see, dear."

Miriam rode in silence for the next ten minutes, but Al could sense her fuming.

"Al, I haven't wanted to say anything...."

"Then don't, dear. Enjoy the scenery."

Suddenly reality stepped in—stepped in with big shoes and squashed the slow moving insect of Al's strategy. His plan born of desperation had pointed Al towards Arizona, or Minnesota, or North Carolina. As they passed yet another shopping center he realized the futility of his plan. There were malls everywhere.

"We could stop at one of these shopping centers if you don't want to go to the mall, Al. Al? Al, you turn this car around!"

She's crazy, he thought again and took a left turn. *Crazy, crazy, crazy!* It was about that time that Fate started playing catch-up. After six more blocks his eye caught the sign and he pulled impulsively into the drive marked Glenn Forest Rest Home. *Crazy!* He saw a glimmer of hope. He got out and sprinted for the door. If he could have himself committed he had a chance. He glanced behind as he entered the doors and saw Miriam getting out of the car.

He ran to the reception desk. The nurse on duty was explaining that it took a doctor's signature to commit oneself when Miriam strode in, eyes blazing. Al stepped away reflexively. "Then call a doctor, please!"

Miriam rushed over and grabbed Al by the collar. She was screaming in his face when the doctor entered the reception area. "Nurse, call Security!" the doctor commanded.

A uniformed officer appeared almost immediately. Al was sagging under the weight of a verbal offensive when the officer and the doctor pulled Miriam from him.

"Are you all right, sir?" the doctor asked. "Does this happen often?"

"All the time, doctor. I'm afraid that someday she'll really hurt me."

"I've seen enough to make a preliminary diagnosis. At best we can keep her seventy-two hours, that is unless we have more studies. What would you like to do, Al"

Al suddenly recognized the two men who had pinned the struggling Miriam against the reception desk. "Doc Ruthruff, Ben, thank you." Al straightened his collar. "Yes, these rages have become insufferable. I suspect an addiction. Please, draw up the necessary paper work," Al shouted over the shrieking of his wife.

Fate has her ways of evening out the bumps and filling in the potholes in the road of life. Driving by Glenn Forest Rest Home had been serendipitous. That two members of Al's golf league had been on duty had been doubly serendipitous. It has to be said, though, that the afternoon spent in committing Miriam took its toll on all three men. The diagnosis of compulsive behavior, violent mood swings, and unhealthy projection had taken a group effort. Afterwards, the three men went out for a beer and then to shop for golf clubs.

Thora Left Me

Thora moved in with me after we had been going together for a month. That was one of the happiest days of my life. Thora moved out on me after we had lived together two weeks. That was one of the most painful things I have ever experienced.

Let me start over; I'm not quite telling the whole story here. Thora and her dog moved in with me after we had been going together for a month. That was one of the happiest days of my life. Thora moved out on me-and left the dog-after we had lived together two weeks. That was one of the most painful things I have ever experienced.

Thora is the kind of soul who is always rescuing terrified bats from the homes of hysterical friends or bringing home stray cats and dogs. That's the nature of how she hooked up with her bulldog, Cruncher, and I suspect it's how she hooked up with me. It was probably that nature that caused her to hook up with the guy she ran off to Arizona with after we'd lived together only two weeks. I can't say that it was her running off that bothered me so much—she snored and I hadn't had a good night's sleep in some time. The painful part of the equation was Cruncher. Cruncher was a slobbering idiot who had at first decided he needed to bite me every three or four days just to keep me in my place. The night I came home to find Thora had left us, he wouldn't let me in the house. I had to sneak in through a second story bathroom window. When Cruncher finally figured out what I had done, he cornered me in my room until he decided he was hungry and could be my friend for the time being. I was surprised. He had eaten so many of my socks in the previous weeks that I wondered how he could ever be hungry again.

Thora left a message on the answering machine—Cruncher tended to eat any notes that were left. He ate newspapers, too. When he heard Thora's voice on the machine he began to howl. In order to shut him up I had to give him the left-over ham I had planned on eating for dinner. I didn't want the neighbors to call the cops again. I settled for a can of garbanzo beans as my repast. The next morning when I let Cruncher out, I slyly determined never to let him in again. Then he began to bark. My neighbors, bless them, are hard-natured people. Cruncher won.

Did I mention that Cruncher slobbered a lot? Have you ever tried pulling on wet socks on a cold morning? Have you ever noticed how disconcerting it is to have long, white, frothy streaks on all of your dark pants? I gave up trying to wash the window in the screen door. I cancelled my newspaper subscription and considered taking *Water Sports Review*. And it was not so long before I stopped referring to Thora at all. I began referencing her only as Damn Thora.

I called the pet store, and a nice man came out to haul Cruncher away. I forgot that Cruncher had played that game before. He was only selectively an idiot. Cruncher bit the nice man and tore his pants. The nice man swore and said I'd have to find Cruncher a new home on my own. Damn Thora!

After a week or two, life with Cruncher began to take on a routine. I'd let him out in the morning and he'd poop in the yard. I'd come home to let him out at noon and he'd poop in the yard. I'd come home from work in the evening and he would go out and poop in the yard. Before bed each night I'd let him out and he would poop in the yard. Needless to say, I started spending a lot of time following him around in the yard. It wasn't just my penchant for neatness that drove me. If I hadn't followed him I never would have had any socks to wear. And one time I managed to retrieve an uncashed paycheck from a steaming pile of poop. Damn Thora! But I was lucky. There was only one tooth mark in the check and it was in the lower left corner where it didn't bother anyway.

Did I mention that Cruncher slobbered a lot? Perhaps his most endearing trait was the way he greeted you at the door and his whole body wagged. Flakes and gobs of spit and slobber would fly in all directions, and if the sun was at the right angle there would be little rainbows everywhere. I grew to love that. Damn Thora!

Cruncher may have shared Thora's duplicitous nature, but the old boy had one clear advantage over her. He didn't snore. That didn't mean that I got much more sleep, however. Cruncher insisted on sleeping beside my bed, and his unusual culinary tastes manifested in an unrivaled talent for flatulence. Some might find green air beautiful as it wafts about in the moonlight. I did not. Sleeping in an army surplus gas mask is uncomfortable, but it was better than not sleeping at all. Damn Thora!

Lest any of you begin to feel the weight of the depression and woe that dominated my life with Cruncher, I must tell you that two events led to a happy ending for the story.

Six weeks after she took off for Arizona, Damn Thora tried to come back. Cruncher bit her! Good Cruncher!

The very next day, Cruncher ran out in the road to chase a school bus. He bit the right rear tire and it blew. The concussion of the blowout killed poor Cruncher. Fortunately there were no children on the bus. I buried Cruncher in the back yard under a pile of his own poop. If it ever all composts, perhaps someday I'll plant a tree on the spot as a kind of memorial. A dogwood might be nice. I almost miss the old boy.

The Question without Answer
A Parable

Three disciples approached their teacher, arguing as they came.

"Who is God?" asked the most forward of the three.

"Tell me first what you know of who God is," replied the teacher.

"God is a being of infinite love, of perfect justice, all-knowing, all-wise."

"You have searched all of your mind and your intellect, and these are the highest qualities you have found? These are your thoughts?"

"They are."

"God is not your thoughts."

"Then what is God?" asked the second disciple.

"Tell me first what you know of what God is," replied the teacher.

The disciple thought for a moment, drawing circles in the sand with his toe as he prepared his answer. "God is perfect forgiveness, perfect compassion, creative, omniscient."

"You have searched all of your feelings and emotions, and these are the highest qualities you have found? These are your feelings?"

"They are."

"God is not your feelings."

"Then where is God?" asked the third disciple.

The teacher raised his head slightly and looked at his young disciple. "Tell me first what you have experienced of where God is," replied the teacher.

"God is here, ever present, walking with us and answering prayers. God is everywhere—both here and in heaven."

"You have examined all of your life, and it is in these times and places you have found God? These are your experiences?"

"Yes, I have experienced God in prayer and meditation, in dreams and intuitions, in joy and in sorrow."

"God is not your experiences."

The teacher led his followers to a large banyan tree and motioned for them to sit down in its shade. "Do not be discouraged. You have done well, all of you, but there is so much more. Our thoughts, our feelings, and even our perceptions of experience are projections of our selves. We examine ourselves and ascribe to God the best of what we find. As has been said, it is, at the very best, through a glass darkly. Depending upon our vantage, God may become presence or absence, love or wrath, creator or destroyer. There is, perhaps, some truth in all of these, but it is dangerous to grab a piece of the truth and cling to it as though it were a whole. Truth grasped in such a manner crumbles into a fine and slippery dust."

The group sat in silence for a few moments, and then the teacher nodded toward a man sitting before an easel in the square. "An artist, like you, is a kind of seeker of truth. Yet how can an artist paint a flower that is forever opening itself? There can be no final brush stroke. That is the nature of your search. Do not despair. Just as the artist must first search for understanding of the anatomy of the figure or tree or mountain being painted, so, too, must you search. That is what you have begun. The true genius of the painting starts when the artist becomes that figure, that tree, that mountain."

Wash the Rabbids

Years ago I spent a winter trappin' in the WannaWashu Mountains. It was strange territory for me, but I was young and always up for a bit of explorin'. I went six months without seeing another human bein', and that was fine by me. I had a excellent season, in fact, muh best ever. By the end, I had enough furs to make me a rich man for the rest of my days, and I was feelin' pretty pleased with myself.

I set out down a strange river, headed east, late in the spring. My canoe was piled high with pelts, and I was towin' a second that was also ridin' low in the water. Traveled six days, so I did, before I saw any sign of human life. There was a little cabin sort a plastered together up on the south bank, and a man was sittin' out front, so I hailed him. I was curious to know how much further I had to go with muh hides and furs.

I tied up to some alders in a little backwater and got out on the bank to stretch. The man never left his chair, jest sat there and stared an' spit. When I approached, I saw he was a hairy old coot, an' I was s'prised that fer a fella who lived on a river, he didn't smell much like he'd ever been near water.

We spoke a little, but that big old cud in his mouth made 'im kinda hard to understand. I'd run outa tobacco three and half months earlier, so I stood around awhile hopin' he might offer me a chew, which he did, but as it had already been used I didn't take it. Fin'ly I asked about the river an' how much farther I'd hafta go to strike civlyzation.

"Pour daysh, thuraboush, butcha wanna wash the rabbids two daysh b'low."

I thanked him and got back inta my canoe, grateful he hadn't ast me tuh supper. ' Twas hours before my smeller stopped whimperin' an' began to behave agin.

Two days b'low that feller's cabin I began tuh listen fer rapids. I hadn't come to 'em by evening, so I pulled muh canoes up on shore and made camp. It was one of those evenings when the crickets an' the peepers make a world of racket, and the sky was brimmin' with stars. I went right to sleep.

'Long about midnight I was woke up to a awful c'motion. Camp was overrun! There was nothin' I could do. I tried ta jump up, but was knocked flatter 'n a week old beer just time an' again. I waved my arms an' shouted, but there was already so much noise it didn't do no good. There was rabbits ever' where, an' they was wild-eyed an' terrible tuh behold. I was staked betwixt two trees an' they began to dance around me chantin'. Sounded kinda like, "Right, right, left, left, forward, back, hop, hop, hop," but I couldn't make heads ner tails of it. 'Long t'ward morning they disappeared. They took muh canoes an' everthin' in 'em—the proof is I'm still a poor man today. I lurnt somethin', though. Never be in such a hurry to end a conversation thatcha don't understand what's bein' said.

Took me three days ta walk outa that place, an' durin' that time I never saw hide ner hare agin.

The Grumpiest Man

My friend Lon is the grumpiest man I know. He's not depressed, exactly; and he's not a pessimist, exactly; and he's not just irritable, exactly. Grumpiness is mostly just a habit. If he was depressed, irritable, and pessimistic, I wouldn't have kept him for a friend all of these years. He can be the kindest, most caring and compassionate person you ever saw, it's just that he manages to be those things in a gruff and grumpy way. In the thirty-odd years I've known Lon, he has never smiled once. Not once!

Being the naturally good-natured person I am, I started trying to be nothing but a positive influence on Lon from the day I met him. I vowed not to be sucked in by the undercurrent of negativity he exudes. Even if I was sicker than a sailor after a weekend binge, I'd find something positive to say when we met:

"So, you look like shit. How ya doin'?" Lon would ask.

"I'm happy as a rat with a cheese ball," I'd smile. "You?"

"Downer than dirt," he'd reply.

It got to be kind of a contest, I guess. I've gotta admit, it sometimes put a strain on our relationship, and since we worked together and hung out with each other often, that could be uncomfortable. I'd have to sit up nights sometimes thinking of pleasant things to say.

I'd see Lon in the morning and smile, "So, how's it goin'?"

"I feel lower than the lint in a snake's belly button," he'd growl. "You?"

"Happy as a coon in ketchup," I'd lie.

I'd run into Lon at lunch and inquire politely about his state, and he'd say, "If I was any worse, they'd have to bandage and bury me. You?"

"Delighted as a dog in a dump!" I'd grin.

At five o'clock I'd see Lon as we were leaving work, and I'd ask, "Happy now?"

"Miserable as a mangy mutt in a pound," he'd moan. "You?"

"Merry as a mosquito at a blood drive!" I'd smile. He'd never smile back.

Lon'd pick me up to go fishin', and he'd ask, "So, how ya doin' this mornin'?"

"Pleased as a pig in a puddle of poop," I'd say. Then I'd query, "You?"

"Forlorn as fading flatulence," he'd grouse.

About noon, if the fish had been biting, I'd say' "So, how ya doin'?"

"Hopeless as a hairless whore," he'd respond. "You?"

"Blissful as a buck-toothed beaver," I'd smile back.

When we pulled the boat out in the evening I'd say, "You seemed to catch your share of fish. So, how're you feelin' now?"

"Day's over. Gotta clean all these fish. Hell, I feel gloomy as a gastric bypass. You?"

"Rollicky as a rogue rooster in a henhouse!" I'd enthuse, though I really was just tired. I didn't lie, though, because I imagined a rogue rooster in a henhouse would quickly be exhausted.

I remember the day Lon had a 290 bowling. Beat me by 112 pins, he did. I thought I had him. "How you feeling now?" I inquired.

"Blue as a baboon's butt! I shoulda had that last strike."

He didn't even smile. Some people are just never satisfied.

Our greetings and exchanges went on like that for years. I'd claim I was happy as a lizard licking lollipops, or delighted as a duck on a dike. Lon would reply that he was depressed as an elevator button, or glum as gum on a hot sidewalk. Then this last week my golden retriever died. Carrie'd meant the world to me, and when I saw Lon I had to admit to him that I was just miserable as a mound of mule mucous.

He put his arm around my shoulder and smiled.

The Letter

As a young man, my client, James, was extraordinarily sensitive. Most folks just thought him shy. He loved people, but he empathized so much with them that he couldn't stand the pain of long relationships. The problems and heartaches of those around him became his own. That fact led, over time, to a series of awkward partings. By the age of twenty-six, he had become so unsure of himself that he allowed himself only pen-pals. They were the only people he dared to value. Today his outlet might have manifested on Facebook, but that was not an option all those years ago.

I became one of those pen-pals. We had a fair amount in common, though I was not the introvert James had become. Like James, I remained single, and I, too, enjoyed the surprise and adventure of correspondence with strangers. We both understood that it's easier sometimes to allow ourselves to become vulnerable with someone if they are not physically present. As the years passed by, I did meet with James twice. Those meetings came about because, through our correspondence, I had become his lawyer and executor. He was fascinating in person, but it was in his letters that he truly shone.

However deep it may bury itself, there is an innate need for companionship found in all persons. Each of us needs at some level to find someone with whom we can open up. For James, that opening happened with Christy. The two became intimate friends—at least as intimate as twenty-four hundred miles and the U.S. Mail will allow persons to be intimate.

James had a ritual with letters he received from those he valued most. Whenever one came, he would save it back from the other mail, set it on the mantle, and spend the rest of the day savoring what it might say. He spent hours imagining the sender and speculating on content and what the writer might be thinking and feeling. With Christy, he fancied that he had come to know every nuance of her thinking. Afternoons after one of her letters arrived would become an intense, sometimes spiritual experience.

In the evening, after all of the chores were done, James would prepare a drink. He would then take the latest letter from the mantle, settle into his easy chair and, after visioning the sender one last time, open the correspondence and devour it. If a letter happened to be one of Christy's, it often would leave him so energized that he would fix another drink to help him get to sleep.

When James composed replies to Christy's letters, the draft often went through ten or twelve revisions. He had not used such care at first, of course, but over time those words became the most important thing in his life. It was not just letters he was creating, he was building his very spirit. The love letters were his masterpieces. The metaphors were ringing carillons. The alliterations elevated the essentials of his emotions. The allusions sparkled like Ali Baba's treasure.

I came to know Christy, too, through what James shared with me. I admit to feeling jealous of such a deep and moving love. I admit that I was tempted to try to insert myself, but such imaginings were never in danger of becoming reality. I had too much respect for the two of them.

The correspondence continued for three years, four months and twelve days before James reached the point of no return. At that time James went to the young priest at the church for advice. The reluctant cleric responded in general terms, but James heard what he wanted to hear. That evening he composed what I can only imagine was the most beautiful love letter ever crafted. In it he asked Christy for her hand in marriage.

When James took his usual stack of correspondence to the mailbox on the corner the next morning, he found he could not drop the letter to Christy in. He took it home that night and re-read each line until he had it memorized and was certain of its perfection. The same thing happened for six days in a row as he struggled with his self-doubt. On the seventh day, James approached the mail box with mixed feelings of apprehension and sadness. Though he was convinced of the perfection of the letter and the correctness of his love, he was torn by his inability to act. The letter to Christy wavered above the slot after all of the others had slid to the bottom of the blue, metal container. It was in an instant that a slight breeze tugged it from his hand and the envelope dropped softly after the rest. Never had James felt such panic.

The time was early spring. Cool spring. Yet James perspired with uncertainty each time he imagined the reply from Christy. When it arrived, he placed it on the mantle with shaking hands and began the ritual of visioning what the sender was feeling and what the contents might be.

That evening James fixed the required drink and settled into his easy chair after the chores were done. The letter and his gaze remained on the mantle.

Night after night, the same routine. He could not bring himself to dare to open the pale blue envelope. A week later another blue envelope arrived. He tossed it in a basket thinking he would open it after the first. The collection in the basket grew.

James stopped answering all of his mail. In the evening he would sit and fantasize and berate himself and fantasize. One spring led to another, and another. Eventually there were no more new letters. Still that one letter stood on the mantle, a symbol of love and the fear of love. It was there when the paramedics carried James from his easy chair to his final resting place thirty-seven years later.

The letter now stands on my mantle, and I sometimes sit at night and look at it. I envision someone twenty-four hundred miles away still wondering how a special love could fall apart, how such beauty could cease to exist.

I was given no instructions, but I know how badly James came to feel about betraying Christy's trust. It ate away at him. I never married, either, and sometimes I daydream of standing in James' place. He and Christy never met face to face. I could do it for all of us.

I have written a letter intended to accompany a return of Christy's letter to her. A dozen times now I have put the two letters in a large, yellow envelope and taken them to the mailbox. Each time I do, I find myself hesitating.

Stuffed

Sometimes it's hard to tell who's the head in a marriage. My friends CJ and Georgia are examples. CJ is a hunter—a serious hunter. His wife Georgia is not enthusiastic about that. Georgia is a vegetarian and a gardener. Other than what might be implied from those facts, they seem to get on fabulously.

As related to me, Georgia and CJ had been married about ten years when CJ bagged a ten point buck and was bitten by trophy fever. Six months later, when CJ brought the mounted head home, the trouble began.

"I will not have a cadaver hanging on my wall and looking at me all day. Period. End of discussion."

"This deer, dear, represents an important moment in my life. When I shot him I became responsible for his soul, in the Native American sense. He has become my friend, and I will look after his spirit for the rest of my life. I call him Cecil. That was not his deer name, but as it was revealed to me, it cannot be translated into English. He is going on the wall."

Georgia told me one time that she had, at that moment, considered an ultimatum: "The remains on the wall or me!"

But she wasn't sure how that might play out, so she gave in—a little. When CJ came home from work the next day Cecil had been decorated with crepe paper and ribbons to the point where not one hair could be seen. He looked like a piñata constructed by a class of hyperactive third graders.

So it went. Cecil was decorated for every holiday in the holiday book, including Tin Can Collection Day, Kamehameha Day, and Groundhog Day. Georgia's dislike of Cecil brought out her creative best.

The next year CJ returned from Wyoming with a trophy antelope. Georgia had by that time decided to fight fire with fire. She'd had a replica of her award winning cabbage mounted and hung by Cecil. To match the antelope she ordered a reproduction of her largest watermelon. She named the cabbage Carl and the watermelon Wendy. She immersed herself in conversation with them any time CJ walked through the room.

CJ started talking to them, too. He claimed they made more sense than Georgia ever had. Other than at moments like those, CJ and Georgia seemed to get on fabulously.

So it went for several years: turkey, tomatoes, black bear, zucchini, bobcat, a forked horseradish....

The fall when CJ returned from Saskatchewan with his mammoth moose, Georgia was ready. She'd grown a thirteen hundred pound pumpkin. It was nearly the size of a Volkswagen beetle. After the trophies had been installed, the living room was no longer navigable.

As CJ and Georgia sat at the kitchen table the next spring, CJ announced that he was going for elephant that year. He was only half serious. Mostly he wanted to see Georgia's reaction.

Georgia didn't blink. "You know, I'm getting tired of picking up walnuts every fall. There are always so many of them, and that old tree is beginning to shade out my rhubarb. What do you think it would cost to have that tree cut down and mounted?"

They sat and pondered their coffee cups.

Finally CJ broke the silence. "I've been thinking about giving up hunting and raising dogs instead."

"What kind of dogs?"

"Oh, I don't know. Something small. Beagles, maybe."

"I've been thinking about a new hobby, too."

"What's that?" CJ asked.

"Oh, raising cats, perhaps." She paused and thought a moment, "Or more likely, bonsai."

For some time they sat and pondered their coffee cups.

"I read in the paper that the museum downtown is looking for exhibit material," Georgia finally offered.

"Do you think...."

"It's worth a try. We might even get a tax write off."

The museum folks were delighted.

CJ still hunts, but he never keeps a trophy. Georgia still gardens, but she's more concerned with nutrition than size. The last time I stopped over we sat in their living room, and they seemed to be getting along fabulously.

Fairyland

I watched her move purposely from machine to machine. She seemed to be winning for most of three hours. I was not. She was certainly in her eighties, and she carried a homemade string purse in which she kept her winnings. She caught my fancy a bit, and as gambling was not going well for me that day, I decided to see if I could figure out her strategy. I eased my way from machine to machine until I was sitting next to her. She pulled a lever, won a small pot, and I used that as a pretext for starting up a conversation. Gamblers are notoriously secretive about their schemes for winning, but May opened up right away when I asked her where she found her luck. I can only report what she told me, but I think I believe her. She didn't seem to be the kind of old lady who could say a bad thing about anyone, or tell a lie even if her life depended on it. She just smiled at my question, her perfect white teeth and deep blue eyes riveting all of my attention.

"Sweetheart, I got lucky four years ago when I finally found myself a man. I need to back up, though, and tell you just how that happened. I've got to say, I hate dentists. I'd minimized the number of my visits over the past eighty-three years. The gambler in me had long figured my teeth would outlast the rest of my body. Well, honey, I lost that bet. The neglect caught up.

"I remember sitting at my kitchen table drinking my morning coffee and waiting for that Senior's Van to pick me up. I was most terrified. Half of my remaining teeth were to come out that day. The other half was scheduled for extraction in another two days. Dentures would follow directly. Well, I was sitting there and my eye happened to catch one of the refrigerator magnets, one that had a favorite saying of mine on it: *When Life hands you lemons, make lemonade.* Well, I figured sucking lemons was about all I'd be able to do for several days. I decided that for the moment, at least, I wasn't fond of lemons. The idea stuck in my head, though, and I figured to make the best of things.

"That afternoon I guess I must have staggered back into my kitchen. The left side of my face was swollen and I had a terrible headache. What I had to show for my day was a little plastic bag containing five old, yellow teeth. Did I tell you I really hate dentists? I was sure there'd be no hiding what I'd been through when I went to Bingo that night. I almost decided not to go.

"Bingo turned out to be awful. I must have explained my poor swollen face to at least fourteen different people. Two tried to reassure me by popping out their dentures and claiming they were wonderful; one just shook his head and told me I looked like hell; three others told me their own horror stories about trips to the dentist. There are a lot of people out there with deep dental scars on their psyches. To top it off, I lost money for the first time in months.

"Understand, I'm on a small fixed income. Paying dentists and losing at Bingo are not in the budget. Anyway, I went home and fixed some tea and sat back down at my kitchen table. I picked up that little bag of teeth. I remember taking them out and rolling them around in the palm of my hand. I figured each of those teeth had cost about thirty dollars to have pulled. I was trying to make lemonade, and I needed to get back some of that money I'd spent at the dentist. I heard you can sell almost anything on EBay, and I considered maybe making a necklace and passing it off as being made of 'rare Alaskan seal teeth.' I also considered using them as bingo markers—maybe they would bring good luck—but I decided, no, there was nothing lucky about them.

"Well, I got ready for bed that night, and it was like I was flooded with memories of being a little girl. The Tooth Fairy. In nineteen thirty I'd gotten a nickel for the last of my baby teeth. I got to figuring that in today's money that must be five bucks or so. Times five! *Hell*, I thought, *I could go to the casino with that kind of stake and come back a rich woman.* It was worth a shot, so I put my teeth under the pillow and went to bed. Lemons to lemonade.

"At first I couldn't sleep. Honey, I remember the same kind of excitement from when I was a kid. It was hard to imagine that the Tooth Fairy would really stop by to see an old maid with only four teeth left in her head, but I decided to go with it. I didn't dare doubt it. I understand the power of faith. So I got up and went to my desk and wrote the Tooth Fairy a note:

Dear Tooth Fairy,

It's been a long time, but I remember that you were always good to me.
It's been a hard life, what with no one to share it with and only a librarian's wages to get by on. Five dollars a tooth would make a huge difference.
Thank you.

Your biggest fan,
May
P.S. If you'd consider giving me an advance on the remaining four teeth, I'd share the profits from the casino fifty-fifty.

"Well, I slipped the note under the pillow beside the teeth. The next morning I got up and went into the bathroom. I checked the mirror, and the swelling had almost entirely gone away. I looked a little toothless, but I just figured that made sense, so I combed my hair. I decided not to bother brushing just four teeth. I put on my robe and went to the kitchen. Half way through my second cup of coffee I remembered my teeth and the note. You ever have those remembrances while drinking coffee? Happens to me all the time.

"I checked, and the teeth were gone. In their place was a crisp twenty dollar bill and a note.

Dear May,

I hope you didn't have your heart set on five dollars apiece for those teeth. Four is a premium price, and only my fondness for you prompts me to go that high. An advance would be in total violation of the company directive. Should you win big at the casino, however, I can find no prohibition in the rules that would keep you from sharing it with me. To my knowledge, no one has ever suggested that before. I could sure use some new underwear and shoes, so any contribution would be appreciated. I doubt it's tax deductable, so you won't need a receipt. Oh, I should add that the whole fairy business bothers me a bit, so please just call me Frank.

"Well, I've gotta say I was stunned. That poor fairy—man...it was a call for action. I got dressed up and called for the Senior's Van. I just knew that twenty dollars would be lucky.

"That night I wrote Frank a note. It was exciting, and I've got to admit that the whole idea of a man in my bedroom left me a bit weak kneed. Before I retired I put sixty dollars and my note under my pillow. I didn't know then if I needed a tooth to make the transition complete, but I went ahead without one anyway.

"The next morning, nothing. But I took my winnings from the previous day back to the casino, and Frank's share under the pillow that night was ninety-four dollars. For my part, I was almost back to even on the tooth score. Nothing happened that night, either. The next day I had my dentist appointment. Have I told you I hate dentists? That night I added my four teeth to the money under my pillow. I determined that I would try to sleep really lightly. I just had to know.

"At about two o'clock I woke when I felt my pillow move just a little. Well, I reached around with both hands and grabbed a hold of a big, hairy arm. I don't know who was more shocked, me or Frank. I said, 'We've got to talk.' You've never seen such a hangdog look on a man.

"I handed him the pile of money, the note, and the teeth. He read the note, counted the teeth, and handed back sixteen dollars. He seemed to be about my age, but a little better preserved. He was wearing blue jeans and a wool shirt, ratty old hiking boots and a stocking cap. 'You don't look much like I expected a tooth fairy to look,' I said. 'Do you always wear that outfit on your rounds?'"

"'Listen, I shouldn't even be talking to you, but you caught me fair and square. First off, I'm no fairy. Secondly, this tooth thing is just another temporary placement. Everybody has their own tooth watcher; it's like a lifetime assignment—you know, like your guardian angel, only different. After a client loses their baby teeth, it's usually pretty boring for sixty or seventy years.''

"Well, to make a long story short, we hit it off. Frank kind of liked the idea of having some income, so we agreed that I'd continue going to the casino. We solved the problem of being able to get together on a regular basis. Now he's my man."

May turned back to her machine and deposited another token. Nothing. She turned to me, shrugged her shoulders, and said, "Well, gotta be movin' on, honey. Nice talking to you." She got up and walked to a machine on the other side of the room. Soon I heard the sound of another jackpot. I hadn't believed a word she said, so I kept my eye on her. Mid-afternoon she went to a table in the lounge. She put her purse on the table, took out her teeth and placed them on top, put down her head, and soon I could see she was sleeping. It was almost no time before a gray-haired man appeared and walked up behind her. He was wearing blue jeans and a wool shirt with the sleeves rolled up. Also brand new sneakers. He shook her gently, and she got up, put in her teeth, and they walked out the door.

Marriage Counseling

"I've never been so lonely as when I was married."

As a counselor I hear that kind of statement all the time. This time it took on a little extra meaning because several months earlier I had counseled my client's ex-wife. She was a talkative woman. In fact, she was the kind of woman I'd had to keep close track of because she seldom stopped talking and often wanted to go overtime in our sessions. She was so sweet that if I didn't have an appointment immediately following hers, I'd just let her ramble on, but heaven knows I always had to be very forceful to bring her to a close. I could not imagine Mr. McElrath ever being married to her and being lonely.

"You were lonely. Say a little more about that."

"No, I never had a cat. I had a dog once, and she was a lot of company, but Sarah never cared much for dogs. They made her sneeze a lot. Allergies, you know."

"I'm sorry. You had to get rid of the dog, then?"

"Yes, we kept her in a pen. Couldn't have her in the house, what with the allergies. Beagles aren't particularly good house dogs anyway."

"So you didn't have to give the dog away."

"Yup, she liked to play. I used to say that was why her legs were so short. She ran 'em right down to the nubs."

"The dog was a good thing, then. But let's get back to the issue. When did you and your wife begin to grow apart?"

"No, I didn't fart. You might want to check the seal on the toilet in your restroom. Looked like you had a little leakage in there. But I'm no plumber. I was a tax accountant before I retired."

"So you liked to work with numbers?"

"Lumber? What would I do with lumber? I was an accountant, for Pete's sake. That had nothing to do with my depression. My wife caused my depression. Damned woman talked almost constantly for the fifty years we were married. Wore my ears out, I use to say. She'd get mad when I said that. Then it got so she never said anything. Just moved her mouth and flopped her hands around trying to mock me. She was a hard, spiteful woman."

"'A hard, spiteful woman;' tell me more if you can."

"No, she didn't have another man. At least I don't think she did. No one would put up with her. I'd a shot 'em both if I caught 'em. Who told you she had another man?"

"I didn't say she had another man. I'm sure she didn't. Were you ever jealous?"

"He lived in a palace? Don't be absurd. Where'd she meet a man like that? Wal-Mart? A yard sale? No, she liked reading tabloids and romance novels, but that's as close to royalty as she'll ever get. I think she had a crush on Charles back before he met Diana. Even she knew that was crazy.

She couldn't even flirt properly. No, I never had to worry about her that way. You just stick with the real problem, young man."

"All right. Tell me about your depression."

"That's right, get back to the session. You have a hard time staying on track, don't you? Sarah was the same way. Blah, blah, blah here. Blah, blah, blah there. Woman drove me nuts! 'Yackety yak, don't talk back!' I think women have a gene for talking. They don't need anything to say, they just say it anyway! Someday, if you want to get rich, find a hormone treatment for that! I used to watch her sleep. It was like she had a spring was getting wound up, and it made so much pressure inside her that if she didn't get fifty billion words out the next day she'd explode. Sometimes she exploded. It was kind of entertaining towards the end. Arms would flail and she'd jump up and down. You never saw an old woman jump up and down like that. Mouth a goin', all lathered up, and nothin' coming out."

"You liked to set her off."

"Cough? Yes, I suppose sometimes she'd cough. Couldn't help it the way she carried on."

"Were you depressed before the divorce, or did that come later?"

"No, I didn't hate her. I loved that woman. It wasn't until she started mocking me and stopped talking to me that things turned sour. All she'd a had to do was say something and we coulda worked it out. But no, she's a hard woman once she makes up her mind. Talk, talk, talk, one day. Stone silence the next."

"Do you have a hearing aid, Mr. McElrath?"

"Why would I need a maid? I can do things for myself."

“I'm sure you can. Mr. McElrath,” I shouted, “do you have a hearing aid?”

“What?”

I pointed to my ear. “Mr. McElrath, do you have a hearing aid?”

“Yes, I have a hearing aid. It doesn't do me much good, but I wear it sometimes.”

“Do you have it with you?” I yelled.

He dug into a pocket and pulled out a tiny hearing aid. It looked like new. I took it from him and examined the case. There was a teeny switch on the back, and I clicked it on. I handed it back and indicated he should put it in his ear. He did as I suggested.

“How long have you had this hearing aid?” I asked in a low tone.

“I got it about six months before the divorce. Sarah insisted. Wrong again! It didn't do any good. She was so smug and sure of herself. I told her. Damn thing cost three thousand dollars and didn't do anything. That place we got it from was just a bunch of get rich quick swindlers.”

“Mr. McElrath,” I whispered, “would you like to get back together with your wife?”

“Not if she's just going to continue to mock me. I still love her, but she'd have to make some changes.”

“Mr. McElrath, if you'll just stick with me a few more sessions, I think we might be able to make that happen.”

PROFESSIONAL

I love it when people say they don't believe in ghosts. It's a challenge, and I like challenges. I earn my keep as a ghost, you see.

I became a ghost in 1912 when I fell off the balcony of this hotel. I'd been drinking a bit, and I was showing off to my girlfriend, Gloria. Well, you know how it is. I was walking the railing and a manager came rushing out down below and he started yelling at me. I lost my concentration for just a moment, and oops....

Mind you, it wasn't the drinking that caused me to fall. It was the distraction. I still enjoy a drink now and then. I appreciate it when people leave their bottles open in the hotel rooms. It's kind of funny when they can't figure out where all their booze went. If that's ever happened to you, maybe you've been host to a ghost.

Sometimes I get a buzz on, and then I like to play tricks. I have a pretty good sense of humor. One of my favorite tricks is to find someone with glasses, but who doesn't wear their glasses all the time. I follow them around, and every time they take their glasses off I move them to some other room. That's always good for a laugh. Maybe you know what I'm talking about.

Another thing I like to do is wait until they're almost asleep and then start making buzzing noises like a fly or a mosquito. It's probably a little mean, but you've got to understand that being a ghost can be really boring at times. Watching someone slap around in the air and then dive under the covers can be sort of entertaining if you can get a rhythm going.

For the first ninety years or so that I was a ghost I didn't pay much attention to people. I was aware of them, but I just didn't bother to focus. Then one day about ten years ago I was crossing the lobby and I stopped to adjust my sheets. They're not really sheets, but you wouldn't understand. Anyway, the hotel owners were sitting there and I heard one of them say something about closing the place and tearing it down. That got my full attention. I've known some homeless ghosts, and they're a sorry lot—living in cardboard boxes and up under highway overpasses. I couldn't just float around and let that happen, but what's a ghost going to do?

I listened some more and learned that their problem was money. Isn't that just like people? The owners were looking for a new marketing strategy, and they brought in a new manager, Matt Aarons. Matt took up temporary residence in my room, and I've got to admit I was skeptical at first impression. He scared me a little with his seeming disregard for the better features of the place. After a few days I decided he was harmless, and so just for the sake of conversation I came up behind him while he was watching television and gave him a wet Willie. A wet Willie from a ghost involves a little green slime, and I can't say Matt was too happy with it. He spent nearly a half an hour cleaning out his ear, and I made it more interesting for him by constantly turning the water off and on in the sink. He was clueless. He called the plumber.

The next evening, just to show him I had his best interests in mind, I spent some time turning his television off and on. There's really nothing worth watching on television, so I figured I was doing him a favor. You can imagine my chagrin when he started cussing. So he missed the winning touchdown—it's only a game. He wound up calling the electrician.

I decided I needed to be more direct. If he was going to share my room, the least I could expect was some civil conversation. When he returned the following evening I greeted him and asked, "So, who is your favorite composer?" I took the fact that he didn't answer to mean that he wasn't really interested in music. I followed him to the refrigerator. "Have you read anything good lately?" I queried. Apparently he wasn't particularly literate, either. We went back to the couch. I tried to start a political discussion, then a religious conversation. I asked about money, sex, and ethics. I remarked about the weather, and I insulted his mother. I'd about decided the man was a moron, and out of exasperation I just said "Boo!"

He jumped about a foot and his face lost all color. "Who's there?" he asked.

With some people I guess you just have to get their attention. Matt seemed a little jumpy, and actually I needed to calm down a bit, too, so I poured us each a drink. Three drinks later and he began to talk. A couple of drinks after that and he seemed to start understanding what I said. We talked about the trouble the hotel was having, and Matt mentioned that the owners were getting closer and closer to the idea of tearing the old place down.

I've got to say, it made me pretty upset. I got up and started to pace. I always pace when I'm nervous. I like to have something in my hands when I pace, so I carefully picked up an urn.

"Think," I said. "Think! We've got to think of something." I kept pacing. Matt just sat and watched me, but I could tell he was thinking, too.

"Can you do that any time?"

"Do what?"

"Make that vase float around in the air."

"Well, I suppose. Of the five senses, the sense of touch is the least reliable for a ghost. Since we can just pass through walls and stuff, it tends to get in the way. We have four other senses that people don't have, so we don't really miss it. But sure, I could probably pull it off most times. Why?"

Matt got up and started pacing, too. "We may be able to save this hotel after all. I'll need your help." At that point we started laying out some plans, and I became a professional ghost. I have a much better self-image now than I ever had before.

A huge publicity campaign was begun. The hotel was advertised as a place where people could come for ghost encounters. Matt hired a couple of gypsy fortune tellers and a couple of psychics and started tours. The fortune tellers and one of the psychics are nothing but fakes, but they're good at what they do. I mess with them once in awhile by hiding their props, but mostly I just let them do their jobs. The other psychic and I have become pretty good friends, and we often meet for drinks with Matt after work.

I have a lot more contact with the guests than I used to have. Every so often I do a little poltergeisting, and I'll give a wet Willie now and then. What's been most interesting to me are those people who don't believe in ghosts. They're more likely than the others to make fools of themselves when they think nobody is around. You'd never believe some of the things I've seen. Whooee! I should write a book. Actually, people can be a lot scarier than ghosts.

Puzzle

It was a dusty room, full of reflected light woven in blue shadows. The old man sitting at the desk didn't look up when I entered.

"Sit down." The voice was deep, with soft edges.

I sat. The chair beside the desk was soft and warm, but it did little to ease my agitation.

"I died," I blurted.

"So you say," came the slow reply. The man continued to look at the large puzzle in front of him, moved a piece into place, and then looked up with a slow smile. "Who are you?"

I gave him my name. He scratched the back of his neck.

"No, really, who are you?"

"I told you."

"What you did was give me a name. 'What's in a name? A rose by any other name would smell as sweet.'"

Ordinarily his response would have set me off, but there was no sarcasm in his tone, and I suddenly felt compelled to tell this old man about my job, my family, my community—my whole life, really. I even told him about the accident.

When I finished he folded his hands in his lap, tilted his head slightly to the left, and peered at me appraisingly. "Now we're getting somewhere. Now do you see who you are?"

I just looked at him. I didn't understand at all what he was after. "I'm me. I just died. What do you want me to say?"

"You're not you." He looked down and shook his head slowly. "You never existed, at least not in the way you think you did. Let's start with that body you think you're wearing."

I glanced down and was surprised I could see right through myself. I looked up and discovered I could see right through the old man, too. Surprising as it was, it was, in another way, just natural.

"Your body was made up of just six elements, at least those six elements accounted for 99% of it. Oxygen, carbon, hydrogen, nitrogen, calcium and phosphorus. Could you have said that the oxygen is you? The nitrogen?"

"No."

"About eighty percent of the body is water, the combination of oxygen and hydrogen. Was that water you?"

"No."

"If you put them, all six, together in a dish along with the other one percent, the potassium, sodium, sulfur, and so on, would they then be you?"

"No."

"Just like the hydrogen and oxygen have to bond together in a special kind of relationship, so all of the elements have to be in relationship to form a body and life. But then you didn't even mention your body when I asked who you were. The body isn't important? You never judged other people by their looks? Their physical abilities? As a teenager, you didn't spend hours in front of a mirror popping zits and combing your hair?"

"Well, I guess I did." At this point I was a little embarrassed, but the old man continued without seeming to notice. He was on a roll.

"When I pushed you to tell me who you are, what did you tell me?"

"I talked about friends and family and my job, where I'm from, things I'd done, pets, groups I'd belonged to."

"Every one of those things pointed to you in some kind of relationship, didn't it?"

"Yeah, I guess."

"What would you be without those relationships? Don't you see? You don't exist. You're nothing more than a bundle of stories you told me, and those stories only arose because of the relationships. Oh, the relationships might change, but you're still nothing by yourself. Just like oxygen isn't a body by itself, you aren't anything by yourself, either."

"I'm nothing?"

"By yourself."

"By myself?"

"That's what I said. So, what does it mean if we follow the idea to its conclusion? It's the same question I was left here with a while back." Just then the old man smiled and stood. He sort of jiggled all over in a kind of glee and said, "I just got it!" He disappeared.

I blinked.

When I opened my eyes I was sitting in his chair. A huge jigsaw puzzle was scattered on the desk in front of me. It seemed to be the universe. I picked up one of the interlocking pieces and began to search for its position. Just as I snapped it into place I sensed the shadows around me move and I heard the door to the room open.

I didn't look up when she entered; I just softly bade her, "Sit down."

"I died, "she blurted.

"So you say. Who are you?"

Conspiracy Theory

I'm not a conspiracy theory kind of guy. I've never taken much stock in stories of the supernatural, either. I want to get that out right away. It's important that you know I never bought into the Kennedy conspiracies, or UFO's, or heard voices or anything like that. It's also probably important that you know that I'm a sensitive guy; my jealous wife died seven years ago; I'm seventy-two years old, and I like to travel. Emma and I used to travel a lot, and I didn't stop when she passed away. I'm from here in Michigan, but until these last two months I hadn't spent a winter here in ten years. Oh, I suppose I could grumble and say it's almost as cold here as Emma was after forty years of marriage, but I'd be kidding, mostly, if I said that. At any rate, she hated winters, and to keep the peace, I always headed us south.

My observations were jump-started last October on Waikiki. I was having coffee with a nice widow on the veranda of the Banyon—that's where I was staying—and I saw a group of elderly women walk by in the street. The woman in the lead had silver hair, but she had streaked it with purple. The rest of 'em had funny colored hair, too. I've seen the gang girls at home color their hair that same way. They were all wearing leather jackets and chains like the gang girls. The youngest of those women had to have been at least sixty-two or sixty-three, and it got me thinking. Groups of women like that make me nervous, but seeing them in leather and sporting spikey, colored hair really set my teeth on edge. They were probably going to “Gang Day” at the Senior Center or some such thing, but one of them looked a lot like Emma. She stopped and glared at me. Did I mention that Emma was always kind of jealous? The idea of a gang-girl Emma starring at me set me to packing my bags.

A month later I was eating at the Clock restaurant on Tamiami Trail in Venice, Florida. I was with a nice woman I'd met at a literary forum they hold at the library. A group of women came in—oh, there must have been eleven or twelve of them—and they pulled three tables together right near our booth. Loud? Why in the world is it that if you put any two women in the same place at the same time they both have to talk at once—and twelve women simply means twelve voices. One of those voices was kind of high and crackly like Emma's. I looked up, and the woman with the crackly voice was staring straight at me. I'd only half finished my country-fried steak, but I had to get out of there. I excused myself. I didn't even wait for a doggie bag.

I moved on to Sedona, Arizona. I like it there among the red rock canyons and monoliths. It was on a Tuesday, and we were about halfway up a trail on the east side of Bell Rock. My lady friend and I had seen no other hikers since we'd left the parking lot. There were little wisps of cloud pasted in an otherwise deep blue sky. As I stepped out onto a wide ledge that traverses a space under a thirty-foot outcrop, a shower of red sandstone pelted down all around us. I guess I must have let out a yell, because a high pitched, crackly voice floated down. "Oops, we're sorry!" I could hear several female voices having a discussion. They all seemed to be speaking at the same time. A minute later the crackly voice called out again, "Are you okay? Do you need help?"

I swear the tone of it sounded like Emma. I replied that I was fine and headed down the trail fast enough that I expect there was a dust cloud behind me. I can't imagine what my friend thought. I just flat out abandoned her, but she had her own car in the parking lot. During that shower of rocks was when I first began to suspect that Emma was following me, and that she'd somehow enlisted the women of the world to help her. It was just the kind of thing she'd try to do.

I moved on to Helen, Georgia. Helen is beautiful in December. It's a little cheesy, as are most towns that have adopted a Bavarian theme, but that doesn't spoil the surrounding waterfalls, wineries and art galleries. There is a museum there that celebrates pottery in general, but more particularly a kind of stoneware jug that is indigenous to the area. Most of those jugs have really obnoxious faces on them, and they're done in a local clay. My new friend, Ellen, and I were taking in the museum. I was lost in reading the history of one of those jugs when I heard voices—female voices. Seven or eight voices at once—a busload. I learned from their conversation with the cashier that they were retired elementary teachers from Ohio. They all had those teacher voices that can put fear into a classroom of hardened, delinquent children, but it was one voice, a high, crackly voice, that most attracted my attention. When I turned back to the pottery I found myself face to face with a pot that bore a near likeness of Emma, only in an emerald green. I was so unnerved I left immediately and started driving toward Branson, Missouri.

While driving down the interstate, I started thinking about all of the spy novels I'd read. I began taking exits and doubling back. I explored back roads and watched carefully for a tail. I wasn't sure what I was up against, but I knew I had to be careful. Finally I stopped and looked at a map. It was circuitous, but I plotted a course using the most unlikely back roads to Branson. I tuned in a country station, 104.3, and began to drive.

On a wine tasting tour in Branson I met a woman from St. Louis who was traveling alone. We agreed that we liked the muscadine wine, and we bought a bottle and went down to the river for a picnic. That evening we went to see Shoji Tabuchi. We sat in the fourteenth row, center, and were enjoying ourselves immensely. Then I heard a high, crackly voice behind me say, "What do you suppose that old man ahead of us is doing with that hussy? Doesn't he just have the nerve?"

What could I do? Where does a person run?

I turned and looked. I recognized the hair-do. It wasn't exactly Emma, but I knew that crooked smile. All of the women in the row seemed to be snickering. I excused myself and headed for the men's room. That was the one place where I figured I might find enough peace to think my way out of my problem. It is an amazing men's room in that theater. There's a pool table, and the faucets are gold, and it's much fancier than any home I've ever been in. I found some comfort in not being followed there, at least by a woman, though I admit to checking under the doors of all of the stalls. Seeing no problems, I went into the stall furthest from the door and sat down. I was a desperate man. I thought a long while, and then, having come up with no escape plan, I went out to the parking lot. As I stepped through the door and out of the air conditioning, I was greeted with the evening heat. Bingo!

Emma hated winters. I got in my car and headed north. I can't prove a conspiracy, but I haven't had a problem going out with any of my women friends since I got back to Michigan. That was two months ago. It's April now, and things are starting to green up nicely. I hate to think of the possibility that I'll have to stop dating until next November.

Lucky Night

I saw her sitting at a corner table. She was hard to miss. She was hard to miss because she and I and the bartender were the only ones in the place. In the back of my mind something stirred. *This might be my lucky night,* I remember thinking. I was new in town, and I'd been waiting forty years for a lucky night.

I looked more closely. The lack of prior planning had ruined more than one previous opportunity. *Get yourself straight before you make your move,* I said to myself. The last time I tried to ad-lib, I wound up blurting out that I was a Catholic priest. I run a service station, but at that moment priest sounded more important. Besides, the woman had looked like someone I'd enjoy hearing a confession from. As it was, I did. Her confession left me hot for a month, but she left the place with a restored sense of her own virginity. I had to be more careful.

I took a seat at the bar. The woman was sitting behind me and to the right. I ducked my head and peered under my armpit so she wouldn't see me looking at her and become nervous. She was wearing dark slacks and a lacy white blouse with the collar button undone. I tried to imagine what another three buttons would do, but the blood was running to my head and I had to sit up again. I was seeing double by that time. Seeing more than what was really there reminded me of the time I'd picked up the girl with three breasts, but she'd turned out to be a drag queen with a weird sense of humor. I ordered another Miller's.

I ducked down and took another peek. She had long, wavy hair, brunette, but who can really tell these days? I don't think women are ever satisfied. I can't think of a single one who doesn't dye her hair—other than my aunt Beatrice. Beatrice only has about three hairs left, so she wears a big, red wig. Nobody would pick up Aunt Beatrice, probably not even Uncle Artie if he had it to do over.

Forty, maybe fifty? It's hard to judge age upside down. She appeared to be about half good looking. Rubber soled work shoes. Probably a clerk in some store.

She glanced my way, and I sat up fast so she wouldn't see me staring. Hit my damned head on the bar. I hoped she thought what I said was Spanish. I ordered another Miller's.

Bartender asked me if I was all right. "Yeah," I said, "I've just been having trouble keeping these shoe laces tied. Tell me, what's the lady over there drinking?"

"Double rum Bahama Mammas."

"Do you know her?"

"Can't help you, pal." In retrospect, I think he really meant to say that he wouldn't help me. I chugged my beer and ordered another Miller's. I had very little to go on. My head hurt, but I dropped a napkin so I could bend down to get it and take another glance at the woman. She was looking at me. I remember thinking, *Maybe she's interested.* I didn't want her to think I was staring, so I stood up fast. In doing so I hit the other side of my head on the bar. I said a few things, but not too loud. I hoped again that she thought it was Spanish.

I had a sense the woman would go for the strong, quiet type. I needed a line, a persona. I had to think. If she'd seen me bump my head I was in trouble. But if she'd only kinda heard what I said...maybe that was it. Spanish. It was like the answer just popped into my head. I ordered two Miller's and a double rum Bahama Mamma. The bartender gave me a look that I couldn't quite fathom, but I let it slide. I had to be cool. I chugged one of the Miller's, stood up as tall as I could stretch myself, and ambled over to her table.

"Hey, Senorita, you look like pretty hot tamale. You wanna take a walk on the wild side?" I said as I put the double rum Bahama Mamma down in front of her.

"Gracias. ¿Cómo estás? You think you're pretty hot shit, doncha? Bien, mantener los pantalones en, bebé." She motioned for me to sit.

I sat down and just nodded. She spoke Spanish. That could be trouble. She chugged the drink, so I chugged my beer and ordered another round.

"Whatcher name?" I asked.

"What's yours, stud?"

It was time to think quickly. If I used a Latino name I was stuck with that persona. Diablo was out. So was Pedro. I panicked. "Aurelio. What's yours?"

"Depends on who's askin' and where I'm at," she replied evasively.

I just raised my eyebrows and nodded my head for her to go on.

"Outa high school I worked for awhile as an exotic dancer in Cleveland. I went as Suzanne there. Six months and I'd developed such varicose veins I had to quit. Got infection and had to have one leg removed just below the knee. Moved up to Jackson after that. You gonna order me another drink?"

I signaled the bartender. My woman was better looking than some, and a missing leg wasn't a huge problem. "So, what did you do in Jackson?"

"I was a dental assistant. I answered to the name Trudy there. At this point she pulled her teeth out and set them on the table. "Took me fife yearth ta pay theeth off, but ain' they beauties?"

I nodded. The barman brought our drinks.

"Afther tha' I had to go to Ann Arbor. They do thome wonderful thinks at tha' hothpital. I went to Ann Arbor, you thee, becauth one day Doc. Johnson—tha' wath the dentihth in Jackson—handed me back a dental pick and I wathn't lookin' and he caught me in the eye." At this point she plucked a glass eye out of her right socket, set it on the table, and chugged her drink.

I chugged my beer.

"I wen' ath Marlene in Ann Arbor. Took me near ten yearth ta pay off thith here eyeball. After tha' I moved around thome, and then wound up in Battle Creek." She stopped and gave me a look with her good eye. "You gonna order me another drink?"

I waved to the bartender. "So wha'd you do in Battle Creek, Marlene?"

She looked lovingly into her glass eyeball. "In Battle Creek I changed my name to Gwen. I met a man named Henry. We fell in love. I wath ridin' on hith Harley when I lotht my left ear." She pulled back her hair and revealed some smooth scar tissue. "I lotht Henry, too." A tear formed in her left eye.

We sat for a minute in respectful silence. I started to stand, but just then the barman brought our drinks. I sat back down and paid him. As the young man walked away, Gwen chugged her drink and nodded at me to do the same. I took a sip and I saw the contemptuous sneer start to form on her wrinkled lips. I was almost beyond performing, but I managed the world's slowest chug.

Gwen looked at my empty glass with a satisfied smile, then turned and yelled at the bar, "Therveza, por favor, para el hombre! An' another drink for me."

"Tho, amigo, leth talk about you. What do you do for a living?" she asked.

It was time to think quickly. The last time I'd told a woman I was a stockbroker she'd looked at the grease under my fingernails and laughed out loud. If I used any kind of Latino sounding job, Gwen'd be onto me in a second—yet it seemed I was stuck with that persona. I panicked.

"I'm a matador," I replied. Thinking quickly, I added, "Mostly I deal in livestock. My days in the ring are pretty much over. I'm in town on a cattle buying trip."

Her one eye narrowed. "The thtockyards closed here fifty yearth ago. You wouldn't be feeding me el feces de Toro, would you?"

I didn't understand her Spanish, but I sensed she was suspicious. "My uncle Juan has a farm about thirty miles west of here." I needed to change the subject quickly. "So, how did you happen to wind up here in Muskegon, Gwen?"

The bartender set our drinks on the table and waited for me to pull my wallet out and pay him. The break gave me a little bit of time to collect my wits.

"Oh, I don't go by Gwen anymore." She chugged her drink and looked at mine expectantly. "I goth a job here with

Victoria's Thecret." She began toying with the second button on her lacy white blouse.

I suddenly lost all of the wits I had collected. Visions of negligees and possible missing body parts flashed through my mind. I chugged my drink.

"So what should I call you now?"

She smiled toothlessly and tossed her head in the way of beautiful women. Her dark hair swirled around her face. "Dulthinea," she purred.

I said, "Excuse me. I need to visit the restroom." I got up and headed for the front door. She didn't say anything, but as the door closed behind me and the cool night air chilled the sweat against my skin, I thought I heard the bartender say, "So, you want another drink, Ma?"

Forty years I'd been waiting, and as I walked away I reflected, *I think this may have been my lucky night.*

A Quilting

By his side sat a brown box in which there was a quilt sewn by his mother. The quilt was a collection of odds and ends from the family history: old shirts, skirts, and other favored items. He had brought it to add color to the hospital room.

He shifted nervously on his bench and gazed up the long corridor of the hospital. He was waiting for his sister. Eight years earlier they had not parted on good terms. Eight years without speaking; there was so much to say. But what to say? He puzzled over the question as a steady stream of visitors and patients filed past. While his mind turned his situation over and over, snatches of conversation and the people walking by began to filter into his consciousness:

"I've never missed one of his games," a woman in a yellow sheath dress smiled to her friend. "I'll just be gone a couple of hours. I promise."

"You know, all they have to do is go over the state line and get them. It's not that far."

"So is he there for you emotionally?" he heard a thirty-something brunette speak into her cell phone as she strode by. "Well, he..." She was down the hall before he could hear more; her tone left him wondering if she was capable of emotional satisfaction.

An old woman in a pink sweater approached from the other direction. She was berating a hospital employee as they walked. "Well, that's crazy! I tell you, they're just crazy..." She was waggling her finger in the air as she rounded the corner.

A young girl in jeans and a tee-shirt that celebrated a high school volleyball championship stumbled by. An older woman—she didn't appear to be her mother—was supporting her and supplying her with Kleenex. Both had tear-filled eyes rimmed in red. "It was just too much. I'm so sorry..."

"My wife has almost decided on paint...."

"I have nineteen shifts to cover during the week, twenty-three on weekends. Once those are filled, that's it." The pear-shaped man was wearing a hospital identification badge, and as he walked he was speaking earnestly with a young black woman who looked disappointed.

"An outfitter is driving him to Boise. From there Ron's friend will fly him to Salt Lake. There's a flight out of there at twelve-twenty if they can make the connections. I've been trying to raise him on the cell phone, but he's got to get out of the mountains first."

"...was just waiting for her kids to get in. I don't know how she did it."

A young Vietnamese man spoke excitedly into a cell phone, "Hello, Grandma? She's here. Six pounds, ten ounces, and nineteen inches long...."

"I don't know if I can do it. They say they're going to let her out tomorrow, but what'll I do then?" The wizened little man with a cane was looking up at the young woman in plaid and speaking without a shred of hope.

"I don't have any idea where those papers might be. Did they have a safe deposit box?"

"The good Lord was definitely on our side this time. I can't believe there were no symptoms. We were so lucky...."

"...got out of his car and laid the rifle across the hood. You should have seen it. That dog spun around in about fifteen circles before he took off."

"How does she feel about it?"

"I really don't want to go, but if I don't, I'm afraid of what could happen. You know how they can be."

"Don't feel bad, Sarah. He's never been able to say, 'I love you.' Any time you say it to him, all he can ever say is, 'Me, too.'"

A man with a drooping black moustache came from the cafeteria corridor. He was dressed in a jeans jacket and a wool shirt. The miserable expression on his face spoke the story before he said anything. "I'm afraid I've blown it, haven't I?"

"Yup," was all the woman walking with him said.

He had seen him at least twice on earlier visits. Wearing a helmet and a white coat with a hospital I.D., a man rode by on an Amigo waving to everyone and stopping often to speak to those who recognized him. His smile was infectious. He clearly enjoyed what he was doing.

"I only packed for five days. It's going to be at least another week. I'm going to have to leave tonight. Do you think Carl would come and get me?"

"...the downstairs bedroom's ready. I think that's best, but I wish we...."

"They say we won't know for at least twenty-four hours. The doctor said the chances were fifty-fifty at best. Maybe we should...."

He stood as his sister walked through the double doors and threaded her way past the yellow signs warning WET FLOOR. He met her silently and looked into her eyes. There was nothing to say. Everything had been said. He simply handed her the quilt.

Alternate Energies

The feeling of distaste and revulsion started at his feet and traveled quickly upward, stopping momentarily at his spleen and then climbing again to settle like a musk ox on his tongue. He didn't like this man standing before him, Michael W. Barrow. He detested him. He despised him.

"Have you finished yet with that report on the Carthaginian Coal Company?"

"No, Mr. Barrow, it'll be about another half hour."

"Make it fifteen minutes!"

"Yes, sir."

He loathed Michael W. Barrow. He imagined him as a lump of coal at the bottom of the Carthaginian Coal mine. He imagined using a pickaxe to extract him. He imagined kicking the lump of coal down the street like a schoolboy with a can. He imagined throwing him into a blast furnace and then laughing maniacally as the flames consumed him.

But, Michael W. Barrow was his boss. Michael W. Barrow was half again his height and probably had double his strength. There was nothing he could do...except wait. And plan. It was his imagination and cunning that would win out in the end.

He signed the report, Elmer C. Gull, and handed it to Mr. Barrow's secretary. Barrow Energy provided middleman services for clients looking for energy sources. They dealt mostly with traditional energy sources, coal and gas, but were beginning to examine some of the alternatives. Elmer was always looking for alternatives. He knew he should be in research and development. His imagination would make him a success. *I should be one of the engineers,* he thought as he walked back to his desk.

He passed Miss Henning's desk. Today she was wearing a blouse with a silvery, metallic sheen. *Hmm,* his imagination began to work. He could feel her warmth as she lay next to him. *Body heat, aaah. If only there was a way to capture that body heat and convert it into another form of energy. A body suit. Outlets. A person could be a walking receptacle and plug in any small appliance and provide his own energy. The suit would require a storage battery.* When he returned to his desk he began to sketch his idea. He imagined Miss Henning in a sleek, form-fitting, silver body suit, but the idea of a Delco battery attached to the backside distracted him so much that he lost his train of thought and put the plans aside.

At lunchtime Elmer walked by himself to Jose Ling's Mexican-Chinese-American Restaurant. Absently he ordered a bean burrito. He began again to think of Miss Henning. He ate slowly, and it was not until he stood up to walk to the counter to pay for his meal that he realized what he had done. Bean burritos always gave him an upset stomach. Caused gas. Cramps.

As he walked back to the office a bus passed close along the curb, growling and leaving him in a gray swirl of diesel fumes. *Bus,* he thought. He passed his own gas, and for a moment the plethora of odors rippled and danced together on the warm breeze. *Burrito Bus. One might go forever powered only by the natural effects of bean burritos. It would be a revolution.* He took the small notebook from his shirt pocket and made notes.

Elmer opened the door to the office building. Suddenly doors all over the city were opened in his mind. *Every time a door is opened, there's energy created in the friction of the hinges. If every hinge in the city were wired, they might add electric power to the local grid with each entry or exit. It's ingenious! I should be in engineering.* He made more notes.

"The report for the Dalmation Dam Project, where is it, Gull?"

Elmer had just returned to his seat. *Damn project!* was what he thought. What he said was, "Did you look in the tray on your desk, Mr. Barrow?"

"Of course I did, you idiot! I want you to find that report, and fast!"

Elmer got up and went into Mr. Barrow's office. "I'm sure I put it here, Mr. Barrow." He shuffled around the papers. "Here it is." It was under the *Sports Illustrated.* The cover of the magazine had the picture of a beautiful model wearing a swimsuit that was at least four sizes too small for her. Elmer couldn't help thinking of Miss Henning. Behind the model in the picture were several large palm trees. *Hmmm,* Elmer thought, *trees store energy in their roots. If we could tap into that energy—like tapping maples for syrup in the spring, I'll bet we could power whole cities.* He was remembering that he had recently read that 38% of the United States was forested.

"Uh, that'll be all for now, Gull. I'll need that report on the Peterson Propane Project by four-thirty."

Elmer wandered back to his desk. Miss Henning was sitting with her legs crossed. *I'd like to uncross those legs,* Elmer thought, and suddenly found himself blushing as Miss Henning looked up. She self-consciously uncrossed her legs and turned back to her desk. Elmer was already thinking about how often people crossed and uncrossed their legs each day. He imagined that if pants could be wired so that the energies produced by crossing and uncrossing legs were captured, civilization might well be able to do away with all coal-fired power plants. And Mr. Barrow. He jotted his ideas in his notebook.

At four o'clock Mr. Barrow came storming out of his office and thundered, "Miss Henning! You misspelled the word *principle* in this report. That's thee misspellings this month. Miss Henning, you are incompetent! Miss Henning, you are fired! You may pick up your final paycheck from the Payroll Department. Please make certain you leave all of the pens and pencils you have been supplied in your desk!" He turned and stomped back into his office.

There was a tear on the cheek of the shocked Miss Henning when Elmer glanced her way. He imagined going to her and comforting her. He would take her in his arms and hold her until the pain went away.

He stood. He envisaged going to Mr. Barrow right then and telling him what a world-class jerk he was. He would punch him smartly in the nose and leave him sitting in a heap on the plushly carpeted floor of his office.

Plush carpeting. Elmer sat down. *Plush carpeting causes static electricity. If there was a way to harness that.... Perhaps wiring in the soles of people's shoes and little batteries hidden in the heels. I should be in engineering,* Elmer imagined. He made a quick diagram.

The sound of Miss Henning sobbing as she cleared her desk drew Elmer's attention away from his notes. Crying women were a form of energy he couldn't fathom. It frightened him a little. Nevertheless, he found himself crossing to her and asking if there was anything he could do. She sobbed even harder. He was frightened even more. *What if someone walks in and finds me standing over her while she's sobbing?* He raised his hand to pat her shoulder, but lowered it and went back to his desk.

Peterson Propane Project. Peterson Propane Project. Peterson Propane Project. Elmer tried to focus. He pulled up the file and quickly scanned the contents. He typed a few sentences and hit Print. He walked the copy to Mr. Barrow's office. Miss Henning was still sobbing at her desk. He delivered the papers and stepped back out. He walked blankly to Miss Henning's desk and reached out and put his hand on her shoulder. She looked up at him. Her face was red and puffy. The mascara that had run down from her eyes put Elmer in mind of Navaho Kachina dolls. Peterson Propane was located on a reservation. It seemed that most reservations these days had casinos. It seemed like the convergence of these facts was more than a coincidence. He didn't normally gamble, but sometimes a person just gets that feeling. "Dinner?" he asked. She wiped her nose. After a long pause she nodded her head affirmatively.

"When you're finished here, stop by my desk and I'll...I'll walk you out," Elmer stammered.

He pondered the idea of a career in social engineering as he skipped back to his cubicle. It had been seven years since his last date. His senior year in high school. He'd thought he'd been scarred for life. He felt the scars beginning to melt away.

Later, as they finished their pasta at a quiet table in a dark corner of the patio of Luigi's Linguini and Libations, Elmer watched as a waiter frightened away the pigeons that were begging from the customers.

"What do you think frightens Barrow?" he mused. He and Miss Henning had been pondering her unfortunate turn of fate.

"His wife. The I.R.S. Liberal judges. That's about it, I think."

Elmer entered the zone. "Who is the most liberal judge you know?"

"Judge Guilford, I guess."

"You were one of Barrow's secretaries. Anything you can think of that the I.R.S. might want to look into?"

"I wasn't really privy to much of that kind of information. Last year Larry Long of Long Industries gave Barrow's wife a diamond necklace as a gift before he sent her and Barrow off to Bermuda on that getaway. I remember, because it was so quiet around the office that week that I actually got some work done."

"Hmmm. Can we find anything against him that might set his wife off?"

"That's easy enough, but what good would it do?"

"Just thinking. Blackmail?" Elmer started to imagine tropical beaches, rum drinks, reggae, and Miss Henning in little more than a sun hat. *Sun hat? Sun hat with solar panels...little fans....* He made a quick sketch in his notebook. Elmer felt his energies rising.

"Well, he does have all those porn sites bookmarked on his computer. I just hate the thought of porn, don't you? We could tell his wife about those."

"Oh, yeah, I don't like porn." Elmer pulled out his notebook and added a bikini to the sketch. "I'm not sure how we could use them to blackmail him into hiring you back, though. He could just erase them if he wanted."

"Oh, don't worry too much about that. I was going to quit in a couple of weeks anyway. I'll just move in with my fiancée a little early."

Elmer felt his energies drain away.

As he walked back to his apartment that evening Elmer kicked at a can in the gutter. He picked it up and wrote Barrow across the label. After abusing the can for a block and a half, he gave one final kick and it rolled up to a sewer grate and fell in. The sounds of the sewer flowing below would once have had Elmer building dams or floating to the sea. Tonight his energy was spent. Tonight he would sleep. Perhaps tomorrow he would show Mr. Barrow plans for adding pedals underneath the desks of the secretaries so they could power their own computers. *Secretaries, humph!* He had some ideas for hiring a new secretary, too.

The Door

Screaming brakes, a cold rain of shattering glass, violent pounding, and the taste of blood-soaked dirt. Dark silence.

Then came a state somewhere between being awake and being unconscious, a state where awareness is both heightened and uncertain. Our car, a red Malibu, had rolled down the side of an embankment and was wedged upside down between three large pines and a boulder.

My first awareness was of an uneven shimmering of light. It was poised just above Andrea in the passenger's seat. I tried to speak. The light gained substance, turned and looked at me. I was aware of the gaze, even though the presence remained little more than a shimmer.

"Who are you?"

He remained silent for a moment, and then his focus shifted back to Andrea. Gradually, I heard the voices of young children, bells and laughter gradually coming closer. The light grew. Andrea murmured and shifted. Then the light and the sounds faded. I knew. I just knew she was gone.

The shimmer moved to hover over Ron, the driver. The presence seemed more corporeal in this new position.

"Who are you?" I tried to ask again. It is difficult to explain, but the shimmer cocked his head as though listening. Slowly he took on a more human form, moving between Ron and me.

"Who are you?" I think the question was more in my mind than on my lips. Then it came to me. "Death?"

There was a faint smile and he nodded his head affirmatively. I started to speak, but he held up his hand and moved to Shawna, who was in the seat beside me. She moaned, and a bubble of blood formed at the edge of her mouth. The form became a dazzling light and reached out for her. I swear I heard a fanfare. Over the odors of oil and rubber and dust, the scent of incense became ascendant. It lasted only moments.

"She's gone?" I asked.

"In a manner of speaking."

The form seemed to hover again between me and Ron. The loss of Shawna and Andrea brought a lump to my throat, and the form shifted in my direction. Then it stopped and turned to Ron. In an instant, it grew to a gargantuan size with devilish horns, dagger teeth, razor spines and claws. Ron shook and screamed as it reached for him. A wall of heat seared through the car. Soon it was over. A laugh tinged with insanity faded into the distance.

I was shaken. "What was that?"

"Each of you meets me on his or her own terms and with different expectations. In your friend's case, there was a lot of fear and guilt. His imagination got the best of him."

"And now? What's happening to him now?"

"I have no idea. I'm only Death."

"I don't understand."

"I would expect that. Your consciousness has been caught in a kind of aberration. You were never meant to see and share what your friends experienced. Soon you, too, are going to have to make a choice. From what I can tell, it would seem you have a lot to live for."

I was still a half step behind. "You have no idea what's on the other side?"

"Well, very little."

"Heaven? Hell?"

"That will be up to you. Everyone carries their hopes, fears, beliefs and questions with them. You may decide they're no longer relevant, or they're false, but they go with you nonetheless. You may abandon some of them pretty quickly, I understand. But you'll keep on. These universes aren't finished creating, you know."

"And you, Death?"

"Oh, you'll leave me behind, too. I'm nothing but a portal." He moved closer and looked into my eyes.

"A door?" I asked. I thought of my three friends, and I already missed them. My mind began to clear. There were still other people I loved, and some business I had yet to do. I wanted to live. The shimmer of a man melted and re-formed in the shape of a weathered plank door.

"Just a door," he replied as the entry closed.

He disappeared. I was left with a striking image: a door, but with a light showing through the crack at the bottom.

The Anniversary

My forty-third anniversary comes in two weeks. That's quite a lot by today's standards, and my wife asked me to write a love poem in commemoration. I declined the invitation, though I know there will be a price to pay. There'd be a price either way. Think about it. Just think about the possible rhymes: forty-third, absurd, nerd, gave me the bird, curd, gird, herd, demurred, yes sirred, and turd. My decline was the lesser of two evils. Instead, I have decided to write the truth and smuggle it out in a garbage can full of fish entrails and zucchini peelings. Forty three years....

When I married Kate she seemed to be a sweet, innocent, engaging woman. You can imagine my surprise the morning I woke up bound in duct tape. I lost all of the hair on my legs getting loose from that. My only sin at the time was a late return after spending an evening counseling my friend Randy about troubles he was having with his marriage. Was I to blame that we were forced to meet in Taco Mary's bar so that we could have some privacy? Was I to blame that Randy kept ordering shots and beers to ease his pain? Now, when I hear someone speak about sleeping with one eye open, I don't doubt the truth of it.

It was about six months into our marriage that we had a bit of an argument about shared responsibility for grocery shopping. I probably said something kind of sexist or condescending. I came home the next night to a dinner of beet and rutabaga casserole. I don't like beets. Rutabagas are not high on my list. Fasting is a good thing. The next night she warmed up the same dish and added anchovies. I hate anchovies. I do most of the grocery shopping to this day. I learned early on that with Kate it is best to say nothing.

Before our first anniversary was even a glint on the horizon in this sea of life, I had learned the hard way. Even if you win an argument with your wife, you never really win the argument. Oh, they're subtle, but take my word for it, you'll pay: withholding favors, redecorating, visits to her mother's, fake snoring, long silences, the absence of long silences....

Elephants do not have the longest memories in the animal kingdom. Point in case: she once made the right call about a wheel bearing going out in the car. I thought it was brakes. Based on that one incident, she has asserted dominance in things mechanical for forty-two years. Would she ever change the oil or wiper blades? No, but to hear her, she knows way more about cars than Enzo Ferrari.

On our second anniversary I bought us each a new bowling ball. It turns out Kate isn't fond of bowling. I didn't fully understand until I came home one evening and found the bowling balls cemented into the new walkway through our garden. My favorite driver and an old baseball mitt added to the motif. Kate, I learned, is not a sportswoman. She does have a bowling pin that has been converted into a lamp. It's not really a lamp, despite the stylish shade. It's a club. I can tell you that much.

By our tenth anniversary I had the scars to count the years. I thought I was doing a good thing when I bought her a new Kirby Vacuum. They're top of the line! Her life would be so much easier. I thought. I did my best to reason with her. With Kate, I learned, it's often best to say nothing. I'm still pushing my Kirby, though I limp on rainy days.

For our twentieth anniversary I arranged a trip to Orlando. A second honeymoon getaway. Kate was not happy when she learned about the time share presentation. The couch in an Orlando time share is not a particularly good place to sleep. The couch when we returned home was not much better. I think Orlando is where I started feeling my arthritis.

For our thirtieth anniversary I arranged a cruise. We were to take a sunset sailboat ride out of Ludington. I figured it was as romantic as anything I could afford. Four foot waves and a twenty-two knot wind were not conducive to romance. Kate, it turns out, is not a sailor. It was months before I got my next shore leave.

Our fortieth anniversary arrived. By that time I had enough scars and assorted disfigurements so that I was running scared. I hired a bluegrass band and invited most of our acquaintances to a party. My thinking was that she wouldn't hurt me in front of a crowd. I helped cook and set up. You would think Kate wouldn't mind doing a bit to entertain our friends. Maybe the twelve hours she had to put in as preparation was a bit much to expect, but it was a celebration. She didn't need to spend the next day sewing all the flies on my undershorts closed or greasing the handles on my golf clubs.

Ask me the secret of living together forty-three years and I can tell you in a heartbeat. After forty-three years you come to feel the rhythms in a person. I got to know the monthlies, and the silences, and the "your turns." It took years, however, for me to understand the rhythm that most worries me now. I didn't recognize it for the longest time, but for many years Kate has used more make-up when there is a full moon. There is a full moon on the night of our coming anniversary. It got me thinking a couple of weeks ago. Then, last night, when I turned out the lights, I'd swear I saw Kate's eyes glowing in the dark. Forty-three years you ask? "Fear will bring you through," I answer.

Hypnosis

The winter of '23, that was the worst winter for snow and bad weather I can recall, but then I wasn't in these parts at that time. I was way up north cruisin' timber and surveyin' sections to be cut. I spent that whole season up there by myself, livin' in a one room cabin weekends, and headin' out on snowshoes the first of each week. I had taken a stack of books with me when I headed north, and I tried to dole 'em out an' make 'em last, but by December I was readin' each of 'em for the third and fourth times—especially the one about mesmerism. That book fascinated me, an' I read it over and over 'til the cover came off. Unfortunately I had no way to try out the theories it presented.

Toward the end of the month I was snowshoein' along and I come across a snowy owl had broken a wing, so I decided to take him back to the cabin. He didn't like me at the start, and I had to roll him up in a blanket and tie a cord around him in order to get him home. Well, after we got back it took awhile, but I finally got him calmed down. I patched him up with a splint, and then I took it into my head to try to hypnotize the old rascal. If you've ever seen the eyes on one a them birds, you know how I come to an idea like that.

I pulled up a chair and pulled out my pocket watch and fixed a gaze on that bird. It was no time at all afore he was sleepin' like a baby. In fact, it was almost no time at all before all I had to do was look at him and he'd take to snoring, just kinda soft like, right on his perch.

Now a creature like that don't like to have someone have power over 'em in such a way, so he got to where he wouldn't look at me at all. I'd sit him in the center of the room and start walkin' 'round and 'round him, and there were times when I thought he was goin' to twist his head off to keep from lookin' me in the eye.

All this went on fer some weeks. Then, one day I come back to the cabin, and it seems that owl had been doin' some thinkin' while I was gone. He met me with a stare the like of which I'd never seen before. I found myself asleep on the floor afore I knew what hit me. The old bird had figured out what I'd been doin' to him and worked the method. He was hypnotizin' me back. We spent the next two days not darin' to more than peek at one another. Those were probably the most restful days of my life, 'cept it bothered me somethin' fierce, the idea of him getting' the best of me, and I wasn't getting' my work done. For all that, he didn't give a hoot for what I thought.

Finally, come the end of March I was way behind on my schedule, and the owl was ready to get out some. We called a truce. End of April I brought him home with me when I come back down here, and that owl proved mighty helpful. Back then it seemed there was salesmen everywhere, and they was knockin' on your door all the time. Every time one of them fellas came to the door, I'd invite 'em in and show 'em my owl. He'd fix a gaze on 'em, and then I'd sell 'em some little thing I had layin' around the house and send 'em off before they ever had a chance to show me their carpet sweepers or brushes and such. I made a lot of money that year off them fellas, that is until word got out and they started just passin' by my door. Then it got kind of lonely agin. Eventually I went out lookin' for company of another kind.

When I brought my new wife home, she made me send my owl off to the woods. She said, "It's me or that damned owl!" It sorta hurt to think she suspected we might take advantage of her. She was prob'ly right, though—two's company.

#11PPS

The lab assistant appeared harried and unhappy as he dragged into the office. His lab coat had been slept in, and his narrow face was unshaven.

"Doc, I'm afraid the DNA tests don't show us a thing. There seems to be no somatic reason behind the occurrences, and the brain scans that have been taken during these episodes don't give us any clues at all. There's no increased or unexpected activity in any region of the brain except for those you'd expect to find in reaction to pain. Fitzgerald and Lake both noted a kind of ghosting, a sort of halo effect on the pictures, but that could be due to almost anything, including mechanical aberration. I don't know what to else to tell you. We've run every test we can think of, and the Psych Department has, too. Short of holding a séance, we've tried everything."

"I know you have. You all have been great, and I appreciate it. Something'll come up. Thanks."

"Do you want me to stick around for anything?"

"No, no. You look like you need some sleep. And when was the last time you saw that new bride of yours?"

"I've been givin' her a break. It's been a few days."

"Better pick up some roses on the way home. Get outa here, now!"

"How about you, Doc? You gonna get some sleep one of these days?"

"Sure, don't worry. I'm just going to go back over my notes one more time, then I'll go home."

After the assistant closed the door, Dr. T. William Tjader pulled a large data tablet from the lower drawer of his desk. He sat for some minutes contemplating the black, unadorned cover. These were more than just medical notes. They were also diary. He took a deep breath and opened to the first page. It was a ten year old copy of patient notes that had become, for him, the beginning of the case.

> July 23, 2104
> Alice Walker, 42, referred from Dr. Ayyangar. Clone #14AWS. Complains of extreme pain, "as though something was pulling me apart." Pain is non-specific, but seems centered in upper body and head. Recurring at greater frequency over the past three years, weekly at this juncture. MRIX, Laserprobe and US negative. Referred simultaneously to Dr. Toaz because of potential suicidal behavior. Clinical observation initiated immediately. Presc.120 mg. of Thyroxolantin per day.

A ban on human cloning had been initiated two years before the technology for human cloning became available in 2020. The moral, ethical and legal questions had been thrown to the United Nations, and the struggle to reach sufficient compromise and restriction had been enormous. During the ensuing years, the severest penalties had been invoked by the World Court on three occasions when the ban had been violated.

Under the guidelines for restricted lifting of the ban in 2060, three laboratories were given the go-ahead to clone twenty individuals each. Each lab was allotted two sets of DNA with which to work, so two sets of ten clones were produced in each setting. By 2063 all of the cloned individuals in the initial trial had been birthed. Ten years later all but one, the victim of an accidental drowning, were doing well and had been assimilated into a community. Alice Walker had been one of those first cloned humans.

With success seemingly assured, the ban was again lifted, and the "birthing" of a second group of individuals was authorized. Dr. T. William Tjader, Clone #11PPS, had been among those individuals. Plans were made that the same process would be repeated at twelve year intervals seven more times before the broader prohibitions were repealed. The fourth generation of cloned individuals was now approaching puberty, and the genetics for the next generation were being planned.

Alice Walker had been the seventh of the cloned individuals to begin complaining of nonspecific pain. The first, Scott Geldhof, had reported the symptoms beginning at age thirty-four. By the age of forty-three, all of the initial group had reported similar episodes.

The doctor flipped ahead to August 23, 2104. The notes detailed Alice Walker's suicide. The autopsy had been performed 8/26, and had yielded nothing unusual other than the cause of death. She had used a large kitchen knife to cut her own throat.

None of that initial group of sixty still survived. Each had taken his or her own life despite everything medicine and psychiatry could do for them. The uproar had been incredible. Last month the total ban on human cloning had been reinstated.

Dr. Tjader glanced through the rest of the pages in a cursory fashion and then picked up his ion pen and began writing another entry on the tablet at the end of the text.

> June 19, 2112
> The second episode occurred today. The pain was incredible, as though I were being pulled in several directions at once. It is hard to describe the sensation. I sense that it was a kind of psychic pain, whatever that is. It wasn't exactly physical, and yet it was. It wasn't exactly psychological, and yet it was. I don't believe I can survive more than one or two more episodes, and yet I know I must if we are to find some sort of relief for others in my position and those generations that follow.

The doctor closed the tablet and returned it to the drawer. Standing, he shrugged his stooped shoulders and then walked to the door. As he piloted home, fragments of the day wandered in and out of his consciousness: the pain, Alice Walker, the reports, snatches of conversation. Suddenly his head jerked up and he abruptly pulled his car to the shoulder of the road. With shaking hands he booted up the onboard computer and called up the directory. Finding an address, he entered it into the vehicle's navigation system and programmed the vehicle to merge back into traffic.

The building to which he travelled was one of the prefabricated plastic models which had been in vogue some thirty years in the past, but it was well maintained and had a narrow strip of immaculate lawn in the front. He walked to the door and pushed the proclamation button. Following the prompt, he spoke his name and business into the receiver. Soon a faint "Just a moment," came ringing back. When the door opened he was surprised to find a woman of about his own age smiling at him. She was dressed in a casual suit and looked, so he thought, perfectly normal.

"Please, come in." She laughed at his hesitation. "My name's Laura Powers, Dr. Tjader," she said and extended a hand. He followed her with a faint blush on his face. After entering an office that might well, he thought, have belonged to any of his psychiatric colleagues, his hostess motioned for him to take a seat. She sat down opposite and looked at him in a direct, matter of fact way.

"What can I do for you, Dr. Tjader?"

"I, well, I feel a bit silly here. Please give me a moment."

"Take all the time you need."

"I'm sorry. I'm a scientist, you see. I don't mean to sound disrespectful, but I never imagined I'd be consulting the services of a psychic. It's, it's just a little out of the range of my training."

"I understand. I'm an engineer by training. You're not the first to sit in that chair and wonder what in the world brought you here. All I can tell you is that it's a gift I didn't ask for, but which I can't deny. There actually has been some pretty good scientific evidence compiled to give validity to psychic abilities, but there are some powerful forces that don't want it to be widely publicized."

"I guess I've heard of a little of that, but since it never touched me personally, it never really sunk in."

"So what brings you here?"

"No doubt you've read about what happened to the first generation of people who were birthed through cloning."

"I have."

"You know, then, that nothing medically or psychiatrically has been discovered to be the cause of all that tragedy."

"So I understand."

"I've been working on the case. I'm one of the second generation."

"And you think I might be of help?"

"Episodes like those which led up to the suicides of the others have started with me. I don't have much time, and I've exhausted every other avenue I know."

"What would you like me to do?"

"I don't understand what you do. I'm open to anything you suggest. I'm willing to pay anything you ask if you can help."

She looked at him with a steadiness that made him want to turn away, but he fought the urge. Finally she pulled her chair up so that they were sitting knee to knee. "I don't charge anything. It's a gift, and it's my duty just to share it. Take my hands," she continued softly. "I'm going to close my eyes and try to see what is behind this. Please, understand that I don't have control over what may happen. I may speak. It may sound like strange voices. I may go into a kind of trancelike state and say nothing. Whatever happens, don't let go and don't interrupt. I'll tell you right now, I'm a bit scared. That isn't a feeling I often get."

"Are you sure you're willing to do this? I don't want to put you at risk."

"You're at risk if I don't try it, aren't you?"

"That's not your fault, Ms. Powers."

"Take my hands."

Laura Powers closed her eyes and bowed her head. The doctor studied her for a minute, decided he liked her, and then tried to clear his mind and be open to the situation. Five, then six minutes passed. The woman gave a low moan and was again silent. After another few minutes she issued a scream that seemed to well up out of untold depths. The next moment she was unconscious on the floor. The doctor checked for a pulse: 226. Her skin had turned pale and clammy. He reached for the communicator on the nearby desk and called the emergency number.

It was four in the morning before they had her stabilized and she could talk. The medical people gave him two minutes.

"Doctor, I don't think I want to do that again."

"God, I am so glad you're all right. I've been about frantic. What happened?"

"I had one of your episodes, and I talked to some of them on the other side. I know what's happening." Her voice was becoming faint, and he had to bend close as she continued. He listened until he could no longer hear what she said. Suddenly she stared up, clutched his arm and said, "It hurt so bad, I...." The monitors went off and the medical team rushed into the room and pushed the Doctor aside.

"She's flat lined," he heard one of the nurses say as another escorted him roughly out of the room.

The next morning the lab assistant unlocked the door and found Dr. T. William Tjader slumped in his chair, an empty bottle of painkillers in his lifeless hand. On the desk was the black tablet set to one final entry.

June 20, 2112
I can bear the pain no longer. Tonight I caused the death of a valiant woman who was innocent in all ways except that she was willing to help get to the bottom of the deaths of all the cloning victims—and I use the term *victims* purposely. What she discovered is that we clones are all the analogues of Siamese twins, but instead of being joined at the head or hip, we are joined to the original DNA donor and all cloned siblings through sharing a single soul. Since that soul has been divided in life and death, time and space, it is pulling each of us back to its center with an unnatural and inexorable power. Only when those of us with common heritage are joined in death can there be any hope of release. God grant that it be a peaceful release. You must, must kill the others. Do not hesitate. The pain is not worth the life.
Dr. T. William Tjader

The lab assistant read the note again and again.

Cats and Romance

"Uncle Ainer, I miss Aunt June. How'd you meet her?"

"You want the real story?"

"Well, yeah, of course."

"Then you've gotta promise never to tell your cousins."

"Really? I mean sure. I just assumed they already knew."

"They know part of it. There are some things I never even told your aunt June, bless her soul! I probably shouldn't tell you, except you're enough like me to appreciate it, and I think I can trust you to keep a secret."

"Sure, I can keep a secret."

"I was twenty-six, and I'd been bummin' for a couple of years by the time I first saw your aunt. I'd ridden the rails a bit and seen all but two of the states. I'd do an odd job now and again to make a few bucks, and then I'd head out on my way. It was something a lot of guys did back in the late forties and early fifties. When I walked into this town on the twenty-third of June, 1951, I hadn't eaten for nearly three days. That was okay; it's the way it was, feast or famine a good bit of the time. I saw this lady standing behind the picket fence gate in her front yard. She was holding a big black and white cat. I was across the road, and just as I drew even with them the cat jumped out of her arms and ran in front of me. The woman hollered, 'Bad cat!' I reached down and scooped it up and carried it back to the lady. She smiled and thanked me and said she'd be eternally grateful. She was not a beautiful lady until she smiled, but my, that smile....

"I stuck around and we talked a little, and I learned she had four cats: Mr. Fluffy, Sir Galahad, Miss Priss, and Lucy. Of course that made me instantly wary. You never quite know about cat ladies. Nonetheless, I learned she was single, and that was good, but then came the clincher. She brought me a piece of German chocolate cake. I think I fell in love with the cake. After a little bit, I continued on into town. There was a help wanted sign in the window at Meade's Lumber and Hardware. I decided it might be time to settle down, at least for a bit. I'd had some pretty good experience in the building trades, and Bob Meade decided to give me a try. I set up camp down along the river about a mile west of town. That meant I'd have to pass the cat lady's place on the way to and from work each day.

"For two weeks I'd wave and say *Hi* as I passed. Sometimes we'd talk a few minutes. They liked me at the lumber yard, and I kind of enjoyed the work. The day before I got my first paycheck, one of the June's cats disappeared. I stopped on my way past after work and did my best to comfort the lady. She let me hold her hand. I'll tell you what, I thought I'd won in Las Vegas. Things were definitely looking up. The only problem was that it was pretty clear these cats were like children for June. She was twenty-eight years old, and cats were her family. I guess I thought that was pretty lame, but then I thought about my own situation. I was living in the woods and only eating about every other day.

"Six days later Miss Priss came up missing. I went by after work and my cat lady was beside herself. I held her and did what I could to bring some comfort. I've gotta say that I had some mixed emotions."

"You didn't like the cats, did you Uncle Ainer?"

"Cats are good, at least if you don't make 'em the center of your life. It was about three weeks later that Sir Galahad went on a quest. By that time I was spending a fair bit of time with the lady. When I got there that evening I took her in my arms and kissed her. She didn't object. I think that we had both come to realize we were pretty much in love. The job at Meade's was going well. They were talking about making me yard boss. I started to really think about the future.

"There was one obstacle. What with three of four cats missing, I don't think Lucy was even allowed to leave the house in the next couple of weeks. June clung to her like life. It got to be a problem. I'd try to make some time with June, and that cat would wind up between us. I was pretty frustrated."

"So what did you do, Uncle Ainer?"

"I bided my time. Then finally Lucy went missing, too. As you know, timing is everything. A week after Lucy disappeared I asked June to marry me. We didn't wait long, and nine months after that your cousin Kathy arrived. David came along ten months later, and Cindy a year after that. Your Aunt June never looked back. She didn't have time for cats."

"Yeah, and I'll bet you weren't too sorry, Uncle Ainer. Come on, you didn't really like those cats, did you?"

"*Au contraire,* nephew. Cats are good, like I said. They taste just about like chicken."

The Perfectly Attractive Man

The fortieth birthday was hard—a warning shot across the bow. The facts of his single life came crashing in. It set him to thinking about the cause of his singleness, and what would make him more attractive to women.

Frank was an accountant with a receding hairline. Somehow hair, bachelorhood, and accounting seemed related. He was not a bachelor by choice. In the past he had blamed his singleness mostly on his mother, but he had long been aware of a gnawing truth that accounting was not sexy. He was also confronting a suspicion that baldness is not attractive—that grayness is a sign of lost virility. No woman, he imagined, could ever be attracted to a balding, gray haired accountant. Frank found himself beginning to notice other men's hair—or lack of hair—or lack of color in hair. Looking at other men felt strange, and it made him nervous, but it seemed suddenly to be important.

Frank was not a man of action, so he thought a lot about his situation. He thought accountant's thoughts, and as an accountant with an accountant's attention to detail, he began to make charts and keep tallies. The first chart had to do with where a man should part his hair. The number of options at first seemed limited: front to back, part it on the left, in the middle, or on the right. Then he started watching other men, and his observations soon took him out of the box. Some with receding hairlines parted it ear to ear and combed it forward. Some with little left on top parted their hair just above one ear and combed it over to the other. Others combed it back with no part or combed it forward with no part. That didn't even begin to cover things like crew cuts, spikes, or completely shaved heads.

Frank bought a pair of mirrors and began practicing his parts.

A second chart listed his observations about hair color. Soon he bought colored hair pieces and began practicing his colors.

It was not long before he began to make addendums to the charts indicating whether the man he was observing was with a woman or not. Later he began making notations about whether the woman appeared to enjoy being with the man. The amount of data became overwhelming. Frank bought a new computer into which he could enter his observations. He began looking for other variables. The possibilities were mind boggling: height, eye color, build, shoe size.... He decided to limit his research to those things over which he had some control. He began anew with facial hair.

Frank purchased moustaches and beards from the theater supply store. He began practicing styles in front of the mirror. Soon he returned to the store for liquid latex and braids of hair with which to create his own styles—or rather reproduce the styles he observed on successful men. He had never had a beard of his own, but he decided it looked sexy. He wore a moustache to work one Monday, but no one seemed to notice. He decided that it must have been because he hadn't changed the way he parted his hair. He went home and practiced with the mirrors.

A sign in the window at Sears where he bought his socks said, **Dress for Success**. *Success at what?* he thought. *Do women really go for the flashy clothes?* He made a note to add the idea to his charts. That day he bought a pair of white shoes and a neck chain, but since he couldn't wear them to work and he seldom went out, they stayed in their respective boxes.

Finally, at age forty-two, with a full hard drive and prominent widow's peak, Frank decided it was time to crunch the data and move ahead. "Fast track! Stand back, ladies!" He pushed enter and listened as the computer clicked and whirred.

Frank felt faint with anticipation as the data spewed forth from the printer. He was about to become the statistically perfect man. It was within his reach! "Step back, Jack, I'm comin' through at last!"

Frank felt his hopes fall slowly—twisting in fickle winds—as he read through the results. No statistical advantage appeared for any style of hair parting—although there was a slight disadvantage to comb-overs. Hair color didn't seem to make a statistical difference in a man's ability to pick up a woman. There was a slight advantage to having a moustache and goatee along with a shaved head, but that only seemed to hold among younger men and could be explained away as a kind of fad. Besides, he would never be comfortable calling attention to himself in that way. Returning to his numbers, Frank noticed that there seemed to be some correlation between clothing and the type of woman a man might be seen with, but that clothes apparently had little impact on success. It then occurred to Frank, as he mused over his charts, that he wasn't sure what kind of woman he wanted to be seen with anyway.

The results were a blow. Two years of data collection had gotten him little more than boxes of hair and a new pair of white shoes. He had to do something—something impulsive. He thought a long time about what that impulsive action might be. Then he went out and got a tattoo. It was a wicked looking skull with Mother inscribed beneath. He didn't wash it off for eleven days.

Ghost of an Angel

It didn't seem odd at the time, though looking back now it all seems a little strange. I smelled it first, I think. Some sort of change in the air—a freshening, perhaps. Then I saw a wisp of something; at least I think I saw it. Maybe I heard it. Can one hear a wisp? It didn't go away. It didn't dissolve like other wisps. It just stayed with me, peripheral, marginal, like a thought that wants to form in your head but which won't quite come together.

I slowly folded my tent and took the mess kit down to the stream to wash. Across the little stream was an old cabin, door and windows missing, roof sagging like the back of a worn plow horse. I'd set up camp late the previous evening and hadn't been inclined to explore. I wasn't too interested this morning, either, but I had time. I had no itinerary but my own, and that was little itinerary at all. Mindlessly, I hop-stepped over the creek on the backs of smooth stones. The wooden planks of the cabin floor creaked as I stepped in. The scent of mold hung vaguely in the still air. Something, a raccoon I imagine, had made a mess in a pile of rags in the far corner of the first room. A piece of stovepipe hung from the ceiling in the other corner. I walked carefully to the door which led to the back room. It hung from a single hinge.

As I entered the room I was filled with curiosity about the history of this place. The feeling was strange, because curiosity was something I had gotten used to living without. Despite the cabin's age, it was clear it had been carefully constructed. Someone's dream. I imagined a couple—newlyweds—coming to this place in the mountains and deciding on both the beauty and the practicality of the setting. My mind on the spirits of this pair, I sat down on the floor in the middle of this back room—obviously the bedroom. Were there children? What had become of these people?

I was startled when I became once again aware of the wisp. "Are you a ghost?" I asked. I think I was amused at my question. Humor had been on the same vacation as creativity and curiosity, and it, too, felt strange. Then an answer to the question came to me.

"Yes."

"One of the people from this cabin?"

"No. They are in another place."

The words weren't something I heard, at least not in the usual way. It was as if I touched them. "Why are you here?" I asked.

"Why are you here?"

"Sort of by accident. I'm just hiking through the area."

"Well, I'm just following you."

"A ghost, following me? What on earth for?"

"Not a ghost in exactly the sense you're thinking of. I was never 'human.' I'm here because of where you're going. I'm here because you're in a state of uncertainty, and you've been floundering around long enough that I felt I had to do something. Besides, I need help."

"Never human?"

"I was what you would call an angel."

"I didn't think angels could die."

"Nothing dies—not really. It merely changes form. Re-creates."

"So you're the ghost of an angel, here because I can't get my act together, and you need help?"

"In a nutshell, yes."

I took my time trying to wrap my mind around all of this. I think I just stared at the hazy ghost for a long time. I'd walked away from everything: family, friends, job, and home. I'd been sucked into rounds of depression—to the point of planning to end my life on this trip. "Help me," I said finally.

There was a long silence. I began to feel uneasy that my request was out of place.

"Have you ever thought about when you were happiest?" It seemed a digression. A loaded question. I looked around the room for clues, but the memories here weren't my own. I found no clues in the dust and shadows. I really couldn't answer, but the wisp gave me plenty of time to reflect.

"It may not be a time as much as a state you were in. A 'zone' some people call it. If I'm right, it was when you were being creative at something, wasn't it? Building that boat, courting your wife, the new project for diagnosis at work...." My angel let the remarks sink in. "All of creation is like that. That's the God in you doing what God does—create."

"And angels?"

"Yeah, we're here to create and support creation. When we stop that, we're done. Pretty much the same as people and other beings."

"So you died because you stopped creating?"

"You were my charge, and you kind of took me with you when you hit the wall a couple of years ago. You pretty much stopped living, too. That was when you gave up on your job, politics, art, people, and life in general. Remember?"

"I took you with me? You were my personal angel? I'm to blame that you're a ghost? I cost you your wings?"

"Don't get into the blame game. The wings thing is a human idea. Actually it was a magic carpet."

"A magic carpet?"

"I'm kidding! We have to be so careful with you people. Yes, everything is intertwined in a wonderful way. You took me with you, but that's the natural process. It's how we grow. If you finally get the picture, I'll be reborn as an Angel First Class."

"You're kidding again."

"Of course. But you need to get back to creating. First get some help—some support. Be kind and patient with yourself, and help others. We're all in this together; helping others can be the first step to helping yourself. It sounds a little trite, but dream your best; share your truth; follow your words with your actions. Your dreams, your thoughts, your words, your actions—they're the palette and the brushstrokes out of which you create your character, and creating your character is what you're here for. Your character reflects through all of creation." There was a smile in the words, but there was no doubt about their sincerity.

The wisp disappeared—my ghost of an angel.

I camped in that spot for three more days. Life didn't come into focus at once, but lying in the cool duff and watching the hawks glide across blue open spaces was a balm. When I felt ready, I checked one last time over my shoulder, turned, and started my way out of the woods.

When It Really Rained

Ah, piffle! You think the rain is bad this year? I remember the time back before you come ta these parts when we had the year of the really big rains.

I was still farmin' then, n' raisin' some livestock on the place down by Tekamah Creek. It started in to rain on the third of April, and I ain't never seen the like—not before or since. Rain got so deep we had ta shovel a path ta the barn every mornin'. There was a special bad day when my neighbor to the south, old Harry Keller, made the mistake a lookin' up. Drowned, right there on the spot. Harry had wanted ta be cremated, but he was so soaked up they couldn't bring it off. Wound up pickling him, so they did.

After about a month a that kind a weather, I noticed there was somethin' strange about the calves that were bein' delivered. Course I called Doc Sterner in, but he already knew what the problem was. Seems calves all over the county was bein' born with gill slits 'cause it was the only way they could survive bein' dropped. Not many folks can say they made a splash like that when they come inta the world.

It's amazin' how things adapt. We had some chickens at the time, an' they was a sorry lot. We ate a few of the least fit, and the rest of 'em took to matin' with the ducks. That was just fine at the time, but the next fall I lost my whole flock when they flew south.

Now I've always been a purty good wing shot, an' my better half likes puttin' a bird on the table now and again. Course there weren't no birds could fly in that rain, but on days when it was comin' down just a tad harder 'n usual, I could step out on the porch an' shoot a bass or a carp as it went by. I never did get so's I could make a shot on the trout, though. They was just too quick.

Folks in town had it special hard, I guess. The ones who cared about their lawns an' that sort a thing had ta mow the cattails about three times a week.

Wasn't much work to be found in those times, neither, though old man Goodman hired a few a the boys who could do carpenter work. Goodman was the richest man in town. He jest had the boys put pontoons on his house, then they cut it loose and he and Norma took off on a cruise. Never seen 'em since, though I understand Lena Green gets a postcard now and again.

That rain was over in forty days, of course. Things started to dry out in good time and get back ta normal—though we was overrun by cats an' dogs fer about two or three weeks after.

A Question of Faithfulness

Frank left Winona fifteen years ago, the lousy S.O.B. He'd just upped and found a younger woman. Eleven good years, and all of a sudden he'd wanted a divorce.

Soon after Frank's departure, Rafael came into her life. Winona loved Rafael almost immediately. He became the only male she trusted completely after Frank, the louse, left her. She'd had him fixed almost immediately, and he seldom roamed very far. But now Rafael was gone. Disappeared with not so much as a word or a meow. She had walked the streets looking for him in his usual haunts, the garbage cans and hedges. She had shown his picture to hundreds of strangers. She had notified the authorities. Winona was lost without her cat. She had, she reflected, become one of those "cat women." She wasn't sure she liked that idea.

A month after Rafael's disappearance, Winona knew she had to get away. There were just too many memories. She'd never travelled, but she had read widely and dreamed clearly. She spent hours going through brochures online and at the travel agency. Somewhere in the back of her mind she imagined a handsome, dark-haired man waiting to sweep her off her feet. She heard castanets and maracas in her dreams.

When she could stand her aloneness no longer, she made reservations for Cancun: Pueblo de Maya Riviera. She'd find herself a Mayan, maybe. A flamenco guitar player, maybe. Mayans and musicians couldn't be any less trustworthy than Frank or Rafael.

Six weeks after Rafael's disappearance she walked through the drifting snow and into the airport. She was slightly mystified by the process of checking in at the ticket counter, but a very nice young man—not handsome and dark-haired, but blonde and rugged—had helped her navigate the new experience. He stood with her in the security line, and she found herself humming. He offered his arm as she slipped off her shoes. He assured her it was all right to put her purse in the gray tub and send it through the X-ray machine. Her imagination overcame her as she stepped into the scanner. She put her feet in the outlines and lifted her arms as directed. It was the first time in a decade and a half, she mused, that anyone had viewed her nakedness. The thought made her giddy, and she gave an almost imperceptible shake of her hips.

Winona was disappointed when her blonde friend walked away to catch a flight to Minneapolis. Still, she had not relinquished the hopes she had set on that dark-haired man. She found a brown, vinyl seat in the brown-walled waiting area. She sat and pondered the brown carpet with swirls in it that reminded her of raindrops in a mud puddle. Soon her mind transported her to Cancun. The palms were waving and the sun was glinting off white sands. She was distracted from her reverie only momentarily as the pilot walked by. He was very handsome in his blue uniform with the wings on the breast pocket and the gold epaulets across the broad shoulders.

Her cell phone rang. It was Alice, her neighbor. "Rafael is back. He looks a little worse for the wear, but he's sitting in front of your door. What do you want me to do?" Winona stood and looked back toward the airport entrance.

Decision time. The cat, or the dark haired caballero? Winona loved Rafael. She stood and began walking back toward the entrance. Her mind filled with happy feline memories: his long soft fur; the purring; how he would rub between her feet as she stood cooking in the kitchen; his curling up on her pillow at night.

"Well, what do you want me to do?" Alice asked again.

"Sun Air, flight 567 for Cancun is now boarding at Gate A-9."

Winona imagined the look on Rafael's face as he sat looking at her door. He would be bedraggled, but not likely remorseful. He had left her. Unbidden, a picture of smiling Frank came to her. She shook her head and imagined the smell of sea breezes. She pictured a mariachi band made up of smiling, dark-eyed men. *Rafael left me. He could leave again—the rat! If a person has any brains at all, she learns from experience.*

She spoke decisively into her phone, "Take him to the pound."

Haircut

You say you're on your way to the barber? Did I ever tell you about the time I had a chance to get a free haircut—I mean from a professional? If you're willin' to take yer chances on a barber you've never been to before, you might have a chance at keepin' your money, too. At any rate, it's an interesting experiment.

On Tuesday I went to my barber in town. I discovered he'd taken off to go fishin'. Bill was always takin' time off to go fishin'. It'd get to be three o'clock in the afternoon, and if there weren't no customers and it was a nice day, he'd jest close up the shop.

The next day I had to go all the way up to Carson City to see about a stock tank, and I figured I might as well stop in to the barber shop there and get my hair cut. There was two guys ahead of me, one in the chair and one waitin'. Well, I don't think that barber shut up more than thirty seconds the whole time he was cuttin' their hair. Now I understand that barbers are about the nosiest people in the world, and I understand that for most of 'em talkin' sports and gossipin' is more of a draw in the profession than whackin' at somebody's hair. This fella, though, was over the top, as they say.

Now that barber didn't know me from Adam, and he was askin' questions even before he got his big ole bib tied around my neck. I wasn't feelin' particularly social that day, an' his nosiness jest sorta rubbed me the wrong way. I made up my mind that other than tellin' him how I wanted my hair trimmed, I was gonna leave that place with him knowin' no more about me than when I came in. The conversation went sorta like this:

"You live around here?"

"Hmmmummm," I answered. I figured he probably knew everybody for miles around, an' he was just warmin' me up.

"Whereabouts?" he went on after a two snip pause.

"Erruhmmmmm."

He tried another tack. "Got the day off work, huh?"

"Mmmmhmmmmumm."

"I'm sorry, I didn't catch that."

"Glummmertkle."

He was gettin' curiouser and curiouser. He started snippin' faster, an' you could almost hear the wheels a turnin'. He started talkin' about the weather, an' football, an' schools, an' politics, and askin' me about most everything except when was the last time I'd had a bowel movement. I give him about the same answer each time, "Ummmemummmstk." Before long he was real agitated, and he started snippin' slower and slower. He was tryin' ta buy some time.

"So, yer wife, she stay at home, or does she work, too?"

"Yup." I gave him a little more there, 'cause I figured he'd seen the ring I was wearin' an' had surmised I had a wife, anyway.

"Ya got kids?"

"Mmmrrennummm."

He whimpered a little, but by this time he was really gettin' on my nerves, too, so I didn't pay him no mind.

"You get ta town here often?"

"Errummnblk."

"Got any relatives come in here?"

"Ummmnnnfarts."

"Oscar Briggs looks a bit like you. You related to him?"

"Ummmenoyeah."

He started shakin', an' I was glad he'd already shaved the back of my neck, but I didn't like the look in his eye. I made up my mind to get outa there as fast as I could.

He made a couple more feeble attempts ta get information, an' then he took the towel off me an' shook it an' sorta kicked around in the hair on the floor. You could see he was about gone crazy.

"Listen, mister," he said after a minute, "I'll let you have your haircut free if you'll jest answer me one question plain and clear."

I put the fifty cents in his hand and jest walked away. I glanced back once, an' he was sittin' in the big chair with a couple of the regulars standin' by him tryin' to console him, I guess.

I heard later that that afternoon he packed up his barber stuff and moved out to Washington D.C., where anybody he asked would tell him anything he wanted to hear. That's what makes them barbers happy, I guess.

I do sometimes wonder what question I woulda had to answer, but I s'pose it's better this way.

Practical Nature

Ginger was a practical woman. Marsh always said he married her because of her practicality. The wedding had only cost one hundred and thirty-two dollars and eleven cents. That was the kind of practicality a man could appreciate.

They'd gone camping on their honeymoon. Twelve dollars and fifty cents in gas to get them to the Upper Peninsula and back. Four dollars and sixteen cents for pasties as they splurged while driving U.S. 2. The rest was incidental. Marshall often bragged to his friends about how cheaply they'd gotten by. He had himself a practical woman.

They'd rented a trailer for the first three years of their marriage. It was a sacrifice they made in order to save the down-payment on a piece of land and their first home in the country. It was to be their last home, too, though they added on four times to accommodate a growing family. Ginger did most of the carpentry and all of the decorating. It wasn't easy on the allowance she got. Her friends Mary and Kate declared she was a wonder.

Ginger loved the country, and their pets. The Myna Bird was a wedding gift from a cousin Marsh had never particularly trusted. The first cat came with the house. He was a tiger with a horribly crooked tail, the product of his trying to sneak in the house while the door was being closed. Marsh had justified the Springer Spaniel he brought home as a hunter and a watch dog.

As the years passed more cats came around, and Ginger raised chickens and goats, pigs and cattle as they were needed to help make ends meet. She raised and canned fruits and vegetables. She sewed the children's clothing. She was, indeed, a practical woman. That was good, because Marsh never did raise the allowance he gave her each week. She just quietly found ways to make do.

It was Marsh who found the Myna Bird dead in its cage. He was on his way to work. "We'll bury him when I get home," he had told Ginger. He spent the day at work dreading the funeral. Marsh was a soft-hearted man, and he was sure Ginger would be devastated. When he got home he expected a tearful ceremony. What he got was a lesson in practicality. After dinner, he finally asked what had happened to the Myna. "I fed him to the cats. Cats eat birds, so I figured we'd save on cat food." Marsh beamed with love.

When the kinky-tailed tiger cat showed up dead on the doorstep a few months later, Marsh was sure Ginger would fall apart with grief. He stopped and had a couple of stiff drinks on his way home from work, and then hurried on to comfort his wife. The household seemed to be operating as normal. After dinner Marsh inquired about the cat. "Oh, I cooked her up and fed her to the dogs. That seemed to be the most practical thing I could do. In the wild, dogs eat cats, you know." Marsh felt a lump of pride in his throat.

The spaniel was twelve when he died. In Marsh's mind she'd been their "first child." "We'll bury her under the lilacs when I get home from work," Marsh mumbled as he climbed into his new pickup and left for his job. Marsh sobbed quietly all that day at work. He stopped by the bar and had several stiff belts on his way home. Ginger had his favorite meal, fried chicken and creamed potatoes, waiting for him when he walked in. "We need to bury Cookie after we eat. It's getting dark pretty early now, and I want to get it over while we can still see."

"Oh, Marsh, I couldn't bear to see Cookie's life be a waste. I boiled her and ground her up and fed her to the goats. It's the circle of life, you know."

"I don't deserve a good woman like you," Marsh responded. "Let's go out and drink a toast to Cookie!" It was the most romantic evening they'd spent since their honeymoon. Marsh even bought their first two rounds.

Years passed. The year after the kids had all gone off, the calf from the previous spring got tangled in the barbed wire fence. "Dumb cow. We'll bury it when I get home from work." Marsh knew that Ginger would have it wrapped and in the freezer by the time he got home. He stopped and had a couple of good belts at the bar after work. He wanted to show the boys his new fly rod, and he needed to make sure Ginger had plenty of time. She was a practical woman. He knew she'd call Mary or Kate if she needed help. It seemed those women were always together.

It was true. Mary and Kate had been Ginger's support group for years. It was not too many months after the incident with the calf that the girls were sitting around having iced tea on a warm, summer afternoon. Kate remarked that it had been a while since she'd seen Marsh.

"Oh, he died last spring."

"Was there a service? I'm so sorry; I didn't hear anything about it. I'd have helped!"

"You poor woman," Mary chimed in. "You should have told us. Did the whole family come home? I'd have brought a casserole."

"No need. I appreciate the offers, and I knew you'd be there for me, but I didn't go to much trouble. Circle of life, you know. At first I just tried feeding the cheap bastard to the chickens, but they quit laying. Too much roughage, I'd guess. But I figured I had to get some good out of the man. After the chickens, I tried feeding him to the cats, but they just gained too much weight. I'm finally rid of him, though. I've got two really fine hogs will be ready this fall. Now if you're serious about giving me a hand, I really could use some help when it comes time to butcher them."

Ginger was a practical woman. That was why Marsh had loved her so.

A Question of Image

I was drawn to the open air booth. It was some of the most unusual work I had ever seen. The gray-haired man sitting there had on a beret and sported a Vandyke beard. He was the quintessential picture of an artist. I asked him about his wares, and he waved me to an empty chair. "It's a long story," he began dramatically, "a story of true love and identity.

"I met my Frances fifteen years ago. She's in the camper there now fixing some lunch. She'd been divorced recently, and so had I. I think I was going through what's called a mid-life crisis. I'd guess that's what it was, but I never really ask those kinds of questions. At any rate, I was trying to figure out who I was—looking for an image, so to speak. At that point I was trying to be the world's greatest lover. Frances is one of those women who'll accept you for who you are. She'd go along with any whim I had, so she wasn't much help in my search except she was kinda pretty. That wasn't going to hurt my image no matter what it happened to be. Thing was, she had this way of keeping a person grounded and humble without really making him feel inadequate or anything. Did I say she's a knitter?

"The divorce Frances had gone through was a bad one. Contentious and hurtful. Her husband had strayed, so to speak. He was off the reservation more than he was on. Now Frances is a clingy kind of person. She just likes to be close, and she's insecure in some odd way. I don't know if that's the result of her divorce or if it was the cause of it. I never really ask those kinds of questions. At any rate, the knitting seems to help her cope. As I was saying, at that time I was trying to be Don Juan. Did you know it's possible to knit and make love at the same time? It wasn't like she had her mind elsewhere, 'cause she'd knit underwear and handcuffs and stuff like that. Pretty soon I fell in love and we got married. It was time to look for a new image.

"One day I came home riding a brand new Harley-Davidson. Frances was almost as excited as I was. I'd gotten matching leathers for us, and matching helmets with radios. Problem was, it's hard to hold on to somebody's back and knit at the same time. Her yarn kept flying away and getting wrapped in the spokes. She solved that by knitting herself a little bag for her yarn and needles—one that would fit over the seat back. Then she'd get on and strap herself in facing backwards. She could knit and see where we'd been at the same time. I had to install new footrests for her, and I suppose she may be the only person who's seen Yellowstone Park entirely backwards. Well, I was still trying to find myself, and riding that way wasn't quite the image I had hoped for.

"I took up fly fishing. Frances would sit on the banks and knit. It was pretty hard on her those times when she'd follow and the stream headed down through a cedar swamp, but she never complained. Her crashing around didn't help the fishing any, though I'd have to admit the trout I have mounted and hanging on my living room wall wouldn't have been caught without Frances. I'd torn my net right off the frame when I got stuck trying to get around some downed trees on a bend. Frances knitted up a replacement for me right on the spot. Where the knitting got to be a bit too much was the multi-colored mohair fishing vest she rigged up for me. I don't know if she did it on purpose. I never really ask those kinds of questions. I just figured it was time for a new image.

"I joined an Alpine club and invested in rope and chalks and carabineers. I was a bit old and stiff for that kind of activity, but I did okay and it was exciting. We tried letting Frances belay a few times when we were short of people and were top-roping a climb. The problem was she'd get nervous or bored and start to knit. A couple of nasty falls, and pretty soon word got around that she couldn't be trusted. She tried to make up for it by knitting everyone little Alpine hats. They were cute, but I don't know that everyone appreciated the effort that went into them. I will say that she did get a couple of orders for the Kevlar climbing shorts she knitted. I was wearing a pair of those on the day I was working on the lay-back you need to get past the overhang on Beelzebub's Belly. It's a particularly tricky spot that comes after what is, to that point, an easy climb. I was stretched out with two points of contact on the rock when I reached for my chalk bag and found it full of yarn ends. What they were doing there is beyond me; I never really ask those kinds of questions. I will say that those knit Kevlar shorts probably saved me some nasty cuts and scrapes, and the doctors were impressed with the colorful sling she knitted me before I left the hospital.

"White water rafting is maybe the most exhilarating thing I've ever done. We tried it, liked it, and I decided I needed to take the training to be a guide. I found an outfit that would take me on and provide training. Before long I'd learned the river and had become really adept at taking on the boulders and wild currents. A couple of weeks into the training Frances and I almost had a falling out when she knitted a life jacket for me and I refused to wear it. It wasn't the jacket so much as the little turtles and snails and things she knit all over it. I suppose to some it was cute, but what kind of confidence does that inspire when you're taking a group of people down class four rapids? The boss liked my work, but on my final training run I lost the raft. It wasn't a rugged boulder or extreme undertow that sank my career, it was holes punctured by runaway knitting needles as we went through the part of the canyon known as Satan's Spout. The owner wouldn't listen to reason and said if I stayed, Frances had to go. Well, when a man's in love, a man's gotta do what a man's gotta do. Winter was coming on, anyway.

"I decided to raise bulldogs. I liked the image—rugged, tenacious. I named the first two Lucifer and Scratch. Did you know that a bulldog will eat almost anything? Did you know there are one hundred and ninety-one yards of yarn in a skein? Do you know what following a bulldog with a pooper scooper as he poops out a hundred and ninety-one yards of yarn through the bushes and trees does to a man's image? Try that not once, but three times. Two different dogs. You have to wonder what makes them do it, but I never really ask those kinds of questions.

"I sold the dogs and took up knitting. It was hard, but when I came upon the idea of knitting rawhide and barbed wire I knew I was on to something. It was an image I could live with, and Frances has been more than supportive. These wall hangings have been very successful, and I've also done well with the leather sweaters. You meet lots of interesting people at these art fairs. I had one fellow bring me a deer hide and I cut it into strips and knit him a hair shirt. We kind of bonded over that one, though I'm not sure why. I never really ask those kinds of questions."

The Review

The corridor was long, and all of those who met me followed quietly as my guide led the way. I wasn't used to dying, and I guess the others probably thought I needed the company. At length we arrived at a room—just an isolated area, really—and my guide motioned for me to sit. I sat, but the rest of the group continued on.

When we were finally alone, my guide said, "This is where you will conduct your life review. You may call for help at any time, but the review must be finished before you can move on."

"How do I do this review?"

"It will just come to you. You'll find you can generally control it with your mind."

"How long will this take? Don't I need to catch up to the others?"

"It doesn't matter how long. For some it's over very quickly. Others take ages. A life, you see, is a collection of moments. Those moments make up a kind of dam of pebbles built across the stream of time. That stream is full of strange currents, pressures, and backwaters. Now is the time for you to inspect your work and evaluate the structure you have crafted."

"And when I come to the weak spots?"

"You're the engineer."

He left me with that. It began almost immediately. My review was not sequential, but there were patterns to it. Friendships came and went; ideas were picked up and discarded. I found myself collecting a kind of inventory, some of it painful, some of it delightful. In time that inventory began to recycle through my mind and I would feel the same experience over and over. I could feel the undertow and called for help.

"I'm getting stuck," I complained as the guide again appeared. "This metaphorical dam you spoke of—I'm dead. What can I bring to it now?"

"I can only say that you still possess the tools. You're still swimming in the stream. You've experienced a good deal. You know that there are moments when time grows dense, like wet clay, and breathing is hard. There are moments when time grows thin as spider webs and life pours through. There are hospital moments, moments of boredom and uncertainty, moments of overwhelming love, conversion moments, moments when the truth or fear of truth is close upon us. As you've found, most of this process goes very quickly, but we all have our individual moments. With virtually everyone, it seems a point is reached where the same moments keep coming round and round again. Those are the issues that are most problematic."

"How do I deal with those?"

"That is a question you are here to answer. You may call for help at any time, but you have to discover the answers on your own."

"Okay. How long have I been here?"

"Twenty minutes, a month, a hundred years, a thousand—not long enough. Does it make a difference?"

"It seems like it should, but I suppose not."

I returned to my work. Time wrapped around me and disappeared among sunsets and whispering breezes. I was enfolded in the scent of loam, the sting of rime, a taste of salt, the lure of money. Hung in those folds of time I found allusion wrapped in illusion, dreams setting in concrete, love, lust, pride and hurt. Eventually I found myself with a two part list. One part held the people and things I loved. I knew that love had to be free, so I could let go of those on that list; at some level I understood that that was the way to keep them. I had also arrived at an inventory of people and things I had injured, and of people and things that had done injury to me. I found myself clinging to old embarrassments and shortcomings. Again I was stuck, looping over and over through the muck of these images while all of the rest of my life became little beyond a murmur of memory. I resisted calling again for help, but eventually even my pride was worn smooth. I called out, and then explained my situation to my friend. I have to admit that I was feeling some frustration with him.

He appeared, and stood, arms folded and looking for all the world like a genie just loosed from a bottle. I think he was amused with himself. "You called?" he asked, smiling ever so slightly.

"I did. What am I supposed to do now? I'm left with a bunch of negative stuff I keep recycling and recycling. I need help."

"I'm sorry, what did you say?"

"You heard me. I need help!"

"Don't we all? People you've hurt, people who've hurt you.... You know the answer. It's in two parts. You tell me. What needs to be done to put those things away?"

I didn't like his attitude, but I knew it was really my own that was holding things up. "I guess I need to forgive. Then what?"

"Brilliant! I knew you could do it! The second part comes after the first, obviously, but it will come more naturally. I'm going to leave you again. You need time. Forgiveness doesn't come in one big event, it takes time and repetition. And remember—I may be going too far in saying this, but I've grown to like you—forgiving yourself is often the hardest, and it's often the first step."

I was smoldering a bit, but my guide had disappeared again, so I had no one to abuse. They weren't making this easy. I started examining motivations, misunderstandings, handicaps, attitudes, biases.

Eventually the weavings of emotions and events became clear. I don't know how long it took, and I surely wasn't going to ask again. I started feeling better, and one by one the issues I had recycled began to disappear. Like most of my other memories, they were still there if I wanted them, but I had released them so they released me. I was feeling pretty good about everything when I heard voices. All of those people who had accompanied me to this place appeared again. My "friend" stepped forward, smiling.

"What?" I asked him.

He put a warm hand on my shoulder and smiled even more. "Congratulations, you've torn down the dam and now the waters can run free again."

The whole group gathered around me. They, too, were smiling. My guide gave me some time to let his words sink in, then, “You thought you were through, didn’t you?” There were a few chuckles. “At least from here you won’t have to go on alone.”

Imitation Heartbreak

I have been in love only once in my life. Oh, of course I fall in love with every pretty woman I meet, but as for real love— it was only that once.

I saw her first at a party given for my friend Matt's birthday. Short brown hair cut in a kind of shag, glasses, a gray pullover—she was hard to miss. She was doing her impressions of a peacock in heat: *Nooo, nooo, nooo!* Arms bent, elbows back and flapping. I noticed that two or three of the fellows sitting around the room began to look uncomfortable. It's hard for some guys to stifle a display when they feel one coming on. I decided that this was a woman to watch.

It was perhaps twenty minutes later, after another glass of wine, that she stood up and did her screaming armadillo. Two or three of the married men looked uncomfortable. Clearly, what she was screaming resonated at some level.

Later she did a snapping turtle imitation that had most of the men in the group checking their flies. Here, I decided, was a woman who could communicate on a primal level. I couldn't wait to introduce her to my animal friends at the park.

I should introduce myself. I am Wolfgang DeMark, and I am a specialist in communication, particularly animal communication. You can read the outline of my dissertation at Demarkishere@biggov.com. I knew this woman could be important to my research. I had to meet her.

I sidled up during the chicken dance and offered her another glass of wine. She clucked and scratched around in a circle. I lifted my head and crowed in a pretend aloofness. She tilted her head and waggled her tail feathers. I could see the research for my doctorate taking a new and interesting turn. “Have we met before?”

“You were better as a chicken,” she replied and then went flapping off.

Stunned by her primitive animal perceptiveness, I went looking for someone who could give me a formal introduction. I spotted Lee Bradley across the room. Lee knows everyone. She’s a retired teacher and had half the world in her class at one time or another. Besides that, she knows and accepts me for who I am. I’m not always great in social situations.

I was just explaining to Lee what I wanted when Matt announced that it was Karaoke time. We listened for a couple of songs, and then Lee dragged me across the room. “Wolfgang, meet Cerise. Cerise, Wolfgang.” Lee pushed us both forward. “Matt, put on 'Muskrat Love.'”

By the time Cerise and I had finished purring and burbling through that song we had everyone on their feet, and I felt I had known her all of my life. It was a seminal moment for me. I felt like I had poured out my soul to her, and I could tell she felt a similar attraction.

Cerise led me to a corner of the room. Her head was bobbing back and forth slightly, and she had a speck of saliva on the corner of her lower lip. She gave me a sidelong glance.

It was mesmerizing, and I knew I would follow her wherever she might lead me. A sudden shudder ran through me as I recognized her expression, but I shook it off. Hers was the unmistakable look of a female mantis, but I wasn't going anywhere.

I remember very little else about the party. Cerise and I were in a world of our own. I learned that she had grown up on a farm. Her closest childhood friends had been woolyhead sheep and pigs. Though she seemed to have some animosity towards deer, she spoke fondly of chickens and woodchucks and skunks. She had grown up and become a teacher. She confided to me that she'd learned classroom control by studying pumas. She felt a particular affinity for cats. That's probably why she would stop talking occasionally and lick herself.

The next weeks were a blur. I introduced Cerise to my research and all of my animal friends at the John Ball Park Zoo. It was amazing how quickly she learned to converse with the spider monkeys, and it was no time before she was chatting with the hyena. Her imitation of the macaw was simply genius. But it was her insights into turtlespeak that were a real breakthrough in my dissertation work. Even after twenty-seven years of research, I'd had no idea what importance there was to the angle at which the head was held.

Cerise and I met daily at the zoo. Those walks we shared are the stuff of my fondest memories. I was particularly impressed to watch a woman her age scramble up a tree and share her bag of nuts. To see her out on a limb was to see the perfect imitation of a red squirrel, right down to the way she would cock her eyebrows when she chattered. It was no wonder I fell in love. In truth, it was as much awe as love.

Perhaps I should have seen it coming. One day as we walked by the pond Cerise looked uneasy. I honked two or three times and the geese came paddling over to be fed. I carried on a conversation with a big gander for several minutes. When I turned around Cerise was studying some goose poop she had on the bottom of her shoe. She had been uncharacteristically quiet. I waddled back to her side.

"I'm not a goose," she declared. "I've never understood geese. It's time you learned that. I'm not a goose—a goose mates for life."

With those words she gave a low warning growl and turned and ambled out of my life. Of course I tried to find her, and when I asked Lee Bradley if she knew where Cerise had gone, Lee shrugged her shoulders and said, "Just hibernating again, I suppose."

The Old Profession

Since you've asked, I'll tell you how I became a therapist. I won't bore you with the back story about my troubled childhood, the usually missing father and alcoholic mother. Most therapists could give you that old story. I'll start at my most desperate moment, the one where I decided that to survive I would become a prostitute. I was on my own. At the time, I had just enough money left to cover the rent for three days and buy a pair of mesh hose and a tube of bright red lipstick. I didn't know then that mesh hose are not an attraction on someone with thighs like mine; I just figured they were part of the uniform.

I had a lot of questions my first night on the corner. What do you do if you're a prostitute, somewhat overweight, homely, and have no skills? What if competition is not really something you're good at? What do you do when all of the good-looking girls have left the street corner? How can a story like this lead to a happy ending?

The other girls weren't too happy to see me. The one who called herself Robyn raised a little fuss, but the others soon quieted her down. It wasn't good for business, you see. They told me I could stay, but I had to go fifty paces down the street. Hookers are a little like cabbies in that they line up and take turns bantering and bartering with the motorists who drive slowly by. They wouldn't let me join the line because they were afraid I'd scare away the customers. That's what they told me at the time, anyway.

By three-thirty in the morning, when I was alone and could finally move down to the corner, I was really getting desperate. I only had the room for three nights, and the first was nearly over. It was shelter time after that. I started wondering if there were unemployment benefits for hookers, but as I had never yet been employed, I figured not. At a quarter to four I began walking slowly down the street. I practiced shaking my booty as I walked, but there was no one to see. I probably wouldn't have practiced if there had been. I'd walked only about a half a block when I heard quiet sobbing. It was coming from the alleyway just ahead. I've gotta tell you, my mind raced through a hundred bloody scenarios, but I picked up an old yellow brick and went to investigate. It was a man, slightly balding and holding a guitar case. He wasn't too old, but I didn't get the impression there was any danger. I cautiously walked to him and put my hand on his shoulder. He didn't respond, so I sat down beside him. We just sat there until his sobbing began to subside. He was shivering in the cool air.

"Do you have someplace to stay?"

He shook his head to the negative, so I stood and held out my hand. I've got to be honest and tell you that right then I'd totally forgotten I was a prostitute. I led him back to my room. To this day I've never seen or heard anything quite like it. He'd been so quiet, but after a few minutes in the warm room that quiet changed to a tsunami of words.

I guess I was a good listener—at least until seven-thirty the next morning. Matt Bliton's story was both lengthy and sad. His long-time relationship with his agent had ended in a huge fight when he found that she was seeing another man. She had thrown him and his instrument out of her apartment, and he had wandered the streets in shock and sorrow. Being able to talk about things definitely made him feel better. He asked if he might come back, and I had to explain to him about my uncertain situation with the rent money. Was I ever surprised when he pulled a checkbook out of his guitar case and wrote a check to cover the lease for three months!

I probably didn't look so desperate the next night. I'd ditched the net stockings. I wasn't so desperate, but one of the other girls was. I wound up talking to Lee through most of the night. In the end I wound up taking her on the bus to a rehab center. It took us most of the morning to get her admitted, but when they finally got ready to take her back, Lee emptied her purse and gave me all the money she had in it. I tried not to take it, but she absolutely insisted. She promised to keep in touch after she got out, and she said she'd need my support. I finally had to take her five hundred and twelve dollars, but as I did so I promised myself I'd make sure Lee was taken care of after she returned.

My third night on the corner was a bust, but because of my taking care of Lee I had gained the respect of the other girls and I spent most of the evening talking with them. Mostly I was a listener, and boy, were their stories fascinating! Especially Phyllis and Shirley's.

On the fourth night I was approached by an elderly man. I've gotta say, my heart jumped into my throat when I was finally faced with the possibility of my first real customer. What should I say? What in the world should I do? I'd sort of been rehearsing lines in my head, but, "Hey, Baby, wanna make a little mojo? Wanna get lucky?" just really weren't in my functional vocabulary. At that moment, "Are you a cop?" flashed through my mind. I had almost decided to run when the man spoke. He was confused. Disoriented. I took his hand and noticed the I.D. bracelet on his wrist. I knew a little about this. I spoke calmly and quietly and took him back to my room. I called the number on the bracelet, and when the lady answered I explained where Mike Von Stratton was. It was the man's daughter, and she promised to be there in minutes. The family had been terrified. Her dad was an Alzheimer's patient and prone to wander, but he had never before disappeared so completely. When she arrived, the daughter spilled out her story. I listened. I answered their questions as openly as I could, and I know I hugged Mr. Von Stratton before he left. The daughter said the family would be back in touch.

On the next night Matt Bliton returned and talked through half the night. Of course I had to be there for him, listening and commiserating. At first he made me a little nervous because he kept stopping to make notes about our conversation, but then he explained he was just putting down ideas for song lyrics. He left my room at two in the morning. There was a spring in his step; his soul was unburdened, and apparently he had a new song in his head.

On my sixth night of street-corner vigil, I was approached by another elderly man. He was dragging a big portfolio folder, and he introduced himself as Rich Travis. He claimed to be an artist. He asked if I would be interested in buying a painting. I wasn't sure about this guy. He had a funny sideways way of looking at people, and I sure couldn't have been mistaken for an art critic standing there on that corner. But I listened to his starving artist story, and I've got to tell you that it was so compelling that I dug into my purse and purchased two canvases for ten dollars each. We went back to my room and I fed him chicken soup. It was, he said, his first warm meal in four days. I could see that he'd been nearly as desperate as I had been. You can't trust artists, though. They're all alike. He asked if I'd like to pose for a nude portrait and I had to slap him. Before long he fell asleep at the table, and when I awoke in the morning he was gone.

Three weeks into my career and I still had not had a regular paying customer. I've got to say, however, that I'd developed quite a following of people wanting to tell their stories and ask for advice. And I was doing okay. Lots of folks gave me gifts. A man from India who missed his family deeply left me a watch that I was able to pawn for two hundred and thirty dollars. An old farmer from the Upper Peninsula gave me his last rutabaga. A teenage runaway that I talked to for hours and finally convinced to go home left me her bus ticket to Peoria and half a box of M&M's. I was able to get a partial refund on the ticket.

The final corner was turned on a Tuesday afternoon when there was a knock at my door. Standing there was Mr. Von Stratton's daughter and a lawyer in a blue pinstripe suit. I almost fainted at the sight of the lawyer, because I figured this had to be lawsuit time. Nevertheless, I finally managed to invite them in. Von Stratton, it turned out, had made a fortune writing self-help books about dream interpretation. The family was so grateful for his safe return that they established a scholarship in my name. I was to be the first recipient.

The girls on the street corner were ecstatic. Trish and Eva both wanted to sign up to be future scholarship recipients. Clarice got the girls together, and seven of them pledged an evening's earnings so that I'd have money for books and fees.

Things just continued to fall into place financially. One afternoon I was stopped on my way out of Psychology 113. A man wearing a purple jacket and an ascot handed me a check and had me sign a paper wherein I agreed to accept future payments. The check was for royalties from a song I had inspired Matt Bliton to write. My account was a bit stretched again two years later when I finished my undergraduate degree, so I went on line and sold the two paintings by Rich Travis to a collector in Oklahoma. The price for the pair was thirty-three thousand dollars. With that money I started graduate school.

I'm proud today that the nameplate Dr. Wanda Walters is now on the door of a very successful counseling practice. I've been able to put my broad experiences to work in a variety of areas, but I never, never accept cases involving problems with a client's sex life. I'm probably not qualified in those cases. I may have made a living as a prostitute for slightly over a month—a virgin prostitute—but it was really just my listening skills that got me by. Usually if a situation comes up, I just write a street corner address on a slip of paper and send the client down to speak with the girls. It seems to work.

Sail Haven

There is nothing like feeling a boat heel hard to the side and having the wind and spray in your face. As a youngster sailing had been the main object of Marvin's daydreams. Not long before he was married, Marvin purchased a used 36 foot sailboat. For years the boat was his escape, his outlet, his kingdom. In that sense, there had probably been times when the boat saved his marriage. There were times, he was sure, when the boat had saved his sanity. He loved to sail alone. Myrna showed no interest in sailing until their seventh year of marriage. Marvin's stomach tightened instinctively when she asked him to teach her to sail. He knew he was in trouble.

He asked why she wanted to learn. At first Myrna said that she just figured it was time they develop more interests in common. Later, after overhearing her on the phone, he figured out that she and some of her friends had decided the marina was a happenin' place, and it might be just the spot for them to meet, gossip, and play cards. It did not bode well. He needed a plan. Marvin watched the forecasts. When the long range forecast for the next Friday called for thunder storms, he found Myrna in the kitchen and said, "Why don't we start those sailing lessons Friday?"

"Sorry, I've got to fold bandages for the Hospital Guild Friday. How about Saturday?" Saturday was forecast to be a bluebird day. Marvin was bummed, but a man can't control the weather.

Saturday came. As they walked out on the dock Marvin had a sudden inspiration. "Watch out for the water snakes," he said calmly. "They crawl up between the dock planks and go for the ankles."

Myrna moved a little closer but did not miss a step. "They can't be too big," she mused. "The planks are really close together."

Marvin began to sense his task would not be easy.

As Myrna stepped onto the boat, Marvin did his best to jump up and down without being noticed. He wanted to create some roll, but the water was too calm and the boat too heavy to set up much motion. It would not be easy.

"When we get ready to cast off, it will take two of us. You'll have to learn to do both jobs. Either you'll have to cast off the lines or you'll have to maneuver us out using the engine and the rudder."

"What does it take to do the driving?"

"You start the diesel and let it warm up. When you're ready, you give the order to cast off the bow and stern lines, and then the aft spring line. You'll turn the wheel to starboard and advance the throttle until the aft comes away from the dock. When you're clear to the aft, call to have the bow spring line cleared and reverse the throttle. Then you'll steer out of the slip keeping to port. Once you've cleared the dock, shift gears and give the throttle a little nudge and proceed at a no wake speed until you're out of the harbor."

"Oh, what does it take to cast off lines?"

Progress, thought Marvin. "Well, when I give you the word, you'll have to undo the bow and stern lines. They're fastened with cleat hitches and the tails are Flemished. Throw the lines on board and you'll coil them as soon as we're under way. Stand by, and when I give the order, you're to unfasten the aft spring line. Place it on board, and then you'll take the bow spring line and tend it as I ease out of the slip. When we get to the end of the dock you'll have to jump aboard. Don't worry, though, if you fall in, hang on to the line and I can pull you out once we clear the break wall outside the marina."

Myrna stood thinking carefully. Marvin noted that he seemed to have confused her sufficiently, and he knew that she hated taking orders from him. Three commands in a row would be a record she'd have to really struggle with.

"I'll do the lines, but you'll have to walk me through it a couple of times before we try for real."

Marvin's heart sank. "Cool. But that was just the beginning. Once we've cleared the break wall you'll have to hoist the sails. I'll be busy at the helm, so you'll have to center the traveler and snug the mainsheet. Then you'll take a winch handle forward to the mast, stow it, and prepare the mainsail. The main halyard is cleated to the starboard side of the mast. Halyards for the jib and spinnaker are on the port. Make sure the lines aren't wrapped on the shrouds or stays. You'll need to attach the D-ring on the halyard to the head cringle. Wrap the tail of the halyard clockwise twice around the winch at the base of the mast. When you're ready to hoist, signal me and I'll point the bow into the wind. The first two-thirds will go up easily, but after that you'll have to use the winch handle. When she's up, wrap the halyard a couple more times and cleat it off. Then you'll have to come back and we'll start with the jib sheets. We've self-tailing winches for those, so it's not such bad work."

Myrna was glaring at him now. Marvin did his best to look innocent. She didn't like taking directions from him, but he knew she'd seldom back down if he challenged her too much. "You're just trying to make this sound hard. All right for you."

After she'd turned on her heel and walked back up the dock, Marvin wondered just how much trouble he was in. His sanctuary was apparently safe for now, but a question about the cost of his victory vibrated in the back of his mind.

The answer to that question came at dinner ten days later. Myrna had looked smug all day, but he knew better than to question it. "I've signed up for the six week sailing class they offer in Mackinaw City. It'll cost $3,550, plus a motel on nights when we aren't on the boat. The instructor is a woman, so I won't have any trouble understanding her."

A sudden tightening in his stomach left Marvin wondering if he was developing an ulcer. He saw his refuge sinking slowly in a storm.

"We should be able to sail together by August. When do you want me to schedule an overnight sail with the girls?"

Marvin didn't respond. In his mind he heard the bubbles as his sanctuary slipped under the waves. He looked up. He conjured a new daydream. In it he saw himself flying in a single seat stunt plane.

LONELINESS

It was through the blur of stale tears that she first spotted the congregation of butterflies. They were small and blue, shimmering over a squat, red stone. Sensing that she needed to get up, to move on, Sheila stood. Mindlessly she wandered in the direction of the fluttering, azure cloud.

As she approached, the butterflies continued in place, seemingly unconcerned when she stopped and watched their aerobatics from just a few feet away. She was exhausted both in body and spirit, and the curious exhibition fluttered only on the surface of her mind.

The death of a spouse is a numbing experience. It had been only six days, just eight since the accident—two since the funeral. Time had been a blur, a swelter of people and responsibilities. Now the isolation of the cemetery was a relief from the constant questions and condolences of relatives and well-intentioned friends. The fresh sod from Mike's grave had stained the knees of her slacks, and loose dirt clogged the ridges in the soles of her sandals. She leaned back on a dark, granite stone and began scraping at the mud under her heel.

Tears welled up once again as she chipped at her shoe. She wondered if the grief were bearable... and for how long.

"The tears become you."

Sheila started at the oddly hollow voice and looked up. There on the red stone in front of her the butterflies had settled in such a way that the nuance of sun and wind and shadow formed the perfect portrait of a man. He smiled.

She moved closer, now aware of each thump of her heart within her chest. She wiped her eyes with the back of her hand and stared.

The mouth of wings opened. "Death isn't at all what you think, you know."

"Who are you? What are you?"

"Who I am is not important. If you want a name, read the marker. I am, I suppose, what you would call an apparition—a ghost—though that word is so full of nonsensical connotation as to be nearly useless."

"Have you seen my husband? His name is Michael. Can he come here?"

"Oh, it takes many years for most to learn to manifest. Most never bother because by the time the trick is learned there is no one left that they know or would even want to manifest for."

Sheila's mind began grasping at possibilities. "Can you carry messages?"

"Loneliness is a powerful motivation! I suppose that much of what we do is out of a fear of loneliness. That certainly has been the case for me." The eyes of the butterfly specter blinked slowly.

"Have you seen Mike? Could I see him?"

"What are you willing to give up?"

It was the classical question, and though Sheila recognized it immediately, she was too tired and empty to appreciate it fully.

"Right now...I'd do almost anything to see him again."

"As I said, loneliness is a powerful motivation. That is as true for me as it is for you." The smile on the blue face widened. "Perhaps you would care to accompany me?"

A rush of cold overwhelmed Sheila, and she stood in the sun rubbing her arms. She was exhausted, shattered, deeply depressed. Without warning, her legs lost their will to stand and she crumpled to the ground. Her head was pounding, and she was overcome with dizziness. Her will to live was gone.

"What are you willing to give up?" the thin, blue voice repeated.

"I'll come with you!" Sheila gasped just before she lost consciousness.

The butterfly smile scattered and then returned. The winged eyelids blinked rapidly several times. "You should know," the apparition intoned, "that things here are highly compartmentalized. You will stay with me, and it's very unlikely we'll ever see your Michael. But, ah, well, you have made your choice, and you'll never need to be lonely again." The hovering blue smile widened. "You can't say I didn't warn you, even if you couldn't hear me."

When the two men from the cemetery crew found the body, they were amazed to see that it was covered in butterflies.

"Do you think maybe she committed suicide?" the younger man asked.

"I don't know; it's possible," the older man replied. "Loneliness is a powerful motivation!"

Marriage Training

My friend Ted recently came to me with a business proposition. "Chad," he said, "I have a young friend who is thinking of getting married. He's as green as a lizard's butt, and I worry about him. Now it occurred to me that you and I have enough wisdom and experience that we could take young men like Ben and give them a proper basis from which to commit their sorry backsides and shoulder the matrimonial yoke. Not only would we be doing a humanitarian service, but we could also make a few bucks."

Now Ted is on his third wife, so he has some insights I don't possess, but I was flattered that he thought me competent to give matrimonial advice. "What are you thinking, Ted?"

"Think about the differences between men and women. With all of this equality crap we hear today, some of that gets lost. Women talk way more; they shop more and seem to enjoy it; they tend to be more open with their emotions; women ask a lot of rhetorical questions; and they think dates like anniversaries are important. Those are just a few of the problem areas. A guy can get blindsided. We can prepare them to be ready for those things."

"Maybe you have some talents I don't have. I'm not ready for those things myself, and I've been married over forty years."

"That's exactly it! You've developed some coping mechanisms, and those strategies need to be shared. I propose that we start with my young friend Ben, and we'll use that experience to build on. It's a place to begin, and Ben needs help. He's like a big bug about to make the acquaintance of a windshield."

"Alright, I guess giving it a try won't cost us anything but a little time."

The next day we got together with Ben in Ted's study. Ted began, "Son, there are some things that you should know about maintaining a happy marriage. You've got to understand how to take care of yourself. There are a lot of men out there who've been emasculated, traumatized, trampled and driven to the very edge. We can't let that happen to you. You are about to become the recipient of the product of an important new business venture."

"I appreciate that, I think. I don't really understand."

"Of course you don't. You're young and haven't had enough experience to understand the ways of the world. Women are not the same as men. They are, in many ways, fundamentally different. They're hardly human is my point! Chad, why don't you start?"

"Alright, Ted. Ben, you may have noticed that women like to talk. I'm not referring to simple conversation. They talk for the sake of talking. It'll drive you crazy unless you know how to handle it. Many's the man has become a lunatic from listening to a woman." We pulled up our chairs and sat close on either side of Ben.

"Listen up, Kimosabe. The solution is simple, but it takes some practice. It's a bit like going to a game in a major stadium. You hear voices all around you—thousands of voices—but you don't really hear any of them. You focus just on the game, except in this case the game is in your head," Ted explained.

"Appearance is everything," I interjected.

"That's right. You find your focus, then you kind of let your neck go loose so your head bobbles. The woman will take the movement to mean that you are listening. It helps if you learn to mumble like a medicine man once in a while, but that's an advanced skill that takes some practice. You see, women seldom expect a real response, and they're not listening while they talk, either. I heard about a woman who listened to herself once, and she wound up nuttier than a fruitcake and in a psych ward. The important thing is to look like you're listening." Ted put a game tape on.

"Focus," I said. "Keep your mind in the game." Then we both started talking to Ben at the same time. It was all nonsense, of course, and after an hour and a half Ben's eyes kind of glazed over and his head began to bobble. The boy was a natural. We figured three weeks of twice-a-days and he'd be ready to withstand the initial phase of marriage. We made a note about our success in our business plan and forged on.

The next day I plunged into the new lesson. "There's lots more to communicating with a woman than you might expect. They each have their own set of cues. You're expected to know these cues, even though they often seem to be the opposite of what is apparent. With a woman *yes* means *no* and *no* means *yes*, but only part of the time. The rest of the time you have to guess. If you just kind of smile and don't say anything, eventually they'll tell you what they really mean. It just takes patience."

"Oh, and it's a myth that you should just say 'Yes, dear,' every so often," Ted added. "That can land you in a pile of trouble deeper than elephant shit on a circus midget if you don't know what you're agreeing to. The flowery sofa and chairs in my living room are an example of that."

Ted continued, "You can't just sit back all of the time, however. For instance, never let yourself be trapped in the position where you have to answer questions like 'How do I look?' or 'Is this dress too short?' Whooee!"

"Be proactive," I suggested. "It's a kind of instinct. Tell her before she asks, and be prepared to lie a little—or a lot. You can't think of it as lying, of course. Lying is bad. Think of it as allowing the survival instinct to kick in. It's been bred into us by God as a survival mechanism, and it's not good to ignore a gift from God."

"Yeah, what he's sayin' is that sometimes it's best to not give her a chance to talk. For instance, never take your wife along when you go to deal on a new car. She'll go on and on about how she loves the upholstery and the cute little dials on the dashboard. Salesmen love that. You'll pay at least two thousand extra for having your wife along. It cost me big time before I learned to keep my second wife away from poker games, too."

That evening Ted and I made our notes. I was beginning to feel better about our prospects for a successful business. Ben was growing up before our very eyes. We were ready for him the next day.

"Remember, dates are important to women. Birthdays, anniversaries, holidays, dumb stuff. You need to keep a stash of things you can use if you forget a birthday or Valentine 's

Day or something. Keep in mind that the more practical the gift the less suitable it becomes. Vacuum cleaners and sets of screwdrivers are out. Jewelry and bath foo foo are in."

"Yeah, and no wheel covers," Ted offered. "You don't know how rejection feels until you've had a wheel cover thrown at you. I could tell you stories...."

At this point in his training we sent Ben out to shop for gifts he could wrap and hide away for use in emergencies. There were so many lessons he needed to learn: how to avoid shopping at the mall, dodging quilting groups and bridge groups and home jewelry parties, making excuses to get out to a ball game, maintaining control of the TV remote, protecting turf and tools. The list grew, and we developed lessons to meet the challenge.

Ted and I think we have a good idea. We're working on new marketing strategies, and Ted's already talking about stock options for the company. We worked on Ben for six weeks, though our curriculum could easily have stretched to eight. It felt good. In the end he was almost as well prepared for marriage as a man can be. Maybe the <u>almost</u> is why he postponed the date for their ceremony, at least for a while.

The Widow's Might

I'm a seventy-four year old guy. I fought in Nam, jumped out of airplanes, been lost in caves, hunted grizzlies in Alaska, and battled wildfires. I tell you this only because I want you to understand that I've been around a bit, and that when I say there's only one thing that strikes real fear into my heart, it's not that I'm a wimp or a sissy. That one thing, you ask? Let me start by simply commenting that there's a big difference between a widow and a widower. I don't make that statement without some experience and a lot of observation. My wife died almost five years ago. My observations have taken place mostly since then, but they're backed up by centuries of examination by scientists and others. I would offer, as an example, the fact that there is no such thing as a black widower spider. The arachinophile who named the black widow was no doubt an astute observer. Widows are legitimate agents of fear.

Walk down the street while visiting almost any tourist destination—like where I live—and one of the first things you'll notice is that widows tend to run in packs. Seldom do you notice one or two by themselves. They form gangs of three to six, occasionally more. You can spot these groups because the individuals in them are less apt to follow the rules of polite decorum and appearance than ordinary women. Among widows you will generally notice more pink hair and plucked and painted eyebrows than in the average population of older women. Cheeks are rouged, outfits often include wild prints, and seldom is more than one gang member quiet at a time.

Widowers, on the other hand, are more solitary. Years of marriage will make a man quiet and introspective. Widowers are most often seen wearing faded old clothes, speaking softly, and seeking out quiet avocations such as fishing and philately.

We men develop particular sensitivity to what women in these widow gangs are doing. Take the other day, for example. I was in Wal-Mart with my friend Dan. We were looking for fishing tackle when a pack of widow women walked by. I was kind of around a corner where I could see down the aisle. I watched them walk by Dan. Now it should be said that Dan isn't a bad looking guy for a man of seventy-two with cauliflower ears, but there was no call for all four of those women to check out his legs as they sauntered by him. The next to last one clearly was checking out his butt, because she made a little patting motion to the woman behind her and I saw her wink. It's no wonder that often we widowers feel violated.

Not all widows are trying to find a man. Only 92.873% fall into the category of man hunters, and it usually takes sixteen to twenty months of widowhood before that urge becomes an urgency. My friend Matt discovered all of this the hard way. He tried to live in a retirement condominium in Florida. What he didn't realize was that those places attract widows like watermelon rind attracts ants. In his experience, an average of three widows a week asked him to come over for dinner; twice a day he'd have women stop by to borrow cups of sugar, and six times a week he'd get invited to bingo or pinochle games. Matt's a bit shy, so of course he never had the nerve to take up any of the dinner invitations, but it made little difference. More often than not, they would bring him a plate of "leftovers" later in the day. Those widow women drove him nuts! Drove him clean back to Michigan, despite the cold winters.

Harvey and I were in the food court at the mall the other day. We'd stopped in for an ice-cream cone. We soon noticed there was a flock of women who sort of circled our area several times. Oh, they pretended to be looking in the windows and shopping and such, but Harvey allowed as how he was starting to feel like road-kill, and we moved on to the tool department in Sears. I was paying for my sandpaper discs when we saw those same women just two aisles over in the appliance department. Now it may be I'm paranoid, and it may be it was a coincidence, but both of us found it just a bit scary. These were widow women, too. You can tell, because when there's a man within a mile they smile all the time and there's a kind of bounce to their walk. For some it's a wiggle, but mostly these ladies bounce.

Fear can cause paralysis only so long; a man can take only so much; a widower can be pushed only so far. For me and Tom and Harv the limit was reached during an incident involving a gang of widows from the Congregational Church. Seven of 'em: Shirley, Carol, Tricia, Sarah, Robyn, Gloria, and Susan—we know all of 'em, 'cause they've terrorized the neighborhood for years. They call themselves a support group, but to look at them you couldn't see how the support was working. Anyway, Tom, Harv and I were sitting in the park feeding pigeons and gloating about the fact that the Redsox had made the playoffs and the Yankees hadn't, when this bunch of ladies surrounded us. They started talking at us about the weather and the sale at Gimble's and a bunch of other foolishness. It was more than two to one. Tom's a few years younger, and there was a momentary gleam in his eye, but after a few more paragraphs of yakking he got to be as scared as Harv and me. Trapped, we were! Subjected to seemingly endless assaults of mundane verbiage! Fortunately for us, fifteen or so minutes into their outburst an ambulance came screaming by. When the ladies turned to watch, Harv made a dash for the pond and Tom and I followed. We were forty-three minutes hiding in the water lilies before the last of those women went away. It was a cold forty-three minutes, but terror makes a man do extraordinary things. I hope whoever the ambulance was after made it, but in any case I'm grateful for their sacrifice.

After we'd gotten dried off and changed, we got back together for a drink and to talk it over. Tom was still shaking, and I think it was more from the close call than from the dunk in a cold pond. I still had a bit of tremor myself. It had been the odds, seven to three, that had been so daunting. That's probably part of why widows tend to flock together—it makes 'em feel confident and intimidating. We naturally got to wondering how they'd feel if the odds were reversed. A plan was born. Wednesday at bowling we got sixteen guys from the Senior's League together and explained the situation. We made ground rules: talk only about sports, tools, or cars. Stereotypes carry their own levels of fear and mistrust, you know. And don't, don't let them get a word in edgewise. Once a widow starts talking she'll begin to feel comfortable and go for the upper hand.

The next morning we spread out over the neighborhood scouting. It wasn't as hard as hunting deer or raccoons. With widows you generally can find them either shopping or eating. We found the serpentine seven waiting outside The Yarn Barn where there was a sale about to start. The sixteen of us surrounded them and started talking. Most of the guys did pretty well at sticking to the script, but I heard a couple of off-color comments thrown in for effect. You should have seen those widow ladies go into a huddle, turn red and white and purple by turn, and try to talk back. I'm sure it was their inability to speak that most broke their spirit. In the end, Harv made a little speech about how widows should not prey on single and widowed men, and how if they ever accosted us again there would be dire consequences. They seemed contrite, and the guys all had a good laugh as the girls left. The ladies didn't even bother to check out the sale. That didn't go over well with the manager, who gave us a piece of her mind, but we didn't care.

Since that time I've felt pretty good about a free and easy future—until this morning. I looked out my apartment window and saw a gang of five widows ride by on Amigo scooters. They were movin', too. Hell's Widows in training, I thought. This could take more than a bowling league of old men.

Processing

It felt as though time stopped, and then it started again when I entered the room.

"Back again? Welcome. I see by the spring in your step that you're ready to take on the material world once more."

It seemed the voice of an old friend I'd never met. My surroundings held the sense of coming home to where I'd never been. They were comprised of a room with no walls and a crowd with no people. I stepped forward.

"Your assignment this time involves a very short turn-around. Your mission is more to teach than to learn, so this will be a kind of vacation."

"No homework?"

"Oh, there are plenty of lessons to learn if you're open. There'll be some trauma, but you won't be making the decisions. You'll have plenty of decisions in the assignment that follows this one."

"Okay, when do I start?

"You've already started. Part of you is in place. Actual conception is in about three minutes."

"So what's the story with the quick turn-around?"

"Abortion. First trimester, this one is induced."

"All right, let's get on with it."

Materializing is a kind of hazy process, like being in a web of cotton and losing reality through the mesh. But the whole sense of bursting from seed into a growing form is exhilarating, and I like that part. There are comforting sounds, rhythms and caresses, a sense of buoyancy and embrace. This time, however, there was soon a horrible sense of depression. There was shock, disappointment, anger, hopelessness; all of those feelings washed over me by turns. They came from outside. I felt them, but with distance and a lack of understanding.

When the moment came, it was a shock. All of the warmth receded, and I felt material life being pulled from me. On one hand, I'd have screamed if it were possible; there was a kind of panic. On the other hand, the events felt as natural as anything I've ever known. It was a time of expansion, then of rest. It felt as though time stopped. It started again when I entered the room.

"Back again? Welcome. I see by the spring in your step you've rested, and that you're ready to take on the material world once more."

It's Not Duck Soup

My Uncle Merlin has never done much travelling outside of his home state of Tennessee. In fact, until recently I've never known him to get more than fifty miles from his place on the flatlands southeast of Memphis. I tried for years to get him to visit Michigan, but he always had one excuse or another. Usually it was dove hunting or quail hunting or turkey hunting, or he had to fetch a new cow.

Duck hunting is my passion, and every time I spoke to Uncle Merlin I tried to convince him it was the greatest sport of all. In his part of Tennessee there just aren't the same opportunities for duck hunting that we get in Michigan. Like I say, I worked on him for years, so I was most delighted when he called and said I'd finally convinced him to try out the hunting in our great state.

I had just the place to take him. One of my friends has a cabin on a private lake—well, more of a pond—just outside of Harrison. We've built three blinds up there, and seldom have we failed to limit out on teal or mallards. The trees are tall all around the lake, and there's lots of wild rice and other vegetation to draw in the waterfowl. With the big trees, we often don't see the ducks coming in until they're right on top of us. It makes for interesting hunting.

It was a Wednesday evening when Uncle Merlin arrived in his '68 Ford pickup. He has an old camper in the bed, and inside that camper it looks like a hunting lodge. Sometimes I wonder about Uncle Merlin. There are a half dozen fish mounts and a deer head on the walls, and a stuffed bobcat and a raccoon on the ledge out over the cab. He showed me six shotguns in the gun cabinet, and he assured me he had ample ammunition for each. Uncle Merlin doesn't mess around when it comes to hunting. I suggested that his 12 gauge Browning semi-automatic was just what he would need.

We started north on Thursday morning. I drove separately because I didn't trust the brakes on Merlin's truck, and I knew I'd have to come back downstate for a couple of hours of work on Friday. Before we got to the cabin, I had a call on my cell phone. One of the foremen had quit, and they needed me back at work immediately. I'll tell you, I was bummed.

I showed Uncle Merlin around, pointing out the blinds and showing him where the canoe was stored. I promised to call him that evening and headed back down to work.

When I talked to Merlin that Thursday evening I had to tell him it would be Sunday afternoon before I could make it back north. He assured me that he was okay, having fun, and not to worry about him.

When I talked to Merlin on Friday evening he asked me where the nearest sporting goods store was. He said he could hardly shoot fast enough to keep up with the ducks, and he was running low on ammo. I was delighted, of course, but I reminded him that there were limits. He said that he was from Tennessee, and that the Michigan limits didn't apply. Besides, there were so many blood-thirsty ducks that a good thinning of the population would only be a healthy thing. Sometimes I wonder about Uncle Merlin. He's prone to exaggerate when he's telling a story. I tried to argue, but he hung up after telling me that he had duck soup boiling over on the stove, and he needed to get ready for morning.

When I talked to Merlin on Saturday he mumbled on about soft bodied ducks and how they made lousy soup. I asked if he'd managed to buy more ammunition, and he said yes, but maybe I should bring more when I came. He sounded tired, and I asked him how it was going. He told me I'd be tired, too, if I'd had to stack hundreds of ducks. Besides, they seemed to be night fliers, so he'd stayed up all night trying to keep up with them. Sometimes I wonder about Uncle Merlin, and I worried that he might be arrested for hunting ducks at night.

Sunday afternoon Uncle Merlin met me out in front of his pickup. He was beaming with pride and could hardly wait to show me his prizes. I was pretty nervous about the law—that is until I saw the stacks he'd made out in back of his truck. Merlin is from Tennessee, so I suppose that he wouldn't know about Michigan. A lot of people don't appreciate Michigan. He hadn't bagged a single duck. I think he was kind of embarrassed when I pointed out to him that he'd spent all of his time shooting down Michigan mosquitoes. Just because it's the size of a duck, and it flies like a duck, that doesn't necessarily mean it's a duck—especially in Michigan.

Dreamholder

He hadn't asked for it. At first it was a gift he didn't fully trust. That is most often the way with gifts of that type. They must be nurtured and exercised and honed.

The man had not been conscious of his gift before his daughter, three years old and completely trusting, wandered in to the living room where he was sitting. She smiled with chubby cheeks and held her tiny dream to him. Later, he would remember wondering what one did when another person handed over their dream. At the time he *oohed* and *aahed* until he thought his little girl was sufficiently impressed, and then, when he was about to hand it back, she ran happily from the room. He cradled that dream in his hands for awhile, and then decided to store it in a safe place until she was older.

He never understood exactly why, but from that time on others began to trust him unconditionally in the same way his daughter had. He accepted each dream that was handed him as a gift, and initially that was all that people seemed to want. He wrapped each carefully so as not to lose any parts, and he was cautious not to betray any of the secret details. He simply accepted each at face value and tried not to read too much into their meanings.

Then came the bad dream. He accepted it from a stranger without question, and reflexively, on recognizing what it was, dropped it so that it shattered into great dark splinters across the floor. Then, as if in a mirror, he stood there looking at the man as they shared waves of shock, anger, frustration and shame. Troubled, he later inquired about the man. He was told of the hurt and abuse of the stranger's upbringing, and the dream seemed less threatening in that new context. He learned the lesson: always hold a dream long enough to see it in perspective. He had since then shattered other dreams, some of them his own, but never was it done in surprise or indignation. It was always in a manner more conscious and worthy than that. And only one person, whom he later recognized to be contaminated with evil, had failed to thank or forgive him for his actions.

His reputation as a dreamholder grew. It was not something he sought, and he had the feeling that if it had been, the gift of it would likely have disappeared. He simply followed the path of his unconscious knowledge, and that hidden source gave him strength when the spirits of lost dreams sometimes called to him in the night—voices too sad to be understood. The voices made him uneasy, for they reminded him of earlier times when he had believed that a song was just a song, and a poem was just a poem.

Each of the dreams handed him was nurtured carefully, stored and retrieved to be examined in its proper time. He carefully acknowledged that a dream left too long unexamined withered and turned to dry dust.

As he grew old, the edges of the dreams he held began to fray. As the distinctions between them faded, he came to see all dreams as one. At first he was disturbed by this, for he worried that his gift had left him. Later he came to see that his younger perceptions were only Truth, who had disguised herself that she might be more alluring to her lovers. One more secret she showed him when he found her out: the dreams he held had been his own all along, for a man is nothing more than the dreams he holds.

When the dreamholder was born again into the journey of death, he once more heard the voices of lost dream spirits calling out. They were closer now. He reached out and picked one from the air. He felt a sigh in his hand, and a smile. “We have been waiting for a dreamretriever,” a voice spoke in his mind. He shrugged, peered into the distance, and took a slow step forward.

It's Not Small Talk

Three years ago I was just a hospital orderly. I might have remained just an orderly except for inspiration that came to me while I was sitting with three doctors having coffee in the break room. What I learned that day has set me on course with the hope of finding a cure for the most persistent plague the world has ever known. That day I was telling Dr. Gilford about how I had just become engaged, and I mentioned how my fiancée liked to talk. It was then that my first anatomy lesson began.

"Women are different, you see. In addition to the obvious differences, some women are also built differently in other ways. For one thing, they have an extra layer of skin called the vocadural. The other layers are involved in respiration, breathing, and they help to release toxins and regulate heat. The vocadural in a woman is more like a balloon. Words build up in a woman, and more and more pressure is placed on the membrane—that is until there is either a release or she explodes. Many of the female fatalities you hear of are actually the result of this process. You've heard the term *femme fatale*; this explosive tendency is what that term originally referred to—literally a feminine fatality."

"That's right," Dr. Wolfgang added. "We run into it in Emergency quite often. Fortunately, we've developed techniques that in many cases allow us to get past the worst of the crises. Keep in mind that it's not just vocadural episodes, but others as well where we can use our technique to good effect. It's been discovered that manually manipulating the jaw of a woman has a cathartic effect on all of the systems. The mere physical formation of words is sufficient to bring about a regenerative response. I've personally seen at least a dozen cases where a woman declared dead has been brought back to life by the use of skilled jaw manipulation. It seems that in some women the will to talk is even greater than the will to live."

Dr. Travis continued, "Amazing, isn't it? I'm finding, however, that there is even more to the issue. You know, I just returned from a conference where research was reported that shows us that the basis for the symptoms we're discussing is often in the DNA. Inside each gene there are sets of switches, the most important of which are the gateway switches for on and off. In gene BS101 of the female X chromosome, the off switch is missing in about two-thirds of patients studied. That leaves those women with a neural inability to stop talking. It seems to make no difference that much of the vocalization is mindless."

"Does this mean that there is no cure?" I asked.

Doctor Wolfgang shrugged his shoulders. "There's been some effort to examine an approach using stem cell therapy, but that's not showing much promise."

"If there is to be a cure, I'm afraid it will have to come from someone younger than the three of us—someone with vision and motivation," Dr. Gilford offered. "Have you given thought to your career...?"

And so began the path I'm following today. I'm married now, and nearly finished with med school. I have the motivation. How could any married man of good conscience sit by and watch his loved one talk herself to death? I also have the vision. In my mind I can see myself somewhere in the future watching the football playoffs uninterrupted.

Hard Gambler

She was a hard case. Gamblers Anonymous had had no luck with her. They're the ones who referred her to me. As a psychiatrist, I have a reputation for success with quirky and unusual cases. I could sense from the start that this one would be a challenge.

"So, Sandra, I think we can help you with your gambling addiction."

"Wanna bet?" She fixed me with a hard, frozen stare.

"Do you want to deal with your addiction?"

"As a betting woman, I'm betting against you, doc, even though I'd like to be on your side. I've already lost the farm, my dignity, my friends, and my job. My pension and Social Security have been garnished until 2049, at which time I'll be a hundred years old."

"So what do you have left to lose?"

"Two cats and the clothes on my back."

"Let me ask again. Do you want to deal with your addiction?" At best I can tolerate cats, but I sensed my opening. I didn't say anything about the clothes on her back. The thought of Sandra naked on the couch in my office was incentive enough for me to overcome my feline phobia. She could keep her clothes.

"Sure, maybe. What're the odds, Doc.?"

"Hmmm. Well, two cats.... The two cats might interest me. I think we can give you pretty good odds. You give me the two cats, and you can have them back when we finally declare the treatment finished."

"I can't give up my cats!"

"We can work out visiting privileges for days when you've been successful. What do you say?"

"It's more than I can bear, Doc. Those cats are all I care about."

"We need something you care about to make this work. You've about used up your options, Sandra. You said it yourself; you literally have nothing left to lose." I was grasping at straws. Even given my work with street people and death row inmates, I'd seldom seen anyone in sorrier condition than this woman. And Sandra made me nervous. They say that in time people start to look like their pets—I had reason now to believe that. Maybe it was the hair, but I think it was the way her pupils turned to slits that most unnerved me.

In the end, she relented. I took the cats home with me. That first night I was awakened when my security alarm went off. When the police arrived, they found Sandra sleeping on the back porch with her cats. The next day I began looking for a safe house for felines. It ended up being a hundred miles away, so we had to limit visitations to once a week.

I sent Sandra off to a Buddhist retreat center. They sent her home. Her insistence on betting about things like the length of meditation, the number of people you could fit on a prayer mat, or the number of goby in the pond was distracting to the monks.

The Mennonites fared little better. They gave up after they caught her organizing buggy races and teaching the boys how to make book on the odds.

In desperation I played my final trump card: the cats. I threatened to sell them to a Chinese restaurant if she didn't shape up. I introduced her to the owner of a restaurant, Lee Wong, who is a friend of mine. He was sharpening a cleaver as we spoke. To reinforce the threat, I started having her listen to Chinese music each night as she went to sleep.

She did fairly well for the first week. Scared straight, I thought smugly. I moved our meetings out of the office and into the community. I've found you get a better perspective on a client's progress when you watch them interact with others in an ordinary way. It was during one of our community meetings when I caught her putting quarter after quarter into a gumball machine. It seemed pretty harmless, but I could see by the tilting of her wrist that it wasn't far removed from the slots. I called her on it, and it led to a long and complicated confessional. It seems that as a child her fondest wish was to put a penny in the gumball machines at the front of the store where her family shopped for groceries. Her very conservative father had never allowed it. Her mother, believing gum to be bad for the teeth, backed him up.

Gambling was her form of rebellion against parents she saw as being oppressive. I listened for three and a half hours as the story poured out. As a youngster shopping with her parents, she tried to sneak away and use the gumball machine. She had been captured by the store manager. He called her parents over the loud speaker system. She'd been grounded for a week. According to Sandra's own diagnosis, it was the start of a neurosis. The next week she ran away from home and headed for the grocery store with twenty-seven pennies in her purse. The cops picked her up on her way. Her parents had reported her missing. They were forced to go to the precinct station to retrieve their daughter and file a report. She did dishes for a month. Was it no wonder, she asked, that she suffered psychosis? I was starting to feel for the embarrassed parents, but I didn't share that with my client. I just listened as she relayed one incident after another.

That afternoon we went out and bought Sandra her own gumball machine. She has complete control over filling it up and emptying it. She really doesn't care for gum; she fills it with cat chow. She hasn't gambled since. I'm willing to bet she's cured.

Old Habits

John wasn't really sure at just exactly what time he died. At first he hadn't noticed the difference. There was no long tunnel with a light at the end, no angels greeting him with soothing harp music. He just continued listening to his wife talk. Habit, he figured later, was what held him in place.

It was his wife, Blanche, who first discovered that he was dead. She had asked him to go and get the load of white clothes out of the washer, and he hadn't complied.

The doctor came later and pronounced John Halliday dead as the result of an aneurism. John had never placed much faith in doctors and their diagnoses, and he figured his wife had talked him to death. There were others who figured the same, but proving linguistic homicide is not an easy undertaking. John was puzzled when the men carted his body away and he was unable to go with it. It was a moment of acute awareness and profound depression. Blanche just kept talking as though he was still there, even though the room was, to any observer, clearly empty. She droned on with speculations about the men who had come to take his body away, observations about how her uncle Bud had died in a similar fashion, and her wonderment over whether or not the minister was really gay. Finally, she turned and spoke to the exact spot where John had stood rooted all through her monologue.

"I know you're there, John. You wouldn't dare leave me. It's time to go to bed now."

John dutifully started toward the hallway. Blanche followed.

"I knew you were there all along!" Blanche shouted. "I just knew it. John, I can see your footsteps in the carpet."

John looked down. He took a step. Sure enough, the thick pile of the carpet compressed beneath where his foot should have been. His depression deepened. John looked furtively around. He spotted the linoleum of the kitchen and jumped for it. There was a puzzled look on Blanche's face. Instantly the depression started to lift, and John smiled. Then, each at the same time, they noticed the curtains at the window had been set into tiny undulations by the breeze from John's jump.

"John! Don't you start playing games with me now! You get right on in to bed!"

John complied. Old habits are hard to break.

Blanche waited until she saw the hollow appear on her husband's bed before she crawled into hers and pulled up the covers. She began to talk. She had always talked them both to sleep, and John knew that she would continue to talk until she began to snore. Later she would alternate between snoring and talking in her sleep: twenty minutes of talk, twenty minutes of snoring. That had been the pattern for many years. What frightened John now was that he didn't seem to need sleep anymore, and he knew he didn't dare to get up. Had he been alive, it would have been the longest night in

John Halliday's life. There was no need for a life review. He was lying next to it.

In the morning Blanche began to speculate on the tax advantages of the new twist in their marriage. She started pulling out insurance policies and ruminating about where they might go with the new found wealth. She made up a shopping list and seemed delighted that grocery costs would be cut by a third now that John wasn't eating. In sum, it seemed to John that Blanche was quite happy with his death and the new arrangement it had precipitated.

In the afternoon Blanche decreed that they would be going to the grocery store. John tried desperately to get out of the trip, but Blanche was insistent. At the grocery store John discovered a new game. He was amused as he watched the reactions of others to Blanche as she stalked the aisles looking for bargains, all the while talking to him about each selection she made. The other shoppers, unable to see John, began to give Blanche a wide berth. A light started to dawn in John's mind. Whenever Blanche would start to slow her discourse, he would rattle some cans or pick up a cabbage to remind her he was there. She would begin anew. In the end, the manager walked her to the door and bid her a good day. John was delighted. She clearly had no idea.

On the way home they cut through the park, as had always been their habit. John decided to test the waters and wandered off behind a bush. Blanche soon tracked him down and scolded him. Later he swung up into a tree, but she heard the rustling and told him to get down that instant. He complied. Old habits are hard to break.

Over the next two weeks John developed a new respect for his wife. Even though he was invisible to her, she had an uncanny sense and could track him anywhere. He had tried mingling with crowds, wading in a brook, hiding in closets, and jumping over lines of grocery carts. Sometimes she was slowed, but she always tracked him down. In the end she would always scold him and he would obediently shuffle off to wherever she wanted him to go. Her tongue lashings became more scathing, and John's depression was deepening. John would lie in bed at night listening to his wife and just know he was going crazy. *There should be some relief in death,* he thought. *I can't stand much more of this. I'm dead, and I'm going bananas. Bonkers!* He had begun to notice a nervous twitch in his left butt cheek. *There has to be a way—Lord?*

As the nights and days pressed on, the kernel of that first grocery store idea began to sprout. Then, one day as they passed the Forty-third Precinct Police Station, the solution blossomed. John planned carefully. He began taking little forays away from Blanche just to make her angry. Soon, almost no one in the entire city had missed seeing her stalking around and talking to the air. It was almost too easy. He'd tried some new strategies, too. He played in traffic, but instead of following him, Blanche would stand on the curb and scold him until he became contrite and came back to her side. Old habits are hard to break. Once, in desperation, he had jumped off a bridge. He was delighted when his wife had called the police to report what happened. There was hell to pay that night, though, and he didn't try that again. He paid the piper, but his efforts helped him devise a plan.

It was on a Tuesday—June 23, at 2:43 P.M. to be exact—that the plan finally started to fall into place. Blanche and John were walking down the street and she was talking happily about the shopping and her mother and the lack of rain. The talk of Blanche's mother put John a little on edge, and the nervous twitch he had begun to notice in his left cheek became almost uncontrollable. Then Fate stepped in. Blanche turned down State Street, and soon the red brick building housing the Forty-third Precinct was almost in sight. John felt the tumblers falling into place. He knew it was time, and drew in a deep, empty breath. He began doing all of the little things that he knew would make his wife agitated. He swung from branches, ran up and down porch steps, and even stuck out his tongue and waggled his fingers in his ears at her. She couldn't see him, but he knew that she knew. Then he ran into the Precinct building and through a door with the name Det. Noah Pawrohl written in a rainbow curve across the window. Soon Blanche was in hot pursuit. John danced on the desk of the startled detective as Blanche warmed up and began giving him what for. He worked to keep the detective between himself and his wife. He climbed atop file cases and swung from the light chain. With a sudden insight, John Halliday found that deep down he was enjoying himself.

The dark-eyed detective walked to the door and motioned for the desk sergeant to come in. The two veteran officers stood and watched in amazement as Blanche shrieked at her invisible husband and chased him around the room. They glanced at each other, and the sergeant went back to his desk to get handcuffs and call for backup. It was just a matter of minutes before Blanche was wearing a new orange suit and sitting in a private cell.

John was a free man at last. He felt some remorse when he thought of the three officers who'd been injured, but he went home feeling a sense of relief that left him walking just above the sidewalk. As quickly as he entered, the peace and quiet of the apartment filled him. He was soon really resting for the first time in forty-two years.

Then Blanche's mother arrived. Her plan was to stay in the apartment so she could be near her daughter in her time of need. "The apple doesn't fall far from the tree," was one of the few truisms John had validated in his life time. He was at the crossroads. He wasn't sure he could stand the struggle involving violent upswings and downswings between heaven and hell. Within hours, John's twitch returned and spread across both cheeks. He was once again descending into desperation. Opal did not put down the receiver of the phone from the moment she arrived at 8:13 A.M. until she finally ran out of people to call at 10:26 P.M. John's ears were ringing.

He hung around the couch that night. Not even habit could bring him to sleeping in his own bed, not with Opal in the room.

The phone rang at 7:00 A.M. sharp. It rang and rang.

"Hello. Yes, this is Opal Lippincot. Lieutenant Wells? Yes. Yes. She what? She's dead? Oh, my God! No! How did it happen? Heart attack? If you people had anything to do...."

Opal suddenly convulsed and slumped to the floor. By the time the men arrived to take Opal's body away, John was again beginning to feel rested. There was absolute silence. No one needed to be answered to. It was heaven, again. John sat down in his easy chair and sighed. All of the tensions drained quietly away.

Suddenly his reverie was interrupted by two voices speaking in unison behind him.

"John!"

He jumped to attention. A sudden twitching began in his cheeks. Old habits are hard to break.

The Right Kind of Music

Sometimes you just have to save a woman from herself. I knew something was up when my wife all but disappeared for the better part of three days. Oh, she was around in the evenings and all, but she was missing sunrise to sunset. Finally I asked her, "What've you been up to?"

I could tell she'd been waiting for me to ask. She jumped up from the table and said, "Wait here." Then she disappeared into the spare bedroom. When she came back she was wearing a big Stetson hat and a white jacket that was covered with fringe and sequins. As if that weren't enough, she was sporting a mini-skirt and net stockings and cowboy boots. My first thought was, "Oh, no, not another mid-life crisis!" She's had a few of those since the kids left home.

Apparently the fact that my mouth was agape was not sufficient response for her. "What do you think?" she asked.

I've been married long enough to know better than to answer that question directly. "Pretty amazing. Tell me, what's up with all of this?"

"Well, the combined ladies groups in town decided we were going to sponsor a benefit talent show to support the Domestic Violence Shelter. Ginger and Lorraine are part of the judging panel, so I know that half the score is going to be appearance. Mary and Pat are also on the panel, so I know that the other half of the score will be creativity. Barb's one of the other judges, so talent will be half of the criteria, too. At any rate, I decided to write and perform a country song. I'm gonna turn loose my inner cowgirl! A lot of women in our group like country music."

"Domestic violence, huh?" I admit several bad jokes passed through my head in that moment, but I know when to shut up. "That's a good cause. But I don't understand about this inner cowgirl stuff. You almost never listen to country music."

"Well, the last few days I've been looking for inspiration—shopping for an outfit. I've been to all the second-hand stores and the garage sales. I found this jacket at Goodwill the first day, and I just knew it was right for me. It was the motivation. I figured that if I had the outfit, the rest would come."

"What about the music?"

"Oh, that's not so important. As long as it's in C, I can play the chords on your guitar. There are only a couple of kinds of country songs; how hard can that be?"

"Yeah, there are cheatin' songs, and drinkin' songs, and somebody shot my dog songs, and I love my tractor songs, but, honey, none of those are you. You can't parallel park the car, much less handle a tractor or a combine; you were drunk once or twice in college, but that's a hazy memory; you don't own a dog, and I don't think there's ever been any cheatin' in our family."

"You just don't know about my inner cowgirl."

"I don't know about your inner parts, but I do know a little about farming and cowboys. I remember that one time we went for a little trail ride when we were on vacation. You could hardly walk for two days afterwards. That's one thing. Then there's your habit of coming in and spraying the bathroom when I'm finished in there. What're you going to spray a hundred head of sweaty, poopy cattle with? I can't see you diggin' post holes or shovelin' out a barn. That's why most of those country singers sound so nasal. What with the smells of a herd or the dust kicked up from a disc or combine, they have to practice while they hold their noses."

"You just don't get it. It's about my soul calling for the freedom of the open range."

"Now think about that life on the open range. No microwave. No place to recharge a cell phone. No shower in the morning. At least you wouldn't have to be after me about leaving up the toilet seat—because there are no toilet seats. You ever tried squatin' in the sage brush? Lots of ticks in the sage brush. Rattlesnakes, too. Your soul might soar free, but your bladder'd be a mess."

I could see I'd pushed a little too far, but sometimes you just have to save a woman from herself. Besides, I couldn't face her practicing country music for a month or more. I'm not that fond of country music. Fortunately I've been married long enough so I know the formula: apologize and create a diversion. "I'm sorry, but look at it this way, honey, you'll just have to do some more shopping."

She perked up a bit with that.

It was a couple of days later when I came home and my wife had on an old felt hat, sunglasses, a flannel shirt, very wrinkled khaki pants, and a pair of dilapidated tennis shoes. "Do I look like a blues singer to you?"

"You do, Honey." There followed a minute or so of silence.

"What?" she finally asked. "There are only a couple of kinds of blues songs; how hard can that be?"

"Yeah, there are my baby's been cheatin' songs, and drinkin' songs, somebody shot my dog songs, and I love my old guitar songs, but, honey, none of those are you. Besides, none of them are ever in the key of C."

"You just don't get it. It's about all the sorrow in my soul calling to be expressed."

"We all have some blues, babe, but you've never really been hungry. You've never had to sleep in a doorway because you couldn't find a home. Nobody's ever abused you, or cheated on you. Besides, you've never been drunk for days at a time, and you hate cheap wine. I'm sorry, but look at it this way, honey, you'll just have to do some more shopping."

She perked up a bit with that.

I was amazed when I walked in a couple of days later and she was wearing a helmet with horns and a bronze breastplate. I just shook my head. I mean, I really like blues, but opera, not so much. What happens when you roll over in bed and try to snuggle up to a cold bronze breastplate? It's no wonder those people sound the way they do. Even I might catch a couple of those high notes. I think I was quiet too long.

"There are only a couple of kinds of opera songs; how hard can that be?"

"Yeah, there are cheatin' songs, and drinkin' songs, somebody shot an apple off my head songs, and I'm gonna commit suicide because my love is gone songs, but, honey, none of those are you. Besides, I don't know that any of them are ever in the key of C, and if they were, they'd be shot full of accidentals."

"You just don't get it."

Sometimes you just have to save a woman from herself, but at times you need to make a concession or two for your own health.

"You're probably right—but those are really cool sandals. I just don't connect with your inner swan—at least not in an ariatic sense. I'm sorry, but look at it this way, honey, you'll just have to do some more shopping."

She perked up a bit with that.

A few days later and I walked in to find a psychedelic hippie sitting on my couch. It was tie dye and beads, ripped jeans and a familiar looking pair of sandals. She had something in her hair to make it look unwashed and stringy. She had a roach clip attached to her collar, even though I was pretty sure she didn't know what it was for. I figured she'd probably had one of her friends help her come up with this outfit.

"So, what is it, acid rock this time?"

"No, silly, I'm going to be a folk singer."

"Most of the folk singers I've known are pretty down-to-earth people. I think you may be a bit off the mark with this outfit."

"Alright, but how about folk music? I can write a folk song. There are only a couple of kinds of folk songs; how hard can that be?"

"Yeah, there are cheatin' folk songs, and drinkin' folk songs, and somebody shot somebody songs, and I love my fishing boat songs, but, honey, none of those are you. You might do okay with some kind of folk music, but you don't run a fishing boat, and you're not out on strike, and you don't make your living from the land. Why don't you go take a long bath, and I'll get supper and then we'll talk about it?"

She put on a pout, but she did as I suggested. To a woman, I think a long bath is almost as good as shopping. When she got out I had the table set with our best china and the silver her mother had given her. There were two candles lit and soft music playing in the background.

As she walked into the room I said, "That's it! That's the look! You just need to be you." I took her in my arms and we danced for a bit. "Maybe you could write a song that's a little romantic."

She smiled. Sometimes you just have to save a woman from herself. I think this was my best save.

Marriage in the Wilderness

My best friend, Ed McRee, was thirty before he married. He didn't wait so long because he was busy scouting the field. His spare time was too involved with the manly arts of camping, hunting and fishing to allow for the more dubious manly arts like dating, seduction, or marriage. Ed was, and is, a complete outdoorsman. Life was good.

Because he entered the field of Love so late, his fall was hard and fast! Like a fight with a cougar. Like Thanksgiving dinner with sharks. Like a canoe over a waterfall. Cupid hit him square. Following that shot to the heart he ran solely on nerve and reflex.

Jan had been raised a farm girl. That undoubtedly led to some assumptions on Ed's part. Erroneous assumptions, as it turns out. They met in June, were engaged in August, and married in September. He assumed he'd found a soul mate, a lover, a camping buddy, a hunting companion and a fishing partner. As it turned out, she was lovely as a lady slipper, but sneaky like a fox, stealthy as a pike, and clever as a coon. In a word, she was a woman. She let him run with his silly notions.

Ed towed his fishing boat behind the car on their September honeymoon. He returned with just a trailer. He took his wife, Jan, camping in October. He came back with the worst case of poison ivy the doctor had ever seen. Ed recovered in time to take Jan hunting in November. It was the first time in fifteen years he didn't bag a deer on opening day.

As Ed's best friend and counselor I heard all of the stories. My wife and I spent a lot of time with Ed and Jan, and when they were together we heard little more than newlywed endearments from them. When we got them apart, it was a different tale.

Ed's version of the fishing story was that he had gotten Jan up at five in the morning the day after their wedding. A sensitive fellow, he wanted to be certain she had fishing success. Jan never said a thing, but hey, they were fishing, so that was cool. Ed caught three medium sized bass almost right away, and he started coaching Jan. About seven-thirty Jan had a good hit. Ed figures it was at least a three-pound largemouth. "Keep your rod tip up! Don't give him any slack!" I could hear his excitement as he told the story. Jan stood up in the front of the boat and worked the fish in. When it was up to the side of the boat, Ed bent down to get the net from under the seat. He swears he doesn't understand what happened, but the next thing he knew Jan banged into him and they both went over the back of the boat. They had been trolling from one spot to another, and with a fish on, the engine was idling. Apparently one of them kicked the throttle and the boat took off on a half-mile trip across the lake. Fortunately they were only in about four feet of water. It was cold water, covered with lily pads. Jan told him later that when he started for the net it made the boat rock and she lost her balance. Ed just looked at the ground and shook his head as he told me that. When they finally tracked down the boat, it was a total loss—a four-foot gash in the bottom and the engine was mangled beyond repair. He managed to salvage three lures and the drain plug.

Ed's version of the camping story was that he had set up camp near a beautiful trout stream. The banks were lined with the gold of fall tamarack, the red of sumac, and the deep green of mature red pine. It was the most romantic place he could think of. The tent was almost level, and the mosquitoes were bearable. Jan was a bit chilled, so she had put on a sweater and gloves and gone for a walk. When she returned she wanted nothing more than to cuddle. One thing led to another. She began to undress Ed, covering him with caresses. He thought the gloves were an interesting part of the game. Then, when things had just begun to progress nicely, Jan jumped up and threw off her gloves. She pulled off her jacket and showed him red splotches all over her arms and stomach. Poison ivy. The next day Ed was covered in terrible places with the itching and rash. He wasn't allowed to touch Jan for the next three weeks. During that period she repeated many times that she never wanted to go camping again.

Ed's version of the hunting story was that he had taken Jan to his favorite blind. For two weeks he had seen a twelve-point buck almost daily from his secret spot in Meade swamp. By 6:30 on opening morning they had walked through the pitch-black, the mud, thorns and bushes, and were seated behind the brush pile Ed had carefully constructed. They were shoulder to shoulder, Ed facing south, Jan facing north-east. Ed spied the buck at 7:15 and nudged Jan so she might also get a look, but the deer had melted away into the under-growth. They saw no more deer during the entire morning. When he sensed Jan was becoming fidgety, Ed explained to her that deer get up and move on approximately a four-hour schedule. "You need to be patient. It's not as good as early morning, but we could see deer any time, especially around 10 o'clock and again around two," he whispered. Ed had counted at least eighteen individual deer regularly moving through the area during the weeks prior to hunting season, and he was sure there were more.

They didn't see so much as a squirrel in the afternoon. By dusk they were both bored silly. Jan complained of both cold and cramps. Citing the onset of a cold, she declined to accompany him on the second day. He didn't miss her. He had thirty-four sightings and took a nice eight-point before noon.

It was two weeks after the hunting experience that my wife Kate came home laughing one evening. She kept smiling through dinner. She giggled doing dishes. I knew better than to ask, and I also knew she couldn't keep her story to herself. Finally she couldn't stand it any longer, but she swore me to secrecy on an oath of certain impending celibacy before she shared the source of her amusement. She'd spent the day doing some early Christmas shopping with Jan, and they'd had some wine at lunch. They'd talked about men and marriage, and eventually Jan had made a confession. It seems that on the morning of her first full day of married life it was not Ed's rocking the boat while fumbling for the net that had sunk the Titanic. Jan had made a prodigious and calculated leap from the front to the back of the boat. To hear Kate tell it, it had been a naval maneuver worthy of Nelson or Halsey. Then, on the camping trip, Jan had donned a pair of gloves and gone out and rubbed them thoroughly in poison ivy. Eventually she came back and smeared the oils all over her would-be lover. The rash she had shown Ed was nothing more than cleverly applied make-up. Kate did report that there was some remorse about Ed's suffering, but "all's fair in love and camping." And as to the fruitless day of hunting—despite being a farm girl, apparently Jan hated the idea of seeing anything killed. She had spent her time blowing on one of those dog whistles that's not audible to the human ear. The clever girl now figured she was free from the burden of ever being asked to go hunting, fishing or camping. Kate thought it quite a fine and humorous story. I laughed in a perfunctory way, but I was sick at heart over the deception.

What would you do? Here I was, my best friend betrayed, and I sworn to silence about the whole mess. I couldn't sit still. This was one of those wars between the sexes. A traitor I am not. I went to Ed as soon as I had a plan. "Ed," I said, "you have been the butt of a horrible joke, the dupe in a dastardly scheme, the victim of vicious machination. Don't ask me to explain, for I have been sworn to silence under a vow of the most onerous sort. Just do as I tell you, use your head, and it will become sufficiently clear. We will undo the damage, and possibly leave you with a happier marriage than you ever imagined."

I have a sister, Sandy, who is eight years younger than I. At that time she was a senior at Indiana State, three hundred miles away. She owed me big-time, as I co-signed several of her college loans. She was a member of the Delta-Pi Sorority, and thus had many attractive young friends. Before opening day in April, Ed asked Jan if she would like to go fishing. She declined, and he went fishing with me instead. The next week I lured Kate out of town on the pretext of visiting her parents. We couldn't have her accidentally running into Sandy. Ed again asked Jan ahead of time if she would like to go fishing. Again Jan declined, and Ed explained that it was okay; he had some buddies he'd go with.

On that Saturday morning seven giggling young women carrying poles and all dressed up in little more than short shorts and fishing vests rang the doorbell at Ed's house. Jan answered, but Ed quickly pushed past her and said, "I should be back shortly after dark." A girl on each arm, he walked them to his truck.

That evening Jan watched as several girls helped Ed from his truck and dragged him to the front door. "We're sorry, Mrs. McRee, but I'm afraid we wore him out." "Fishing takes more than just a good line, you know." "He put up a good fight!" "He has allure, but not the staying power."

That was two years ago. Jan has never been introduced to my sister, and it is unlikely they will ever meet, as Sandy has now moved to Oklahoma. Good things have happened in the interim. In these past two years, Jan has never missed an opportunity to go hunting, fishing, or camping. Life is good.

Bypass

I went in thinking the operations were almost commonplace these days. Two stents and a bypass. A piece of cake. I filled out endless paperwork and signed in about eighty-six places. Then Dr. Rau came in and asked if I had any questions. As he left he said, "Of course every surgery has its risks." I knew doctors say that just to cover their backsides. Just minutes later, two nurses came and wheeled me down the hall. I remember joking with the anesthetist, and then suddenly my memories stop.

I awoke sitting across the desk from a man in a white shirt. His sleeves were comfortably rolled and his tie was loosened.

"So what's going on? Where am I?"

"Go over, take a look, and you tell me." The man smiled.

I stood and walked slowly to the window. I pulled at the blinds. The panorama was a huge surprise. The scene was more than visual. As it came into focus I could smell and hear and taste whatever I looked at. I knew thoughts. I felt emotions. The person closest to the window was a young girl who winked seductively and smiled at me. I quickly diverted my gaze. Just beyond was a man in miner's garb digging for gold with a battered shovel. Beside him stood a man in a dark suit; I knew him to be a stockbroker, and he was carrying a soft leather briefcase. Next was a man in a blue sweater. He was sitting in a chair, leaning forward with his elbows on his knees and his hands over his ears. His red-faced wife was standing over him berating him mercilessly. My eyes wandered next to a dark-haired woman sitting on the edge of a bed reading a letter. She was in tears, and she kept wiping her nose and eyes with a wet handkerchief. Somehow I was aware that it was a letter of unrequited love, and as I watched her I felt an almost boundless loneliness.

"Wow! I give up. Where am I?"

"Keep looking. You've always given up too easily. This should be within your ability."

I looked back. I was uneasy about reading people's thoughts, and I tried my best not to let it happen. Emotions, mostly it was emotions that flooded in. There was a frustrated young man sitting at a bus stop reading the Help Wanted ads in a wrinkled newspaper. A well-dressed woman leaned against a nearby wall and glared at him. She was jostled as a drunk stumbled by, and her glare turned to a new target. A crowd gathered and a man in academic robes strode by purposefully ignoring them. A woman with tattoos on her arms and neck elbowed her way through.

"These aren't happy people. I still don't understand."

Look more deeply," he said.

I saw a man bound in chains that I sensed he had originally forged for others. His gaunt, gray face was twisted in anger. A woman in a tattered dress hugged a scrap of bread to her chest and refused to share with anyone around her. Her fear and resolve poured through me. An elderly white couple huddled in a corner trying to get as far from a group of young black men as they could. The young men jeered and laughed and made lunging moves toward them. I watched as a priest performed rites for a dying woman. Neither was comforted. He dropped his crucifix at the moment of her passing.

"I still don't understand."

The man sighed and reached over to untie his shoes. He put his feet up on the desk and leaned back. His face was inscrutable. His feet were cloven hooves.

"Hell?"

He nodded his head. "Look even more deeply."

I looked. A flame burst up in the distance. I choked at the smell of sulfur. I watched a man burn at the stake. I watched it again and again. I watched soldiers in strange uniforms raping frightened women. Men and women were herded in chains like cattle. Unspeakable cruelties. It was like an endless loop, but I was mesmerized for a time. Finally I turned back to the man at the desk. His white shirt was now covered in soot, as were his face and hands.

"Satan?"

"Right, or Beelzebub, the Devil, Scratch, or a hundred other sobriquets. You can just call me Lucifer if you like."

"How about Sir? Forgive me, but I'm not sure I want to be on a first name basis with you."

"Not to worry. So, what do you think of my place?"

"I don't quite get it. The fire and brimstone sort of meets expectation, but I don't know about the rest."

"Oh, each of these people makes their own hell. It isn't all necessarily unpleasant. And I'm a pretty nice guy at heart."

"I suppose I'd expect you to say that. How does that square with the man burned at the stake or the slaves being whipped?"

"Not my fault! Not my fault at all. I'm kind of like a mirror. People look at me and they see what's inside of themselves. Sometimes we get a good laugh at that. Sometimes it's enough to make even a mellow person like me mad as hell. Don't think I enjoy that, though I do get a certain kind of satisfaction with some, seeing their own nastiness bounced off of them."

"Doesn't it get kind of old—burning people up and drowning them in sorrows?"

"Oh, no, there's enough turnover so there's always a new challenge. No, this job can be almost as creative as God's. In fact, God and I have worked out a pretty dynamic partnership."

"You're kidding! God just lets this go on?"

"You're imagining that eternal damnation stuff, aren't you? I think the church has brought me more good folks than any other institution, and just because of that kind of thinking. Judgmental thinking like that will land you here in a hurry, and yet most religions rely on it to keep people in line. Grace and forgiveness are unlimited, but they require two-way activity. The people here can leave any time they want. What keeps them here is mostly fear. Anger, sorrow, prejudice, greed—it all amounts to fear. They have to work through that. Learn to forgive themselves. Forgive others. See the connection between all things. It's a process."

"So, is that why I'm here?"

"Nah, you're just kind of on loan. It's almost time for you to go back. You have real potential, though. I look forward to maybe seeing you again."

A jolt of electricity brought me up off the table. Later the nurses told me I'd had them pretty worried. I'd been clinically dead for almost three minutes. What I remember most is the smell of sulfur.

Caterwaul

As a boy I loved to visit my Uncle Chris. As long as I've known him he's been a long-legged teddy bear of a man with huge, bushy eyebrows, a rosy nose, and a dog by his side. Uncle Chris liked to kid around, and he always maintained that his dogs were easier to get along with than his wife, but he never would have said that if Aunt Minnie had been there. She'd have invited him to go out and sleep in the dog run with his "other girls." She'd have made him do it, too, though they both would have had a good laugh about it later. After my Aunt Minnie died, Uncle Chris lived alone for years. Well, not exactly alone—there was always at least one dog.

Uncle Chris has been a dog man for most of his life. He loves to tell stories about his German Shorthair, Sukie. Sukie apparently was the consummate pheasant dog. "Pointed like a pregnant maiden with a plethora of perpetrators," he'd say, and then he'd shake his big head in disbelief. And there was the Golden Retriever named Tiz, who could find a downed duck in the middle of a thousand acre swamp during a driving blizzard. And among others there'd been three or four beagles and a coon dog named Sam. Sam, he claimed, would climb the trees right after the coons, and then he'd drop them down into a gunny sack if it was held out for him. There was a spaniel named Dolly that Uncle Chris claimed was the best damned trout dog within five-hundred miles. Claimed he'd made a special harness so he could just drop her over the side and she'd start diving for fish. He declared he and Dolly caught more trout in one season than all of the other members of the rod and gun club combined. A major tragedy in Uncle Chris' life came when he lost his Dolly. One day, according to the story, instead of just putting her over the side he tried to troll with her. "Drowned," was all he'd have to say before a tear came to his eye. He had at least two different friends who would back him up on that story if he was ever questioned. His friends will swear to almost anything he says, however. Uncle Chris is a good storyteller, and he mostly tells the truth, I guess. He'll growl and bark and hold a point and ruffle his eyebrows so that you feel like you're right out there in the field.

All of Uncle Chris' dogs really have been well trained. He claimed he and Minnie never had kids because dogs were lots easier to educate. I think he mostly said that for my benefit, but I've never been sure. My Uncle showed his dogs off regularly at the Springville Kennel Club. His dogs didn't win any prizes for conformation or best of breed, but they always, always took top honors in obedience and field trials. It was a special point of pride for Uncle Chris that his dogs continuously beat out dogs belonging to people who "got all uppity" about the purity of the breeds they showed, and some who even hired professional trainers. He had a long-running though mostly good-natured feud with the leaders of the Kennel Club about just what a good dog was.

Before Uncle Chris retired he was a mechanic and owned his own garage. At the garage they referred to him as the Jack man. He'd been a Jack man for as long as anyone could remember. Just a little Jack and ice and he could sip and sail through the most stressful day. It never seemed to affect his work, and he was the most beloved mechanic in town. Not only was his work excellent, but he was known as a sympathetic counselor. He hated to give bad news about transmissions or cracked blocks, and he often would temper the blow by sharing a bit of his Jack.

It may have been the drinking that led my mom to forbid me from spending any time alone with my uncle when I was a boy, though no one had ever once seen him even slightly impaired by it. He was a generous man, and maybe mom just figured he'd be a little too generous with her boy and his Jack. Maybe it had something to do with the way he changed after Aunt Minnie died. Mom used to say Uncle Chris became a curmudgeon then. I didn't understand what she meant until years later, but I took it at that time to be an affirmative statement—despite the way she wrinkled her nose when she said it. I just figured it meant that he was an independent sort of guy. At any rate, I loved my uncle, and by the time I was twelve I'd worn mom down in her determination that I shouldn't spend too much time with him. I have to admit now that time showed she was probably right in regards to her fears about his generosity.

It was my Aunt Jo who set up Uncle Chris with a cat. At the time, he'd been about a month in mourning after losing his last retriever to a speeding motorist. I was never quite sure of Aunt Jo's motives. Maybe she just hated to see her brother suffering. Maybe she thought it was ridiculous that he seemed more torn up about losing a dog than he had been years ago when he lost Aunt Minnie. Or it may have been that because she's his sister, sometimes she just likes to set him off to see what he'll do. She should've known that Uncle Chris would figure that replacing a good dog with a cat was about on par with exchanging a favorite Harley for a case of hemorrhoids. Personally, I think she probably did know.

Aunt Jo first saw the kitten on one of those Humane Society shows where they talk about the stray cat or dog or parrot of the week. She put in a call to the TV station immediately. Later Jo put that long-haired yellow kitten in a box with a warm batch of brownies and left them on Uncle Chris' doorstep. Brownies with black walnuts are one of the few things that Uncle Chris can't resist, and Jo counted on that.

When he found the cat, my uncle made phone calls to his sister that involved a bunch of threats about cat soup and making his own guitar strings. The next day Uncle Chris became a recluse. He went to his cabin up north. No one had any idea what happened to the cat. He totally stopped communicating with his sister, and he didn't come home for either Thanksgiving or Christmas. Finally he allowed me to spend Spring Break with him.

I was relieved when I was introduced to the cat. My mother and aunt had each pleaded with me to find out its fate. "This is my cat, Erwaul," my uncle growled. That was all he'd say on the subject, but I could see that he'd grown kind of fond of his feline companion. My uncle and I spent most of that time rabbit hunting and fishing, but Uncle Chris would disappear for about three hours each day. All he would tell me was that he was preparing a surprise for the folks down home.

It was a glorious Spring Break, but there were two things that marred that vacation for me. The first was that stupid cat, Erwaul, who was a terror in the morning. He'd growl and stagger and blink and moan. It was a pitiful moan.

A gut-wrenching moan like what you might expect from a wino waking in a cold cell. In the mornings, I learned quickly, it was best just to avoid Erwaul. I can show you my scars. The second thing was an incident, but it also included the cat. It happened the day we stopped back at the cabin for lunch and then went back out into the gleaming March sunshine to return to our fishing. Uncle Chris started up his truck and it made a terrible yowling screech like a fan belt tortured into meltdown. He shut off the truck, and when we looked under the hood we discovered that the cat had crawled up on the warm engine block and gone to sleep. It now had a bobbed tail. There wasn't much we could do. Uncle Chris put a bandage on the stump to stop the bleeding, and when he doused it with Jack to keep it sterile, the cat took off and I didn't see him for the rest of my stay. I can't say I missed him, and I didn't worry for long because Uncle Chris reported that the cat was still around—he was just a bit jumpy.

When my uncle finally did return to town, it was for the April meeting of the Springville Kennel Club. The members spent that evening planning their Spring Show. Uncle Chris announced that he would be entering the novice obedience trials, but he refused to answer the questions his friends had concerning his new entry. When they checked his entry blank they found that the new dog's name was Erwaul, the age was ten months, and the space asking for breed simply said In. Following the meeting Uncle Chris went back up north.

Uncle Chris came to the dog show carrying a curtained cage. My mother and aunt and I sat in the audience through two early events before we finally got to see the first eight entries in the Novice Obedience program. When it was Uncle Chris' turn, he opened the cage, reached inside, and snapped a leash on the collar. He then proceeded to the center of the ring. At the end of the leash strutted Erwaul. His little stub of a tail stood proudly straight up, and the hair on his head had been plastered with Butch Wax and was parted neatly down the middle. He wore a red bowtie, and in homage to Sukie, Uncle Chris had used Crayola markers to give him the colorations of a German Shorthair. The crowd was hushed. Uncle Chris and Erwaul went through the entire routine. Erwaul sat, he lay down, he stayed, he responded when called. In the end the only thing the judges could fault him for was that he staggered a little at heel. Needless to say, Erwaul swept the competition, and when the results were announced the crowd went wild. Erwaul and my uncle returned to the center of the ring where they took a bow. Uncle Chris commanded Erwaul to sit, and then to speak. Erwaul responded with what was to me a familiar, yowling screech.

Later, protests were filed, but it was discovered that the entry forms did not specify dogs as the only species eligible to compete in the obedience portion of the competition. That oversight was changed by a narrow vote at the next meeting of the club. Uncle Chris claimed, with some backing from outside sources, that the motion passed only because some of the members were afraid of losing to a cat in the upcoming summer field trials.

The Springville Tribune gave the obedience trials front page treatment. When the story hit the streets, all of the cat lovers, especially the old lady cat lovers, held back nothing in their rush to say "Gotcha!" Soon people were referring to my uncle as "the cat whisperer." He claimed he had three proposals of marriage within a day. When he wasn't cussing, he would feign modesty and refuse to speak of the events, though you could see that at some level he was pleased. Nevertheless, he was, in his soul, a dog man. He became a house divided against itself. He condescended to a couple of interviews with magazines and newspapers, though his answers to their questions were so sufficiently vague that they soon stopped contacting him.

I learned his secret when I went to see him at his cabin that summer. Soon after I arrived we went out and sat down on the patio. Erwaul climbed expectantly into Chris' lap and looked at the tray on the table. The customary bottle of Jack was there, along with several glasses. Always a generous man, my uncle had early on offered to share with Erwaul whenever he was having a little nip. Erwaul became a most consistent beneficiary of this generosity. He even had his own shot glass—with an English setter embossed on the side. He also had his own morning hangover.

After we'd settled down, my uncle told me his story. It had taken time and patience far beyond what he had ever put into a dog. "You know I've never had much use for cats, but Erwaul here has been more than I ever expected a cat to be. You know, I think he'll hunt." He ended his story by bending over, stroking the cat, and then making a pronouncement I certainly never expected to hear. "A drunken cat is almost as good as a dog." Then he added, "It's probably just as well that we didn't get to do the field trials. Damn cat can't hold a point without falling over."

Fish the Currents

My friend Gary has a dilemma. It's his wife Jo. She likes to fish. Now most men would think they'd died and gone to heaven if their wives wanted them to go fishing. Jo might be a legitimate exception. Jo is a talker. I've seen her sit in a boat by herself for hours and carry on a continuous conversation. To add insult to injury, she always catches more fish than Gary does. Just to boot, she refuses to clean them. She says, "Cleaning fish and taking care of the boat are Gary's jobs: catching fish and cooking are mine."

What would you tell the man? He came to me for advice. "This is serious. I need to have some time to think," I told him. It's one thing to figure out what to do with your own wife, but it's entirely different to figure out what to do with another man's.

Think, I did. The next time we were together I asked him what he really wanted. "Is it that you want Jo to shut up and act like a real fisherman? Do you want her to stop going fishing? Are you just mad because she's a better fisherman than any of the rest of us?"

"I'll have to think about it," Gary moaned.

I figured it was a bit of all three, but each answer might imply a different solution. Even if we had to go for the whole tamale, a bite at a time might be the prudent approach.

"I've thought about the problem," Gary said after shutting off his band saw the next time we were together. He took the beer I offered and continued thoughtfully. "Getting Jo to shut up would be about like trying to stop Niagara Falls with a bathtub stopper. I've got to be realistic. I started fishing mostly to find peace and quiet, but I don't necessarily want her to stop fishing. Maybe if she'd just hold it to once or twice a season. That's not likely. And hell yes, I'm mad because she's a better fisherman. For all those classes and books and videos I've invested in, I might as well have bought ballet boots and tried to join the Bolshoi!"

By the time Gary finished his response to my questions, he was sweating and shaking. I handed him another beer. I've found a beer in hand is one of the best counseling tools. It changes focus enough to have a calming effect.

"All right, let's start with the basics," I said. "What about the old snake in the boat trick...?"

We discussed it at length, and Gary wound up with a much more positive feeling.

The next time I saw Gary he looked glum as a goose with a knot in its gaggle.

"She swamped the damn boat. I lost $400 worth of tackle. And then she said she wanted to do it again because both her analyst and Sarah Self-help on TV have said that a person has to face her fears. She made me spend the next three hours trying to catch another damned snake. Now she has one for a pet. It's not the same snake it once was, though. Talked its ears off, she has."

I handed him a beer.

"What about coating her line with Tabasco sauce or dog doo or something to drive the fish away?"

We talked it over, and Gary went away with a much more positive feeling.

According to Gary, he spent the next week doing tests trying to find what it is that smells and tastes most disgusting to a fish. He spent hours sneaking tidbits in to the fish at the community aquarium. His final analysis: the three things that most repelled fish were Ban Underarm Deodorant, D-Con Rat Bait, and garlic cloves. He'd been thrown out of the aquarium after his wife's deodorant stick so upset a school of perch that they stampeded willy-nilly and set up such a vortex of currents that the plastic feed container was swept off the hook and immediately swallowed by an astounded looking giant clam. His final decision was a 40/40/20 mixture—light on the rat bait because it was the most difficult to use. He promptly began applying his concoction to his wife's tackle.

Gary was amazed when Jo continued to catch more fish than he. A difference, however, was that he continued to catch bass and walleye, while she began to catch catfish. Now I happen to agree with Gary in his conclusion that a catfish is about the lowest form of bottom feeding scum. "And they are the worst damned things to clean I've ever seen. You have to hang them up and pull the skin off with a pair of pliers. They don't taste all that good, either—like having a mouthful of muddy mush."

"Alright, so we've got to admit she's a better fisherman and move on. Would it be enough if we could get her to stop talking?" I asked while handing him a beer.

"My idea of heaven on earth!" Gary replied while twisting off the cap. "But you might as well try to invent a car that would run on used dishwater and earwax."

"Have you tried snacks? What about something that requires a lot of focus to eat—pomegranates or artichokes, say?"

"Think about it. If she were eating even a tiny fraction of the time she spends talking, I'd have a wife the size of an NFL tackle. Talk about intimidation...."

"Okay, okay. What about giving her options? Shopping, bingo, tour guide, self-improvement classes, Wal-Mart greeter, auctioneering school?"

"Shopping, bingo, poker—I'd be broke in three days. I tried sending her to auctioneering school in Kentucky ten years ago. I thought maybe I could harness some of that vocal talent and come out a buck ahead. As an auctioneer, she kept outbidding the customers in the crowd. It wound up with her being sent home at my expense and with $3,405 of purchases on the MasterCard."

"I get the point. Well, what about making her uncomfortable as possible in the boat—spiked seats, hooking the battery up to her seat, putting dry ice under the seat to make it frosty cold?"

We discussed the possibilities at length, and Gary said he'd have to think about it. In the end, though, I thought he went away with a much more positive feeling.

I saw Gary again several days later. There was a desperate look in his eye. I couldn't decide whether to laugh or cry when he told me his story, but the look on his face caused me to lean toward crying.

"Like you suggested, I hitched the battery to her seat. I made sure it wasn't too strong a current—took me nearly seven hours to do the wiring. When I hit the switch, I saw her sit up and smile. She sat there a minute, smiling, and then she started looking anxious. She kept alternating between smiling and looking anxious. Turns out that little current was doing strange things. She couldn't decide if she wanted to make love right there in the boat or pee. I was getting' my hopes up. In the end modesty won out and she demanded that we go back so she could pee. Story of my life, I tell ya. I don't know that I even care to go fishin' anymore."

What could I say?

The next time I drove past Gary's house I noticed his cars were both in the drive, but his fishing boat was missing from the side yard. I found him in the garage working on a complicated looking bunch of wires and switches.

"Where's the boat?" I asked, hopping up to sit on the workbench and handing him a beer.

"Sold it!" he responded glumly.

"What? You loved that boat!"

"A necessary casualty in a war of attrition," Gary averred.

"Explain."

"Since the last time we talked, I concluded that Jo was never going to be quieted. She means well, and I guess I knew what I was getting into back when we got married. It's just that she didn't know she liked fishing back then. And you know I could never deny anyone the joy of fishing! It's just that I reached the point where the joy was fast departing for me. I was desperate."

"Desperate enough to sell your boat and give up fishing?"

"Desperate enough to sell my boat. She hasn't completely driven me away from fishing yet."

"I don't follow."

"I traded the boat in. Go look behind the garage."

There were two one-man kayaks. One pink and one green. I had to admire his thinking.

"So how's it working?" I asked as I walked back into the garage.

"She paddles as fast as she talks. I still don't catch as many fish as she does."

"I'm sorry." What else could I say?

"It's not all hopeless," Gary said slowly. "I've learned a few things from all of our efforts."

"Like what?"

"Patience, for one. Humility. And then there's some promise in fishing the currents...." He pointed to the wiring on his workbench.

"You know I'm no electrician. You'll have to explain."

"I like seeing her smile. I'm rigging up a battery to hook to her side of the bed."

A Matter of Taste

I'm not the easiest woman in the world to get along with. I admit it. I also admit that I've made a mistake or two along the way. The biggest mistake is about two hundred pounds. He's also the reason for my not being easy to get along with. I'm married to an idiot.

Larry has never had much sense of taste, except in me, of course. It wasn't until after we were first married that I began to see clues about his lack of fashion sense. We went to pick out wallpaper. There were at least three floral designs that would have been outstanding in our living room, but Larry claimed to hate floral prints. It turned out that his dislike extended to floral print drapes, too. He was kind of attracted to some animal patterns. We wound up compromising on some dull stripes. I was still pretty easy to get along with at that time.

Over the years we've had differences over a lot of things. You wouldn't believe what I've given up: dust ruffles, throw pillows, sofas, some beautiful blouses and skirts, movies, make-up, favorite television shows (he's such a prude), flower beds in all the right places, year-round Christmas decorations, pajamas with feet. The list goes on. Buying new cars has been a nightmare; I want an automatic with high mileage, and he wants a stick with lots of power. And then there's style!

The suffering doesn't end there. I don't just give up floral prints and ruffles and chick flicks. I have to live with a lot of his junk. Oh, he'd tell you he's made a lot of sacrifices, too, but he's got his trophy deer head and horse collar mirror and beer can collection and a bunch of other ugly stuff.

I admit I lost it recently. I love the man, but I had to draw the line. A gorilla nearly ended our marriage. A nine hundred pound gorilla beating his chest. It was eight feet tall and made out of some sort of resin. Very life-like. Larry brought it home from an auction and stuck it out in front of the house. He put it right down by the street beside the driveway. He was so proud! He called all the neighbor guys over to show it off. I told you he's an idiot. He said never again would anybody have to wonder where we lived. He was right.

The next day I managed to knock it over as I was backing down the driveway. It took four tries. I was hoping that if I left it in the street the city might tow it away because there's a hydrant there. It didn't happen. When a man with a wrecker finally showed up, he helped Larry bolt the gorilla to a concrete pad they'd buried in the ground.

My neighbors thought it was funny. I was the laughingstock. I lived with it a few days. Then I started making inquiries into how to procure dynamite and build bombs. Before long I started getting hints that Homeland Security was watching. Subsequent to my going on line searching for information about acid, I had an agent make a call. She turned out to be nice. After she'd seen the gorilla and heard my story she suggested that an explosion probably would not make the neighbors or local law enforcement happy. Acids could be dangerous to handle, and the EPA would frown on their use. She suggested I look into finding a flamethrower. My estimate of Homeland Security went way up. She asked me to keep her posted. It seems she's married to an idiot, too.

Flame throwers are expensive. I only needed it for one use, and I was afraid if I left one around, Larry'd try to light the barbeque with it or something. I went to the surplus store, and I finally talked the young man there into letting me rent one. He agreed so long as he could come along and watch. He was pretty excited about it. He struck me as the kind of kid that makes mothers turn gray, but I was a desperate woman.

Whew, I've gotta tell you, a flamethrower has quite a kick. It took about a half an hour and a lot of adjustments, but I managed to craft that gorilla into an iridescent boulder that looks very nice beside the driveway. I figure that someday I'll plant flowers around it. Several neighbors complained about the smell, but they were wise enough not to make too big a fuss to a lady carrying a flamethrower. One of them even saluted before leaving.

I got to feeling a bit of remorse that afternoon. I don't particularly enjoy seeing a man cry, so I figured I might better go visit my sister for a few days. I let Rainey, my neighbor next door, know where I was going, and asked her to keep me posted on what things looked like on the front.

That first evening when Rainey called, she said that most of the guys from the neighborhood were sitting around the rock drinking beer. She said it almost appeared to be a wake of some sort. Larry called that night and left a message that a nine hundred pound gorilla was nothing. I wasn't sure what he meant by that.

The next day Rainey reported that some sort of construction had begun around the entrance to our house. That worried me. With Larry, things can escalate pretty quickly. He doesn't have the same good sense I have.

The next report I got wasn't much help. Rainey said she couldn't figure for the life of her what the guys were putting together. There were cement mixers and scaffoldings, and a bunch of folks were running around looking very busy. She said the guys in the neighborhood were all involved, plus a couple of contractors, and that none of them were talking. It didn't bode well, but I knew enough to stay away.

The next day Rainey called and said I'd better come on home. The construction was finished. She wouldn't tell me what they'd done. Said it was better that I just saw it for myself. She also said that she was thinking seriously of putting her house up for sale, but that she was afraid all of the property values were now down the tubes. That really did make me worry. I headed for home right away.

I admit it was a shock. Much bigger than the gorilla. My entryway had been turned into a triceratops head, big beaked mouth open, horns pointing to the sky. I have to admit that it's an interesting artistic statement, but I can't say the setting pleased me. I gathered up the girls from the neighborhood and we made a couple of pitchers of Margaritas. We sat in the yard and discussed the options. Several were afraid their husbands were contemplating similar construction projects. We concluded that all men are idiots.

In the end we decided to fall back on the age old solution, but with a twist. It's worked for centuries, so why not now? We went to work with our own craft project. By four o'clock we had crafted a triceratops egg that was six feet long and almost four feet high. It took eleven of us to hoist it into

Larry's side of the bed. It's the couch for him tonight, but if he's good, and if the triceratops moves down the road and feels no further need for incubating, the egg might go away.

Decisions

No woman is easy to live with. It takes a facile liar to successfully live with a woman, which is why most men, even the most honest among us, are liars. Show me an honest man, and I'll show you a man either between relationships or involved in an unhappy one.

My Emily is more difficult to live with than most. Oh, she's as sweet as can be, and I love her with all of my being—most of her, anyway. The thing is, Emily is indecisive about everything. That was certainly not what first attracted me to her. I'd like to say it was her mind that first attracted me. It wasn't. I'd even like to say it was her sweet nature. It could have been, but it wasn't. She first attracted me with a set of the biggest endowments I'd ever encountered. I soon got beyond that initial attraction, but they've always loomed somehow in the background. Or foreground. More about that later.

For many women, the time they take while shopping is as much from a love of the process as it is indecision. With Emily it's a bit of both, but it's mostly indecision. A man learns to live with—at least tolerate—that kind of indecisiveness. There is a Walter Mitty gene on the Y chromosome that allows men to survive while sitting outside the changing room in a department store. And men learn that there is only one way to answer questions like "Do you think this makes me look fat?" or "Do you like this color on me?" Those are slam dunk, don't-hesitate-to-lie questions.

Emily just loves to shop, and it's led to some unpleasant scenes. For instance, that's why I hate Christmas. I don't have any theological hang-ups; I hate Christmas because Emily likes to shop—and because Emily insists that we shop together. After three hours of pondering which pair of earrings to buy for Aunt Wilma and another two hours wrestling with the decision of which barbeque set to get for Uncle Chub, I'm ready to go crazy. I hiss, "Make up your mind, woman!" but she's used to it and just ignores me. Emily can ignore almost anything when she's shopping. Once a man had a heart attack in the next aisle. The EMT's came rushing in and a big crowd gathered. Emily didn't even see it. I took it as a lesson and try never to have a heart attack while shopping with Emily.

As I say, Emily has trouble with decisions. I don't know what color Emily's hair is. More often than not it's more than one color, and it goes well beyond those streaks that are so stylish these days. The woman can't make up her mind, and when she asks, she'll never get a straight answer out of me. After all of these years I'm as confused about some questions as she is. Of course I always tell her I love the current tint.

Some would say Emily is creative, but indecision lies behind most of what she does. As an example, I could explain that we dine on a lot of strange dishes. If she can't decide whether to cook a tuna casscrole or fix Tex-Mex, we wind up with tuna-noodle burritos. If she can't decide whether to fix something Italian or something German, we wind up with sauerbraten pizza. Of course I always claim it's delicious, and generally it isn't as bad as one might think.

I remember an important Christmas party my company held. After weeks of shopping, Emily decided on a red, black, and green sheath dress. It was stunning on her, and very Christmasy. Of course she didn't have shoes to go with it. She bought six pair of heels, and in the end she wound up wearing one green and one red shoe. Of course I told her that her choice was a knockout.

Decorating our home has been a nightmare. Each room has come to be made up of little specialized nooks. In the living room my easy chair and the surrounding accoutrements are Scandinavian modern—all chrome and glass. Emily's area is antique oak. The entertainment center is a collection of Louis IV pieces. There is an oriental nook complete with Noh masks on the wall. Another corner is filled with animal décor. I can't begin to describe our bedroom and the bath. Of course I always tell her that her decorating is brilliantly bold.

With Emily, things as easy as choosing a movie can be horrifying experiences. For that reason we often binge, seeing two or three movies in an evening, or buying five or six books or magazines at a time. We've almost completely stopped taking vacations, and our car is eight years old and has 213,000 miles on it because I can't face shopping for another one with her. But, these instances pale to nothing. About a year ago Emily started having backaches.

After seeing the doctor, Emily began to contemplate the idea of breast reduction surgery. It was not a decision I wanted to be a part of, and of course I told her I wanted only what was best for her. The surgery was scheduled and cancelled at least a half a dozen times. Eventually she was referred to a different doctor. Finally a date was set, and imagine my relief when my job called me out of town. Emily assured me that everything would be alright. Her mother would come to stay. As they say, the apple doesn't fall far from the tree, but I was glad she would be there for Emily, and delighted to have reason to high-tail it out of Dodge.

When I returned, Emily's mother happily babbled on about how easy and successful the surgery had been, and then rushed off to attend some sort of outing with her Red Hat Society. Emily convalesced for a couple of days, and I slept on the couch. When I called from work in the afternoon she said she had a surprise for me and that I would need to help her make a decision. You can imagine my trepidation.

When I walked in that evening I noted that Vivaldi was playing softly on the sound system. My spirits rose. Vivaldi usually means that Emily is feeling romantic. "Fix us each a drink and I'll meet you in the living room in a couple of minutes," she called from the bedroom. I couldn't help but smile.

Several minutes later Emily entered wearing nothing apparent but a silk robe. She had a seductive smile, and I could suddenly feel my heart beating in my chest. I was probably grinning. She stopped in front of my chair and slowly, sensuously, opened her robe. Vivaldi hit a crescendo.

"I couldn't decide," she said. "The doctor assured me we could match them up any time. Which do you like best?" She turned and gave me a profile with a perky C cup, then turned again giving me a profile of the double D I'd loved for so long. Of course I was speechless.

"Well?"

"I love them both," I stammered as diplomatically as possible. I was in a world of hurt no matter what I said. "What do you think?"

"No, I want to hear what you have to say," Emily responded in her firmest tone. She gave me the profiles once more.

"Let's think about this for awhile. You said they could be matched up any time. It's too big a decision to rush into." My mind was a blur as I weighed the pros and cons. Perky C's meant a whole new wardrobe. That meant more shopping—endless shopping. On the other hand, I was aware of what time and gravity can do even to granite overhangs, and I wasn't unmindful of her aching back. We decided to give the decision a week.

After just a couple of days I knew we had to be quicker with our decision. The seamstress wanted $350 for a custom made bra. Besides, I noticed that each time she got up from her seat, Emily was starting to walk in circles, always to the right. Then a detective at the department store eyed Emily suspiciously as we left. I hated it, but I couldn't blame him. It probably looked as though she had a television stuffed in the right side of her blouse.

I kept asking her if she had reached any conclusions. She said her conclusion was that I should decide. It was the most decisive thing she'd ever said in her life. I asked about her back. She said she couldn't tell, what with the new strains it was under. I asked about her self-image. No problem, she said, there were advantages and disadvantages either way. She was determined to make me happy. I just longed for the old days. I tried praying. I felt forsaken. Obviously I couldn't ask my guy friends. It was too embarrassing to bring up with the ladies.

Multiple choice: C or DD? I'd always been better with essay questions. In the end, I chose the path that had gotten me through all of my really tough classes in college. I flipped a coin. Two out of three? I knew what was right, but without some negotiating it would be a really painful choice.

After dinner Emily sat slumped to the right in her chair. Her eyes had a far-away look, and I figured my negotiating position would never be stronger. I also knew intuitively that this was not the time for a man to slide by with a lie. "Emily," I began, "I love you, and you know that the size of your breasts does not make a bit of difference to me. It really doesn't. They could be on your back for all I care." I was instantly sorry for what I had said. She seemed to be considering it seriously. I hurried on. "I think it should ultimately be your decision, but I'm willing to make it if you will grant me two concessions. They're related."

"What are the concessions?"

"Not until you say okay. You'll have to trust me."

She thought about it for a long time, and for a bit I began to despair. She got up and walked around her chair, twice to the right. "Alright," she said with resignation, "let's hear it."

"Okay, but I want to say again that if you have any feelings to the contrary, you should go with them. I'm concerned about your back, and to me you look terrific either way. Go with the C's."

"Okay, what are the concessions?"

"I know that this decision will mean a whole new wardrobe. The concessions are that you must stay within a reasonable budget, and that I not be involved in any of the shopping."

She looked at me gravely for a long time, smiled, and got up and left the room. "I'm going to stay with my mom for a couple of days after the operation," she informed me as she left. I cleaned up the dishes and wondered what manner of trouble I was in.

Several days later I picked Emily up at her mother's. Her mother answered the door with the usual *What have you done to my daughter now?* look, and left me standing there. A few minutes later Emily came bouncing into the room with a big smile. There were the beloved DD's restored to their usual place. "Let's go shopping!" she grinned.

The Connoisseur

Thelma was the town librarian. You should know that Otter Branch was not much of a town. For that matter, Thelma was not much of a librarian. But, she was an inexpensive librarian with credentials. That was enough for the town council. There had not been one new volume added in the eighteen years since she had taken over the position of Head Librarian at the Otter Branch Municipal Library. In fact, if you didn't credit a few donations, fifty-two volumes had disappeared from the shelves in that time. Thelma did not believe in change.

"I'm happy with who I am, thank you. If I were to change, I might not like the person I became."

Word had it that Thelma had been left at the altar in Lelanau just before coming to Otter Branch, and that she had not dated since that time. Her car was eighteen years old. Her sweaters were eighteen years old. She did her hair up in a bun. Her little house was immaculate. Thelma's one vice, so far as anyone could tell, was raspberry wine. Often on a summer evening she could be seen sitting in the lawn chair in her front yard and dozing under the influence of one of the some two hundred bottles she produced each season.

Over the years several dozen complaints had been made with the Town Council about the lack of updates in the library. The Council was always content to avoid spending, and the reply from the library was always the same.

"This new literature is full of sex and violence, and the young people of this town certainly deserve better. The books we have now served all of you well, and they will serve your children equally well."

To quell the unrest the last time it surfaced, the council had voted on a compromise and sent for a newer edition of *World Book Encyclopedia.*

Max Reynolds had never read an entire book in his life. His home was a scandal of old cars and cats and hunting dogs. Max had only two virtues, if in fact such things are virtuous. He made the best moonshine in seventeen counties, and he never welched on a bet. Max was an uneven poker player at best, but on one Friday evening he won big. Later, after the mayor and the Henning twins had left, Rick Gilford and Luther VanderBean were standing around shooting the breeze, putting off facing the music they'd hear when they wandered home.

Speaking to no one in particular, Luther said, "I'll bet you fifty dollars that you can't get a date with Thelma the librarian, and another five hundred that you can't get her into bed with you. I'll give you one month." It had been a long night for Luther VanderBean, and he was not into making any more bets that he had any chance of losing.

"Hell, Luther, you might as well try ta get a fella ta bet you that he can jump across the Mississippi River at Memphis," Rick said. "Only a fool idiot would take that bet!"

Max stood listening. He was feeling lucky, and when he was feeling lucky he generally went with his feelings. The problem was that his feelings could turn on him faster than a sick stomach, so now he stood and contemplated for a bit before speaking up. Finally he said, "Well, I've been called a fool idiot before, and mostly it was true, I guess, but I think with some modifications we might be able to work us out a bet."

"What kind of modifications you want?" Luther growled.

"Well, double your money for starters. One month will do for a date, but I'll need three to get her into bed."

Luther stroked the stubble on his chin. He thought about Thelma. She was tighter than rusted lug nut, and he figured there was no way he could lose this bet. "Two months. How'll I know you've done it, though?"

"Three months, and you can just ask her."

"You mean she doesn't admit to it and I win?"

"That's it."

"Done!"

As he walked home Max experienced a sinking feeling. He began to worry about a change in his luck. He began to worry that maybe he'd let the liquor talk for him again. He began to worry that maybe Thelma really did wear that iron chastity belt he'd heard of from other would-be suitors.

When the sun rose high enough to shine through the top pane of the dirty east window, Max rolled out of bed. He rolled out and lay on the floor thinking. His head hurt. Thinking and hangovers were bad bedfellows, and bedfellows were on his mind. Finally he struggled up and filled a jelly glass with cold water from the pump. He dumped it over his head. He filled the jelly glass again and drank it down without breathing. It dizzied him, and he staggered to a chair. Drastic action was called for.

When Max walked into the library he'd had a bath and his hair was parted for the first time in three weeks. The last time had been for Wilbur Winchell's funeral, and he'd only parted it then because he'd been a pall bearer. "Afternoon, Thelma."

"Afternoon, Mr. Reynolds. I don't believe I've ever seen you here before."

"No'm, I don't guess you have. But I'm a practical man, and I need some answers. Everyone tells me you're the smartest person in town, and so I've come to you."

Thelma blushed. "I don't imagine that's true for a minute, but tell me what you need."

"I need me a book that will give me a really good recipe for raspberry wine."

"I believe you've come to the right place." She smiled and came out from behind the librarian's desk.

Hot damn! I got her where she lives, Max thought. Thelma seldom smiled. Max felt the luck coursing through his veins.

Thelma walked halfway down the aisle and turned to her left. She pulled a small, dog-eared book from the bottom shelf and came back to Max. "This is the bible for winemakers, Mr. Reynolds."

He picked up the volume and slowly read the title: Slobovitch's Practical Guide to Wine and Beer Making. "Now I hear that you make the finest raspberry wine in the county, Miss Thorgood. Is the recipe in here as good as yours?"

Thelma's eyes narrowed. Max felt the luck melting out of his legs. "My recipe is none of your concern," Thelma growled.

"That was only meant as a compliment, Miss Thorgood. I wasn't tryin' to pry or nothin'. If this book'll give me a start, I believe I'll do just fine. I have some small experience with making beverages."

"So I understand, Mr. Reynolds." She opened the book, pulled out a card, and stamped the date firmly inside the cover.

"If I was to bring you a sample of my raspberry wine in, say, a week, do you think you could try a sip and maybe give me a pointer or two to get me headed in the right direction?"

"Good wine takes months to make before you even think of bottling it. A week won't get it out of the primary fermenter. This book is due in two weeks."

"When I bring the book back, then, would you at least try it?"

"Two weeks, Mr. Reynolds." Thelma went back to her desk and began shuffling through papers.

Max thumbed through the pages of the book. He was looking for inspiration. Thelma had shut down on him like a seized up Ford V-8. As he stood looking at the pages he suddenly felt the luck tickling the hairs on the back of his neck. Long ago he had learned to listen to that siren call, and long ago he had learned that a man had better trade on what few strengths he has, or he'll get nowhere.

"You a bettin' woman?"

"What?"

"I asked if you were a bettin' woman."

She stared at him with those narrowed eyes. For a moment he was afraid she was going to fly across the room at him, so he seized the initiative. "If, in one week, I can bring a bottle of acceptable raspberry wine that I have made with my own two hands, will you go out to dinner with me?"

"The chances of your bringing in a bottle of acceptable wine that you have made yourself are just about as good as the chance that I would go to dinner with you. About half the chance of a snowball in a sauna!"

"So it's a bet, then?"

"Not on your life. There's nothing in it for me except the possibility of a bad taste in my mouth."

Max smiled. She was a wagering woman. "So what would you suggest?"

Thelma thought a moment, then suddenly the crinkles around her eyes softened. "I walk past your place sometimes, and I am always deeply offended—deeply offended—by the junk cars you have sitting around in your yard. I'll tell you what, you clean those up if you lose and you've got a bet."

Max swallowed hard. Those cars were dear to him. He felt like a mother in danger of losing her children to a dread disease. He smiled weakly. "Done," he said, and he turned and walked slowly from the library.

On his way home he stopped to watch a group of neighbor boys playing baseball. Between innings he called them over and offered to pay them a dollar a pound for all the raspberries they could pick for him before sundown. The game ended immediately. Those were princely wages in those days, even for a raspberry picker.

As he passed the mayor's house he saw that the mayor and Luther VanderBean were talking. They called him over. The mayor looked at Max with what could only be interpreted as sympathy. Luther laughed and asked, "So, I see you're all slicked up. How's the project with Thelma coming?"

Max spat in the grass and said, "You be at the restaurant next Saturday night and you'll see."

Both of the men were laughing as Max walked away, and he felt like a man in the bottom of a deep hole that was caving in around him—except he had an idea. Sometimes it is a simple idea that can make a man. On the way home he stopped at Gilford's IGA and bought a bottle of the cheapest wine they had. "Just for the bottle," he explained to Rick as he checked out. "You know me. I figure wine is for sissies and girls."

That evening there were fifteen different boys who delivered raspberries to his door. The change in the old sock he kept under the cushion of his chair was all but used up. Well after dark he sneaked out to the rusty '47 Desoto that sat near the gate and lifted the hood. Pulling the air cleaner housing off the carburetor he reached inside and pulled out a pint of his best moonshine whiskey. He'd been saving this bottle. It was 180 proof and fine as chicken whiskers. It broke his heart to mix it with raspberry juice, but he did it. He experimented into the night until he had just the right combination of sugar and juice and whiskey. Damn, he thought, that might just do it. A fellow who liked sweet drinks could just about like this stuff.

The next day he tried his blend on Christopher Henning. Chris liked wine. He never had been able to hold real likker. That was why Max had never really trusted him. Wine was women's drink. Chris took the cup from Max. Two sips and he had a smile on his face and was headed off to pick another fight with his brother. Max took that as a good sign.

Saturday at closing time Max showed up on the library steps. He'd stopped at the Woolworth's and bought a couple of nineteen cent wine glasses. As Thelma locked the door he said, "I've got something for you to try."

"Oh, Mr. Reynolds, not here. This is a library, and I have a reputation to uphold."

"Oh, your reputation has been on my mind. I thought maybe we could walk down to the park. It's on the way to Wood's Inn. I figured we could have dinner there."

"I don't think so, Mr. Reynolds, but if there's no one else around the park, maybe that's as good a place to stop as any. Have you figured out what you're going to do with all those nasty cars you're going to have to move out of your yard?"

Max just smiled and held up the wine glasses in a salute.

Max filled each glass up to the rim. There was, he thought, enough alcohol in each to bring down a mid-sized bull.

"Mr. Reynolds, you must never fill a wine glass full. You need to leave space for the wine to breathe, for the bouquet to develop. It is part of the pleasure of drinking a fine wine."

"Forgive me," he said, and he drank off the top half of his glass. "Is that better?"

"I am shocked, Mr. Reynolds, but yes, that's more like where you need to start."

Max nodded to her and motioned she should do likewise. Thelma hesitated, but followed his lead. It was the smoothest wine she had ever had. Smoother than a mossy rock in a cold spring. They sipped at the rest of what was in their glasses and soon Thelma was begrudgingly commenting on the fine qualities, the clarity, the legs, the unusual nut-like fruitiness of the potion in her hand.

Max was feeling a bit light-headed. He'd seen a lot of big men go down under the influence of as much likker as had been in those glasses. Thelma didn't show any outward signs that she was drinking, but she took Max's arm when he offered it and they walked on to the restaurant. It turned out to be a pleasant evening, and Max was especially gratified to see the look on Luther's face. Before he deposited Thelma at her door that evening, he asked, "Do you suppose I could come over some time and try some of your wine?" She'd said yes. He had his foot in the door.

The next Saturday Max sat on the couch in Thelma's living room and sipped at her wine. It wasn't whiskey, but he'd gotten a head start before coming over, and now he had to admit to himself that this was pretty good stuff. At one point Thelma went to the kitchen to look for more snacks. Max dropped a peanut and went fishing for it under the sofa. His hand brushed up against a book, in fact a stack of paperback books. He pulled one out and looked down. As he looked at the cover it felt as though his heart had fallen down and tangled with his intestines. There on the cover was a beautiful woman with her mouth open in a lonesome way. Her blouse was gaping, and the fullness of her breasts was almost completely exposed. Max shoved the books back under the couch. His heart was pounding, and he felt desires rising within himself that he had not recognized in years. Thelma found him strangely quiet most of the rest of the evening.

Thelma was a secret reader of bodice rippers. The discovery had surprised Max so much that he walked around for the next few days in a fog thicker than ninety weight gear oil. He felt his old world slipping away.

The next Saturday evening Max was waiting when Thelma closed the library doors. In the past she would hardly have spoken to him. Now they had something in common. Good wines.

"I've got something I want ya to see," Max blurted. There was something adolescent, something anxious in his voice that piqued Thelma's interest. She took his arm. When they got to Max's place she could not believe her eyes. There was not an old car in sight. The dogs were penned out in back, and the cats had disappeared. There was even evidence of recent landscaping.

"This is absolutely amazing, Max."

"I hoped you'd like it. Will you come inside and have a drink with me?"

"Well, I'll certainly drink to this wonderful change, but I don't think I'd better go inside. How about we sit in the porch swing?"

Soon they were toasting the new look of the neighborhood. An hour later Max broke out another bottle. At midnight they woke the mayor with their singing.

It was the following Monday afternoon that Max dragged Luther up the library steps. Once inside Max said, "Okay, you go ask her. I'll wait here."

"I can't do that!" Luther said glancing over at the librarian's desk. Thelma was glaring at them. Luther figured Max was setting him up to be killed so he wouldn't have to pay off the bet. "What would I say?"

"Ask her if she's been to bed with me or not," Max said. "I'll wait outside."

"SSSsssh!" Thelma hissed.

Luther was shaking. Thelma's reputation was absolute. "You stay right here, Max! If I'm shot I want a witness. I heard she keeps a pistol in that top drawer."

"I wouldn't be surprised. You wanna just pay me and be done with it? Chicken?"

"In a pig's porky proboscus! You just stand right here." Luther turned and marched to the Librarian's desk. Thelma stood and met him with a scowl. Luther swallowed hard. Years of grade school training came flooding back: images of female teachers grabbing him by the ear and towing him to the office, knuckles black and blue from where the ruler had landed, the stinging embarrassment of standing at the board with his nose in a chalk circle. Now he faced Thelma—perhaps even more fierce than the lot of teachers had been in the past. He felt his knees shaking.

"I have a question."

The crinkles around Thelma's eyes deepened. "Yes?" Her tone was accusatory.

Luther began to sweat. He felt Max's eyes in his back. His muscles tensed as he estimated how quickly he could make it to the door. He put his hand in his pocket and fingered the bills he would have to turn over if he didn't ask. Luther wanted to cry, but he pulled himself up, took a breath, and blurted out his question.

"Max said he's been to bed with you. Is that true?" He winced as though waiting for a blow.

"Well, what kind of question is that!" Thelma seemed to be looking through him. She waited for an answer. Luther turned red. Perspiration popped out on his brow. He couldn't speak, so when no answer was forthcoming, Thelma said, "Of course we've been to bed together. The mayor married us last Saturday, not that it's any of your business."

Luther was stunned. He turned and looked at Max, who nodded assent. Luther turned red and blue and red again by turns. He pulled the wad of bills from his pocket and threw them to the floor. The words he bellowed as he plowed out the door were unintelligible.

Thelma and Max agreed that the money would send them on a nice honeymoon. They would leave right after she placed the order for new books. Thelma had enjoyed making out the list of new literature. It was a new activity for her, and it reflected the new person she felt she had become. She liked that person.

The honeymoon was something Max was looking forward to with great anticipation. When she had come to him that first night, her hair down around her breasts, her sultry eyes full of eighteen years of passion gleaned from cheap novels, the moment had overwhelmed him. Now Max felt lucky, and he knew it was a luck that would stay with him. He had a new appreciation for the world, and he certainly had a new appreciation for raspberry wine.

About the Author

Richard Tipton grew up mostly in Montana, but settled in Michigan after transferring to Western Michigan University and subsequently marrying a Michigan girl. He received a Masters degree from Central Michigan University, and taught high school Speech and English for many years in Ionia, as well as extension classes for Montcalm Community College.

Richard has three children. He divides his time between his home in the woods and a cottage on Mullet Lake. In addition to writing, he enjoys oil painting, sailing, woodworking, travel, and a host of other activities.